She ran lightly down the steps into the garden, a fairy-tale creature in a gossamer cape, flitting through the darkness, while he stood transfixed, watching her.

"I need to clear my head."

"I can imagine." She strolled back to the foot of the steps. "The scent of flattery can be very strong."

Alexander laughed. So she thought him under Mrs. Hart's spell. He came down the steps, stopping just in front of her, taken with the bright glitter of her eyes. He reached for her.

She twisted in his grasp and staggered against the rough wall of the garden. His hands trapped her there. For a moment there was only their breathing—irregular, mingled, charged with longing, filling the garden.

"I'm not interested in Mrs. Hart," he said. He traced a line under her chin, feeling the silky skin beneath his fingertips.

He brushed her mantle over her shoulder. "All this"—he gazed at the white glimmer of her flesh—"was hidden from me until tonight."

He bent and kissed the base of her throat, drinking in the scent of her. He tilted her face, kissing his way up her neck to her ear, her cheek. There he paused.

"Kiss me, Ophelia."

Kate Moore

A Prince Among Men

AVON BOOKS ◆ NEW YORK

This is a work of fiction. Names, characters, places, and incidents either are the product of the author's imagination or are used fictitiously. Any resemblance to actual events, locales, organizations, or persons, living or dead, is entirely coincidental and beyond the intent of either the author or the publisher.

AVON BOOKS
A division of
The Hearst Corporation
1350 Avenue of the Americas
New York, New York 10019

Copyright © 1997 by Kate Moore
Inside cover author photo by MGM Photography
Published by arrangement with the author
Visit our website at **http://www.AvonBooks.com**
Library of Congress Catalog Card Number: 97–93178
ISBN: 0–380–78458–0

First Avon Books Printing: November 1997

AVON TRADEMARK REG. U.S. PAT. OFF. AND IN OTHER COUNTRIES, MARCA REGISTRADA, HECHO EN U.S.A.

Printed in the U.S.A.

WCD   10 9 8 7 6 5 4 3 2 1

For Kevin and Allison,
my best works.

She took a servant when she took a lord,
a lord in marriage, a servant in love.

—Chaucer

A Prince Among Men

Prologue

~~~⌒⌒~~~

1796

With Napoleon's defeat of the Piedmontese and Austrians, King Lorenzo di Piovasco Mirandola of Trevigna thought it prudent to assess the strength of his tiny kingdom. What he saw sobered him. Everywhere the arts of war had been neglected. Peace, which Lorenzo had striven to preserve, had made the nobles prodigal and the bandits voracious, and divided the cities into factions. His mild rule appeared a failure, but he wasted no time in self-reproach. Though the power of France might crush Trevigna as easily as the press crushed the olive harvest, he boldly began a campaign to restore the vigor of Trevigna's institutions. He made only one concession to prudence, which was to send his ten-year-old son and heir to England to be educated in safety, far from the reach of Bonaparte.

Alexander and Lucca were to be punished. All the boys said so, but the arrival of Donna Francesca made their punishment a certainty. They sat on a hard bench in the dim cloister opposite a gothic door. The heavy door, darkened with age and crossed with antique iron bands, suggested the entrance to a castle dungeon rather than the office of the headmaster of a modern English school for young men of birth and fortune. Yet if their classmates were to be believed, behind that door lay indignities worthy of the Inquisition.

The October morning was frosty, and the fresh scrubbed faces of the two boys smarted. Their collars, damp from contact with still-wet slicked-down hair, sent involuntary shivers down their spines.

The taller of the two boys, a lad with huge dark eyes and the nose of a Roman senator, betrayed a certain miserable anxiety by scuffing the toes of his shoes across the stone floor, until his companion spoke.

"Hush, Lucca, I can't hear a word if you scrape the floor that way."

Lucca immediately stilled, giving a heavy sigh, his breath a fleecy puff in the frigid air.

The shorter of the two boys, Alexander, whose fair looks suggested Eros outgrowing babyhood, leaned forward on the bench, listening intently, his cherub's mouth pursed, his remarkable blue eyes fixed on the door. Though the heavy door muted the voices on the other side, Alexander recognized the value of this rare opportunity to hear what the adults were saying. He realized now, as he had not a few months earlier, that these solemn conversations affected his future directly.

At the moment, he could think of two punishments he most wished to avoid—being sent away from school, and being separated from Lucca. A flogging was nothing. He'd had one or two already and discovered he could bear them very well if he concentrated on some future pleasure, like the promise of a good horse to ride at Christmas.

He inched forward on the bench. While he judged it wise to listen closely, it was beneath his dignity to cross the corridor and press his ear to the door. There were four voices on the other side, all fairly easy to distinguish. The first was the headmaster's, with a smooth, placating cadence to it that he never used when addressing the boys. The second voice, Aunt Francesca's, embarrassingly loud and shrill, could be heard clearly. The other two were Mr. Keane's and Mr. Nevil's.

"Have you dared to lay hands upon the Prince of Trevigna?" Aunt Francesca asked.

"Regrettably, we are facing that step," the headmaster answered. "Unless his majesty can be prevailed upon, perhaps through your influence, to moderate his behavior. Here the masters must govern. The nature of boys, royal birth not withstanding, is such that we must be permitted to apply the necessary discipline for unruly behavior."

"To lay hands on a prince who will one day rule a kingdom older than England is an unpardonable offense."

Alexander could see Aunt Francesca saying this. She was as tall as the mast of his first boat, and she could give a fellow the *malocchio*, the evil eye.

"I regret to inform you, Donna Francesca, that his majesty has had some difficulty adjusting to the rules of school life."

"The Prince of Trevigna does not misbehave."

"Mr. Keane," said the headmaster. "Your report."

A high, thin voice spoke. "I'm sorry to say, madame, but his majesty made faces at the food and comments in Italian for the benefit of his servant. There was no mistaking his disparagement of our very healthful and substantial fare. Furthermore, his remarks precipitated an unseemly display among the third formers. Throwing peas."

Alexander heard Aunt Francesca snort, like a horse smelling bad hay.

"Mr. Nevil, your report," said the headmaster.

Mr. Nevil's booming voice made Lucca start and look up. Alexander put his finger to his lips. "In the classroom his majesty looks down his . . . grand nose at his masters. In the midst of the Greek lesson, he rent his gown in a fit of temper over a correction, an absolute breach of necessary authority."

There was a silence behind the door, and Alexander guessed Aunt Francesca was unimpressed.

The headmaster's voice came again. "These acts of rebellion might have been overlooked, had his majesty not engaged in a brawl with his classmates."

"A brawl?" Aunt Francesca's voice was slow and gathering power like a wave about to pound the shore. "The Prince of Trevigna does not brawl like some wharf rat. He is a sweet-tempered, biddable young man, conscious of his duty to his station."

"Madame, are we speaking of the same child? Perhaps his new surroundings have brought out hitherto hidden aspects of his character."

"Impossible."

"I assure you, Donna Francesca, that his majesty has bloodied the noses and blackened the eyes of several boys, and even threatened the servants. With his size and strength, he could seriously injure someone."

"His size and strength?" Aunt Francesca's tone had changed to one of surprised suspicion. Alexander's grip on the edge of the bench tightened.

"Madame, he is a full head above his classmates."

Aunt Francesca spoke briefly and pungently in Italian. Lucca's eyes widened appreciatively as she called the headmaster an ass with shoes and a coat.

"Are you blockheads not able to see the difference between a prince and a serving boy?"

By straining, Alexander could hear the faint reply.

"Madame must explain."

"You idiots have mistaken Lucca Gavinana, the son of a sailmaker from Laruggia for Alexander di Piovasco Mirandola, a prince with a six-hundred-year-old name."

Alexander could not help the slight slump in his shoulders. Aunt Francesca's announcement put an end to his disguise. It had been a lark while it had lasted, his time as an ordinary boy. He tried to picture the faces of his masters. He knew Mr. Nevil must be looking particularly green, as he was the one who had flogged Alexander for the episode in the Greek class.

"An understandable confusion." The smooth voice of the headmaster came again. "Master Lucca is the taller of the two and of a proud demeanor. It was he, of course, who seemed to have more difficulty adjusting to the discipline of school life, so naturally we assumed—"

"Surely you noted the difference in their work, their English."

Mr. Keane entered the conversation again. "If madame will examine the two copy books, she will see that both boys perform extraordinarily well."

There was a little pause during which Alexander held his breath.

Then Aunt Francesca's voice came again, distinctly. "I recommend that you gentlemen examine the books carefully yourselves. Any fool can see that they are written by the same hand, Alexander's hand."

There was a silence of an awkward duration.

"Are you in the habit of mistaking fireflies for lanterns? You cannot tell the difference between a serving boy and a prince of the blood?"

"With all due respect, madame, it is your brother's opinion we must consider. He has entrusted the boy to us. Now that we know the true prince, we require only that you remove Master Gavinana, and we will proceed with our business, which we know very well, instructing the minds of the future leaders of society."

"Remove Gavinana?"

"If he is not to be a pupil, he may not remain. We practice equality. The only deference here is due not to rank, but to learning. All our students are scholars under the guidance of masters. To have a boy among the others with a personal attendant is against the principles of the school."

"But the prince must have Gavinana. He must speak his language daily, the tongue of Petrarch, Boccaccio, Dante. And he must govern at least one subject to remind him that he is a prince and will one day be king."

"Madame, these are our rules. If your brother is not satisfied with this form of education for the prince, he is free to take the boy elsewhere."

Alexander stiffened, instantly alert, drawing Lucca's glance. The discussion from behind the door was beyond Lucca's minimal comprehension of English. He knew only that they had caused trouble for the adults of the school. Lucca, Alexander thought, was lucky not to be aware of this most dreadful possibility.

Alexander prayed his aunt would not let her pride speak. He did not know which he feared more, being separated from Lucca, or being cast out of the school. He held his breath. It would be like her, to turn on her heel and tell these paltry Englishmen that the Mirandola did not need their school.

The silence this time was awful, and when it ended, Alexander was sweating.

Then Francesca spoke in her more feminine voice. "Well, gentlemen, you must keep Master Gavinana enrolled. You have no objection to two purses from my brother, I trust?"

Alexander grinned at his friend. Thus, unfortunately, both boys were smiling broadly when the heavy door swung open and Aunt Francesca's tall form appeared. Her stern eye fell first on Lucca, with the swift intensity of an eagle's swoop. Lucca froze.

"You impudent, ungrateful dolt," she said in blistering Italian. "Nothing is worse than a foolish servant. Your pride has brought this embarrassment to the prince. It is your duty, your privilege, to serve him in all things. You will be respectful to the masters and students, take any punishment intended for the prince, and study until your brains turn to mush in your thick noggin."

Francesca turned to Alexander. He was shaking with relief, but he kept everything inside. "And you, sir, do not deceive me. You speak English perfectly well, and yet you did not correct the misapprehension of your masters."

Alexander refused to hang his head. He was guilty, and he must take whatever punishment Aunt Francesca meted out.

"Never forget," she went on, "your station or your dignity. Your father depends on you. He sends this book to remind you." She thrust a small leather volume at him. "You are Mirandola, the shepherd of the people, bred to rule, to put Trevigna ahead of all else, to serve her in every action of your life. The petty concerns of schoolboys are not for you. When Trevigna calls, you go, consenting, even to death. Remember."

She made him a curt bow, as a man would, and strode off down the hall, the stone echoing with her sharp footsteps. There was no embrace, no touch.

Alexander stood stock still, clutching the book from his father, not daring to look at Lucca until she was truly gone.

At the other end of the hall, she paused, glancing back over her shoulder. "If your marks are high enough, Alexander, there will be a horse to ride at Christmas," she said in English.

The door at the end of the hall closed behind her, and Alexander grinned. Whatever the masters did to them, he had it all now—school, and his friend, and the promise of a horse.

1816

"I can't do it," whispered Lucca.

Alexander did not look up from the papers on the desk. "You must."

"Majesty, it is your best evening coat, wool as fine and soft as silk, the cut a work of Michelangelo." Lucca's voice was pleading.

Alexander pushed back from the desk and looked up at his servant. "We have no money," he said patiently.

Lucca shrugged. "The English king does not pay his bills. Why should we? I will send the man away."

"Lucca," Alexander said. "We agreed to sell the coats a fortnight ago. I had your promise at that time."

"But that was before anyone came to buy them." Lucca wrinkled his nose. "*Madre della Virgine*, the man has no shoulders!"

Alexander turned back to the letter he was writing. "Then the coat will improve his appearance."

He managed a few more lines before he realized Lucca remained standing in the doorway.

"To sell your coats in a common shop!" Lucca shook his head. "It is beneath you."

"We've slept in barns and fields, and worn the boots of dead men."

"In war. In London you must preserve the dignity of your state."

Alexander put down his pen, the point he was trying to make in the letter had escaped. "Unpack the royal plate, then."

"Majesty, could we not remove to a hotel?"

"No." Alexander rolled the cuffs of his sleeves over his wrists and fastened them properly. "The plan depends on secrecy." He stood and lifted the coat off the back of his chair. "If the foreign secretary finds me before I refill the treasury of Trevigna, I'm powerless." If he let them, the English would put him in a toy soldier's uniform and prop him on a dying throne, so that the royal navy would have a handy port from which to fight the Turks.

Lucca hung his head. "All this I know, but what will Donna Francesca say? What will she do?"

Alexander's glance sharpened. "You haven't told her where we are?"

Lucca's great dark eyes had a wounded look. "I had to tell her you were hiding. How could I lie and say we were still at Windsor? She already knew you'd sold the horses. Like Christopher

Columbus, she discovers everything," he concluded bitterly.

Alexander donned his coat. "You've heard from her, then?"

"She is going to find you a wife."

"A wife?" Alexander felt himself go very still. "Why?"

"So that when you are crowned, you will have the nobles' support."

Alexander stared at the papers on the desk, letters inviting free men of Trevigna to give up being subjects, to regard themselves as citizens, to come together to draft a constitution for a new republic.

"Majesty?"

"Sell the black coat. Charge the man a king's ransom, if he'll pay it, but sell. You do want to eat, don't you?"

"Yes, Majesty." Lucca bowed, and retreated.

Alexander gripped the back of the chair, the papers a white blur on the desk. Bonaparte moved armies and changed the face of Europe. Alexander wrote letters to make one nation free and just.

He snatched a blank sheet, scrawled a message on it, and slipped out the door.

Chapter 1

❮❮❯℃❯

For a moment as it rose, a dazzling morning sun gilded the rain-dampened rooftops of London. Lady Ophelia Brinsby slowed her steps to watch, and the shining deception vanished, leaving a vista of cold, gray slate and sooty chimney pots. With a shrug, Ophelia lengthened her stride, swinging her riding crop.

Two horses, her black mare, Shadow, and her brother Jasper's new chestnut stallion, Raj, stood saddled in the stableyard. Ophelia halted. The stallion was a beauty, but no one had saddled him in a week. Her groom, William, wouldn't dare. Raj had kicked a stall to pieces and proved once again that Jasper was no judge of horseflesh. This morning Raj, the terror of the stableboys, nosed the ground for bits of hay, his tail flicking lazily as if he were the tamest gelding.

Ophelia drew closer and peered under Shadow's black belly at a pair of buckskin-clad legs and handsome boots. Someone was inspecting the mare's right front foot, murmuring soft, indistinguishable phrases.

"William?" she asked.

The voice stopped. Shadow swung her head around to give Ophelia a belated whicker of greeting, and a man stepped into view. He was not William. He was nothing so ordinary and discreet as a groom waiting to accompany a lady on a Monday morning ride in the park. Ophelia could not check the upward sweep of her gaze from his boots to the curly-brimmed hat set on golden-brown curls.

The man looked back, his bold gaze a blue flash, in which surprise vanished into amusement without a trace of humility. Ophelia had the strangest impression of authority, perhaps in the way he held the two horses with a careless touch on the reins, as if he owned them.

The moment stretched. A helpless, awkward, loose-limbed sensation, like being tossed from a horse, washed over her and left her clinging to her riding crop.

Her cheeks heated. Nothing was more tedious than a handsome man, puffed up with conceit, expecting everyone's admiration.

"I'm not a toad." A wry smile lifted the corners of his mouth and gave a sharper gleam of intelligence to his eyes. She tried to identify their unusual color, but nothing familiar, not the sea or sky or thrush eggs, had the intensity of that blue.

She broke the exchange of glances, taking a deep breath. Across the yard three men were polishing her father's black chaise, its ducal coronet gleaming a dull gold in the early sun. Only the stranger was out of place in the ordinary morning routine of the stable.

"M'lady, yer 'orse is ready."

Her gaze snapped back to him at the accent, different from his first words, at odds somehow with his appearance. Shadow nudged his hand, seeking attention.

"Who are you?" Ophelia demanded.

"Yer new groom, m'lady."

More likely the man in the moon. The blue eyes were full of amusement and curiosity, which ought not to be there in a proper servant. Besides the man made a fashion statement her brothers would envy, with his well-cut coat, brown silk waistcoat, and gleaming boots. "Does your tailor know you've taken the position?"

The bold blue gaze shifted away, concealing some truth, and Ophelia's brain began to work again. "Where's William?"

"Sacked, m'—"

" 'Miss' will do, thank you," she told him coolly.

"Yes. *Miss.*"

She spun away, controlling an impulse to administer a blistering setdown. All her arrangements, the fruit of weeks of cajoling her former groom, undone. She made herself walk calmly across the yard toward Clagg, the head coachman.

As Clagg explained her father's orders, she tapped her riding crop against her skirts. The gist of his long-winded speech was that she was not to leave the park.

"His Grace's orders, miss." Clagg offered to accompany her himself if she preferred.

She shook her head, smiling to reassure Clagg that she was ever His Grace's dutiful daughter.

Ophelia had learned that the key to any deception was to look as ordinary as possible while doing the unthinkable. And now that she knew the trick, she meant to enjoy as much freedom as she could within the confines of society. One season of polite simpering and dutiful attendance at vapid affairs had convinced her that London's elite had little to offer a woman of sense. Across the park on the other side of London was the superior society Ophelia meant to enjoy. And no mere groom would stop her.

She made her way back across the stableyard, taking time to observe her new keeper from under lowered lashes. He was taller than most grooms, not short and wiry, but lithe and broad-shouldered, with the sort of build her mother preferred in a footman. But he lacked the vacuous look most footmen wore.

William had been plain, greedy, and not particularly clever. With his readily obtained aid she'd contrived to circumvent her father's rules. Those efforts were now wasted. She would have to start over with the new man, and he looked far too intelligent to manage easily.

Still, he'd chosen the showy chestnut stallion instead of one of her father's well-behaved geldings, so he must think highly of himself. Vanity was always a good starting place when one wanted to manage a man, and handsome men seemed to possess more than their share of that universal male failing.

At the mounting block she had to look up to meet the new man's eye. Her patience abruptly deserted her. To spend another fortnight or two flattering a man in exchange for a small measure of independence galled her. She decided on a direct attack.

"I don't need a keeper."

The words obviously jolted him. There was a quick flash in the blue eyes and a stiffening of his shoulders. "The 'orses need a run," he said, his humble accent at odds with his proud bearing.

She gave him a measuring look. "A run? Or a tame trot in the park?"

"The park is all I 'ave t' offer, miss."

She tapped her crop against her boot tip. "I don't suppose you'd consider a bribe?"

He nearly choked. "Not on the first day in a new position."

She gave him a sidelong glance. The accent had dropped away, but his gaze didn't waver. She shrugged, and he turned and brought her mount.

She made a fuss over Shadow, petting the mare and cooing endearments in her most treacly voice.

He regarded her with narrowed, untrusting eyes.

She smiled sweetly. If he thought she was a docile nitwit, she stood a chance of escaping. If he stuck to her father's orders, she'd be little more than a dog on a leash.

She went back to thinking of ways to use his obvious vanity against him, and a strategy came to her as they neared the square. The stallion was likely to balk at the first sign of city traffic, and it was the easiest trick in the world to make it look as if Shadow had run away with her rider. While the new man worked to control Raj, she and Shadow would escape. Her cheeky new groom could then go home and confess that he'd lost his charge or search for her in the park. Either way, he would discover he could not control her, and she'd be free.

When the bare plane trees of the square came into view, she twisted her left hand in Shadow's mane. Only Shadow's pricked ears showed that the mare felt the signal. From the street to their left a coal cart rumbled into view.

Ophelia waited, listening for Raj's first snort of alarm. When it came, a high-pitched squeal, she pressed her knees to Shadow's flanks and leaned forward. Shadow leapt into a canter headed straight for the coal cart and the narrow street beyond. Ophelia brought her crop down on Shadow's hindquarters. The mare spurted forward, bearing down on the cart. Then came the pause, the gather, and the soaring jump, just like a double oxer on a cross country run.

Shadow landed hard on her off foot, regained her balance and flew on. It was so easy that Ophelia could not resist glancing over her shoulder. Before her startled gaze, her new groom turned Raj in a quick double and sent him streaking after them. Ophelia leaned forward, urging Shadow on, reckless now, sending vendors scrambling out of their way.

A wide boulevard lay ahead, but hooves pounded just behind her. Shadow seemed to sense the stallion and slowed, matching her pace to his, tossing her head. Ophelia's groom leaned forward, snagged Shadow's bridle, and brought the impromptu race to an end. Ophelia gasped at the effrontery.

The horses blew and danced as they came to a halt, jostling each other, wheeling, hooves ringing sharply against the cobbles. The movement brought Ophelia's knee into glancing contact with the stranger's thigh, lean and muscled, controlling the stallion with easy power. A surprising rush of warmth flooded her body, and her gaze met his equally startled one. He'd lost his hat, and the morning sun lit the gold in his hair.

"Yer may not want m' company, miss, but yer 'orse deserves better from yew," he said.

"No one has stopped a horse under me since I was six."

He released Shadow's bridle. "Time, then. The 'orse could 'ave been killed with such a stunt."

There was definitely something unservant-like about him. He should be jumping to do her bidding, not correcting her on points of horsemanship. Under her resentment was the thought that he'd certainly been equal to Raj and he had worked some magic on Shadow, as well.

"Shadow ran away with me."

A short, sharp syllable of derision escaped him. He leaned forward, his eyes fierce. "Ye set 'er at that cart as cool as ice."

Her cheeks felt on fire. He'd spotted her trick. How? Her signal to Shadow had been subtle and quick, and besides, he'd had Raj demanding his attention.

"How did you get Raj to move like that? It took five men to get him in his stall."

He shrugged. "I've been well trained, miss."

"Where?"

He looked away, an instant concealment. She

was too familiar with evasions not to recognize it.

"'ere and there," he said.

"What's your name?"

Evidently, his excellent training didn't include courtesy to a mistress. He stroked Raj's neck, and Ophelia's gaze followed the soothing motion of his gloved hand, an odd tension building in her as she waited for his reply. "Alexander, miss."

"Like Alexander the Great?"

A quick affronted look passed over his face. "Just Alexander."

She would have to try a new tactic. Her father always advised his children, "Treat servants distantly, but generously, and they'll do anything for you." Her mother's theory was that servants were replaceable, interchangeable parts in the machinery of the household, the footmen always called "James," the cook, "Sophie," the housekeeper, "Mrs. Watkins." Sebastian, her nearsighted oldest brother, never even saw the servants. Only Ophelia and Jasper saw people. Winning them over was a necessary part of life if one wanted to enjoy any freedom at all. In Ophelia's experience, bribes and flattery worked best.

"What you did with Raj was not mere training. You have a talent for understanding horses."

He veiled his gaze. "Earns me a situation is all, miss."

"You could look higher than your present situation. At one of the hunts your talents would be in demand."

"Tried 'igher, miss. This suits me." There was something like irony in his expression.

"Then you're more fortunate than I." The words drew a quick, penetrating glance from him, and Ophelia turned Shadow toward the park again. Ophelia kept the restive mare to a walk, trying to think how to regain control of the situation. Alexander saw through her, and flattery wasn't working.

At the park gate, she stole a glance at him. He rode a proper length and a half behind her, just as if he truly were her humble groom, but he was too handsome not to be vain. Most of the men she knew, whatever their rank, swelled visibly at a few compliments. Invited to describe their own cleverness, and a little pause was invitation enough for most, they were apt to give orations, run for Parliament, write their memoirs. William had always been ready to tell her how he'd bested some fellow groom in a game of cards or a wager.

She glanced at Alexander again. He was dressed in brown. His hair was brown, but the word was inadequate. *Brown* was a fine term for potatoes or dust or dead leaves, but the gold in his hair seemed to draw the morning light.

There were few other riders about. No one to report the lapse to her mother if she rode side by side with her groom. She made Shadow fall back. Alexander tensed visibly. She offered him her treacly smile.

A few paces further she gave Shadow a hint, and the mare pranced restlessly. Alexander noticed at once, his blue glance questioning. Ophelia halted her mare.

"Shadow's cinch is bothering her, Alexander. Would you see to it, please?"

Plainly, he did not believe her, but he dismounted and secured the horses' reins to the iron railing separating the path from the dry, dead grass. He looked up at Ophelia, a challenge in his odd blue eyes. A random phrase came into her head from a book of travels she'd once read about the Mediterranean, where hot blue seas lapped fabled isles.

He didn't like taking orders from her. Fine. She didn't like her father's putting her in the charge of a stranger as if she weren't a rational woman capable of governing herself. She freed her foot from the side-saddle's stirrup as he reached up to help her down. Every day she gave her hand to footmen, ascending and descending from carriages, but she hesitated, recalling the hot shock when her knee had brushed his thigh a few minutes earlier.

He saw it, of course, and his full, finely drawn mouth, which she really hadn't noticed before, curved up in a slight smile.

She gritted her teeth, planted her hands on his shoulders and slid into his grip. His hands closed around her waist. She had a sensation of truly falling, her blood rushing.

In a blink she was standing on firm ground in possession of about half her wits, with a furious fluttering in her breast like the beating of a trapped moth's wings. He was taller than she'd thought. She was at eye level with the careless knot of his cravat, and when he swallowed, the bob of his Adam's apple evoked an answering bob low in her stomach. His hands tightened once at her waist, then fell away.

He turned to Shadow, biting the tip of one tan

glove, pulling it free with his teeth, and running his bare hand over the mare's flank. Gently but firmly he tested the cinch and the balance of the saddle. Ophelia could not look away from the hand sliding over the mare's sides.

"It's fine now, miss," he said, his attention apparently absorbed by the task of putting on his glove.

"Thank you," she said, surprising both herself and him.

She stepped up to remount, and he seemed deliberately obtuse about her intention. She raised her brows, and belatedly he linked his hands, but when she placed her foot in them, he froze, seeming paralyzed. Then, with a phrase under his breath, he tossed her up and turned away.

She was grateful for Shadow's steadiness. Alexander's grip on her foot sent some sensation sizzling through her, and in the aftermath her arms and legs were limp like the padded limbs of china dolls. She recognized the mortifying symptoms of her susceptibility to a handsome face. She should get as far from him as she could and insist that her father find her a groom more to her liking, one who was as plain as porridge.

But if she quit, he won, and there was no hope of escape. She allowed Shadow to walk half the length of the park before she said she thought it was not the cinch after all, but perhaps the stirrup.

He halted Raj.

"Beg pardon, miss, but yer the picture of comfort in the saddle."

"Nevertheless, I would like you to check the stirrup." She lifted her foot and pulled aside the heavy blue skirts of her habit. He dismounted and approached her side, stopping with his nose not six inches from her thigh. She had the strangest sensation of heat where his gaze met her person.

Taking a deep breath, as if he were making a great effort, he lowered the stirrup below her reach. She shook her head and removed her glove to point. He raised the stirrup so she could rest her chin on her knee. Her mouth twitched, but she merely asked him to try again. He returned the stirrup to its original position. She opened her mouth to suggest another change, but a quick, sharp glance made her say she thought the adjustment perfect.

She had initiated this game, and he dared to play. She could not reproach him for it without acknowledging her tactics.

When he was back on Raj, she allowed them to go at least a dozen yards before she dropped her glove. He swung down, hanging from the saddle, and scooped it up without dismounting.

Ophelia simply stared. Had the man come from Astley's Circus? She stretched out her bare hand to receive the glove, conscious of his gaze on her hand, as if he meant to memorize it. Perhaps she was taking this thing too far. He was nothing like William or any other servant she'd had.

"Thank you," she said.

They started again, Shadow lifting her head, eager for a run. Ophelia patted her mare's neck, in apology for keeping them from their usual gallop, but she didn't mean to give in. They reached the banks of the Serpentine.

"I'd like to have a look at the water, if you don't mind, Alexander."

"The 'orses would like a run, miss," he said through clenched teeth.

"Do you think the horses should be consulted? An odd view for a groom to take."

"A 'orse should do what 'is master tells 'im to."

"And a servant? Should he do what his mistress commands?"

"Foolish commands do no credit to either. Miss."

Ophelia studied him. There it was again, the too precise speech of his other voice. "You don't speak like a servant."

The blue gaze slid away from hers. "My father was an educated man."

"Then you needn't put on an accent for me." She didn't mean to sound irked.

"Yes, miss." The blue eyes were amused.

"You think me quite spoiled, don't you?"

"I heard you were good to your horse," he said, dropping the accent so completely, she blinked.

"I am."

His stare challenged her.

"Only . . ." She smiled. "When my groom is a proper servant." She didn't wait for his assistance but slid from the saddle and strode down to the water's edge.

Once the girl strode off, Alexander could think. He had misinterpreted what little talk there'd been in the stable about the duke's daughter. Clagg had told him his duty was to accompany the young lady and keep their ride to the park. He remembered Clagg's words. "She has a good seat and never abuses her animal." He had added, with a shrug, "She's spoiled some." It was Alexander, who'd interpreted these remarks to mean he would be escorting a rebellious hoyden of twelve or thirteen. Her habit of riding at sunrise had also suggested a young person, not a lady of fashion who could go from the opera to a ball to a midnight supper in an evening.

The truth was something else. The girl was probably twenty, and though she wasn't a beauty in the common way, the size and brilliance of her dark eyes had already interfered with the measured beat of his pulse.

He hadn't fooled her, exactly. Her eyes were shrewd and clever rather than sweet, and she'd seen through his accent quick enough. He figured she didn't have enough information to unmask him. And she'd been preoccupied with trying to shake his company. Her grip on the riding crop was firm, and he suspected she had little experience in having her will crossed. He didn't know where his own boldness had come from, but challenging her had seemed instinctive.

She stood at the water's edge, looking down, idly stirring the reeds with her riding crop. Her riding habit was the blue of deep ocean when you were nowhere near home. The jacket nipped in at the waist and buttoned up to the lace at her chin, and the slimness of that waist made her vulnerable somehow, in spite of her haughty manner. But he shouldn't be thinking that. He was the lady's groom and he wasn't going to get himself sacked, as his predecessor had been.

The job had given him the perfect hiding place. A week before, he'd been running like a fox from his particular hounds and found this stable a handy covert. He wouldn't be flushed out of it because the duke's daughter was confined to the park.

Of all the pleasures of his former life, he'd missed horses most in the weeks he'd spent at his desk in the room above the tailor's shop. Then, when his plans seemed to come to nothing and his choices disappeared, he'd wandered the long rows of stables behind the great houses of the West End. There he'd come across Raj, blindfolded and held down by four grooms, idiots with neither sense nor kindness. Enraged at the indignity of the stallion's treatment, Alexander had interfered. His success with Raj earned him a job offer on the spot, and in a moment of madness he'd taken it.

Since then, he'd been talking to the stallion, stroking him, teaching the skittish horse the sound of his voice and feel of his hand. Raj didn't like the city, and he didn't like the clatter of wheels, the surprise of traffic coming from every direction at once. It was plain that the tendermouthed, high-strung stallion had been abused.

Raj he understood; the girl was a puzzle. Spoiled, yes, but something more. When she'd not been looking, he'd caught a glimpse of a face bleak with disappointment. It was not the look of a spoiled child denied her way. He stole another glance at her.

Ophelia welcomed the coolness of the morning mist against her heated face. Her pulse drummed in her ears. She hardly understood herself this morning. It was true that patience was not her strongest suit, but she'd lost control of a perfectly simple situation. Alexander had made her incautious and had muddled her mind so that she'd hardly been able to come up with a single strategy for getting free. She gazed across the water through the trees. In the distance, riders cantered along the Row; and further south, carriages moved along the Kensington Road, where she'd be if William were still her groom.

Just a few miles beyond the park, her friend Hetty would be sitting down to good coffee and hot biscuits. In Hetty's morning room, Ophelia had a remarkable degree of freedom. Society expected one to choose friends for their titles or wealth or fashionableness. Society expected one to keep a mask in place everywhere, a brittle, polished shell of indifference, but at Hetty's, Ophelia could laugh or frown or say what she pleased.

Eventually, her senses calmed and she could hear the bird calls from the reeds. She could prolong her ride perhaps an hour more, but when it was over, she'd be stuck at home for the day, where she could predict the remarks of every one of her mother's callers. Where all the talk would be of slights and miseries, hem lengths and trim, scandals and suitors. Where ideas were like boxes instead of like doors.

Ophelia looked up to find her new groom watching her. He stood by the horses, keeping them company, his shoulder against the stallion's. She wondered if all his sympathies were reserved for horses or whether she could just tell him how she depended on Hetty. Would he listen and say, "Of course, miss, no harm in that, let's go"? She dismissed the fantasy. Servants were often as snobby as their employers. Most would not want a duke's daughter to have friends among tradesmen.

She trudged up the slope to the horses. Somehow she had to get the man on her side. "Shall we ride?"

He linked his hands to toss her up. She willed herself to think of him as a ladder, a mounting block, a convenience, but the peculiar melting sensations took hold as soon as her foot touched his hands. She smelled a spicy scent, felt the strength of his arms, and landed slightly breathless in the saddle. She hauled Shadow around and concentrated on working the horse through her paces.

Neither spoke again until they turned toward home.

"Feeling better, miss?" he asked.

"A gallop in the park is not freedom for horse or rider."

"But there is freedom somewhere beyond the park?"

She wouldn't meet that perceptive gaze. She expected Raj to balk or shy at the increase in traffic as London woke up and went about its business, but Alexander kept the stallion moving steadily toward the stable.

Ophelia studied him surreptitiously to see if she could detect the secret of his success with the horse. All that she could see was that he was very sure of himself. And he thought he'd won in their encounter.

With his flashing eyes and proud assurance, Alexander had upset one of the fundamental certainties of life. Servants served—instantly, impassively, unobtrusively. They bowed and scraped and kept their opinions to themselves. They could be managed.

In the yard she dismounted without his assistance, tossed him Shadow's reins, and went in search of Clagg, cornering him as he prepared to mount the box of the ducal chaise and drawing him across the yard.

Alexander was rubbing the horses down with brisk efficiency.

"I want Shadow exercised thoroughly," she said. "And groomed. No half measures. Her coat needs the dandy brush. I'd like her mane thinned, her hooves cleaned, and her fetlocks trimmed. And here . . ." She went on giving orders about tack, grooming, and feeding. She took Clagg to inspect the mare's stall and kicked aside the obviously sweet, fresh bedding. "I want this stall cleaned down to the dirt. It's too damp."

Clagg gave Alexander a swift questioning look, but said only, "Best get to it, lad."

Ophelia waited 'til the coachman was out of earshot. She wanted to hear Alexander grumble, or at least see him glare at her, but he merely moved steadily from task to task, watering, brushing, offering grain and hay.

"Perhaps you're not suited to be a lady's groom, Alexander."

"If you mean I understand horses better than ladies, miss, you're right."

Chapter 2

The two things Ophelia most disliked about her mother's gold drawing room were the gilt friezes and the dog. Pet, her mother's brown and white Welsh corgi, lay pressed against Lady Searle on a yellow brocade sofa and appeared in three larger-than-life portraits of the duchess on the silk-hung walls. The dog pricked his ears at Ophelia, regarding her with the malice of a long-time enemy. Ophelia murmured the appropriate excuses for her tardy appearance and kissed her mother's cheek lightly, ignoring Pet's raised hackles.

"Walking sausage," she mouthed at the animal.

Lady Searle's usual coterie of late-morning visitors had gathered—Lady Pomfret and her daughter Anne, Lady Clermont, two gentlemen who purported to be Ophelia's suitors, and Lady Searle's sister and nieces. Besides these few, Lady Searle's drawing room generally attracted people who wanted something from the duchess. As Ophelia moved to join Anne Pomfret, whom she actually liked, her cousins Cecile and Emily intercepted her.

"Ophelia, did you hear that your beau deserted you?" Cecile asked.

"I have no beau," Ophelia answered carefully.

"She means the gentleman who was so interested in you last season," Emily whispered, as if Ophelia had forgotten who her suitors were.

Cecile leaned forward conspiratorily. "George Wyatt's pursuing a carpet heiress from Finsbury Square."

Ophelia had to be grateful that her cousins were as tall as they were tactless. They blocked her from the others' view, so there was no one to observe the instant of her unsteadiness and recovery, the first of the new season. Last spring Wyatt had trifled with her, and the more malicious of London's gossips would no doubt watch her reaction to each mention of his name.

"I wish her well." Ophelia fixed her smile and took a step toward the tea table.

"You do?" asked Emily with a puzzled thrust of her chin.

Ophelia nodded. "Tea?"

"I suppose you'll keep Lord Dent to yourself, then," Cecile said, trailing after Ophelia.

"Plain, stupid men are the best sort." Ophelia held her cup to a footman who poured for her.

"She doesn't mean it, does she, Cici?" whispered Emily.

Cecile rolled her eyes. "*Of course* she doesn't mean it." She turned back to Ophelia. "You don't need a rich beau, so you should leave Dent to one of us."

"You're welcome to him, I'm sure," said Ophelia.

Cecile wrinkled her brow.

"Really. I make no claim on him." Ophelia stirred the milk in her tea.

Cecile looked suspicious. "Then you won't mind if Emmy tries to fix his attention this season?"

"Not at all." Ophelia smiled at Anne Pomfret across the room. Anne's mother tended to take over her daughter's conversation, but sometimes Anne and Ophelia managed a good talk.

Not this morning. Before she could escape to Anne, Ophelia was intercepted by Robert Haddington. His favorite topic was his carriage, and to stem the flow of details about the suspension and balance, she agreed to go driving with him on Thursday.

An hour later the others had gone and Aunt Augustine was chronicling her miseries in detail, implying that suffering such as hers could be relieved only by whatever favor she had come to beg. Cecile enlivened the conversation by picking at the trim of her bodice, while Emily smiled fixedly, her lips lightly parted, as if by opening her mouth she might better take in what was being said.

Ophelia sat at the end of the sofa occupied by Lady Searle and Pet. While her aunt spoke, Ophelia entertained visions of her new groom laboring over his tasks. Not that anything she had commanded him to do was that arduous, but the number of interruptions in a busy stable would keep him running from chore to chore. Each time someone in the household called for a carriage,

Alexander would have to stop the extra work she'd given him to help roll the vehicle in or out of its house, or to open the gates. Very likely he would think twice about opposing her will again.

She smiled to herself and received a glare from Aunt Augustine.

Inevitably as Augustine's miseries came to light Ophelia regretted the friezes and the portraits. She had long since memorized the static pattern of golden gryphons with their raised paws holding her father's coronet. And not even Reynolds' art could render Pet appealing.

Lady Searle and her sister had once been considered a matched set, with golden red curls and hazel eyes, but married life had pared the duchess to the bone and puffed Augustine like a meringue. At forty-five she clung to youthful curls and styles, so that as her indignation grew, her red curls trembled and her generous bosom quivered.

"What else are servants paid for, if not to come when the bell rings?" Augustine asked.

"You've not lost your housekeeper again, Augustine?" Lady Searle scratched Pet's ears.

"Lost! If it were only that. I think she's taken some of the silver, and I have such a large dinner party planned. I don't know what I'll do." Augustine's not-so-secret wish was to outdo her sister as a hostess.

Her hint for assistance so moved Lady Searle that she offered Pet a bit of scone. "Use a reliable agency and you won't be reduced to counting the plates when your servants leave."

Augustine, who was leaning forward, sat up sharply. A look of annoyance flashed in her eyes and was suppressed with scarcely a shake of her curls. "They're all alike. I'm sure I've had house-keepers from every reputable agency, even from Dalworthy."

"Never from Dalworthy, Augustine. You wouldn't be in these circumstances again if you had."

Ophelia wondered where Clagg had found Alexander—not from a reputable agency, surely. Her aunt's account of the sly housekeeper prompted an alternate vision of Alexander. Perhaps he wouldn't move dutifully from chore to chore. Perhaps he would simply shove his hands in his pockets and seek a position elsewhere. His talent with horses could win him a situation anywhere.

Ophelia straightened. The thought of his walking away from their conflict was somehow unsatisfying.

Augustine's bosom quivered. "It's that dreadful annuity for Edgar's mother that limits us so. She'll live to be a hundred, I'm sure, before we ever see a farthing of the Payne money. If I weren't capable of economies, who knows what deprivations the girls would endure?"

"The girls look well enough." Lady Searle did not confirm this opinion by so much as a glance.

Aunt Augustine straightened and looked pointedly at Ophelia. "In fashion and air, I daresay, they're the equal of any girl in society."

Lady Searle's head came up. "Not in that particular shade of pink for Cecile. She looks quite like a confectioner's box. She would do better in . . . russet or bronze."

They all looked at Cecile, whose full mouth

was flatly sullen. Lady Searle was right, of course. Her one talent was an unfailing sense of fashion.

Augustine produced a square of linen from her bag, dabbing at her dry eyes. "Oh dear, sister, what's to become of my girls if you don't help us?" She sniffed. Aunt Augustine always referred to the duchess as "sister."

"It will take weeks to replace Mrs. Walters, and I will hardly have time to spare for anything else. It really is too hard. And the girls should not suffer for it. They need a grand ball. You must be planning a ball this season, sister . . ."

"Me, give a ball?" Lady Searle's hand stilled, and Pet's ears twitched. He wiggled slightly, and she resumed her strokes.

"It's so easy for you, sister. You have a lovely room and an army of servants. You dictate the guest list to your secretary. He arranges the cards. And it's no trouble to send a note round to Gunter's for refreshments."

Augustine returned her handkerchief to her bag. Ophelia thought it the shrewdest move she'd ever seen Aunt Augustine make, but she doubted her aunt would trick the duchess into revealing her entertainment plans. Still, Augustine had enough sense to know that now was the moment to wait.

Lady Searle's hand moved slowly back and forth across Pet's belly, lifting white tufts of fur between her fingers. Pet arched his long stomach appreciatively. There was no danger after all to his idle, pampered life. Lady Searle would continue to caress him and feed him treats. She lifted her hand suddenly, and Pet's eyes opened. He fixed Ophelia with a hostile stare.

"Well, Augustine. A ball. You know, I hadn't thought of it." Lady Searle held out her hand to end the visit. "Do you go to Talhurst's tonight?"

"Could you get us a card?"

"Of course."

Augustine rose and bowed and took her sister's thin hand. The girls dropped curtsies to their aunt.

"Remember, dear, bronze," Lady Searle said to Cecile.

When they had gone, she turned to Ophelia. "At last. It's so wearing to listen to her. Ring the bell for me, dear."

Ophelia rose and crossed to the bell pull.

"Augustine is so transparent. As if she could vie with me on what Edgar has. Really, it's a kindness to spare her the attempt."

"Are you giving a ball, Mother?" Lady Searle's entertainments were usually on a more exclusive scale.

Lady Searle's hands lay perfectly still in her lap. Pet snored lightly. "Yes, for Princess Charlotte and her betrothed."

"Mother, that's an enormous undertaking."

"A princess marries only once. It would be appropriate, too, if you were to use the occasion to announce your own betrothal. A compliment to the princess, following in her footsteps."

"My betrothal?" Ophelia was aware of a squeak in her voice.

"This is your second season. Searle and I agree it's time you settled on someone of a rank not indecently below your own. Searle will drop a delicate hint here and there with whomever you like."

"I don't like anyone."

Her mother gave her glance that warned against being tiresome. "That's not the point. If you don't want to end like Augustine, you need someone like Wyatt or Dent."

"Dent?" Dent, who never had an idea unconnected to his worth.

Lady Searle stood and clapped her hands for Pet. The corgi yawned and rolled to his feet. "Or Wyatt," she said mildly. "You must marry."

Wyatt, who had opened Ophelia's eyes to the hypocrisy of society, and who was now courting the carpet heiress . . .

Lady Searle drifted toward the door, Pet waddling in her wake, while Ophelia tried to summon her wits. Her parents were entirely indifferent to her happiness. They would give her to Dent or Wyatt without distinguishing between the two or recognizing the unsuitability of either man. She didn't know what to say.

"Mother, did you know father sacked William?"

"William?"

"My groom."

Her mother looked puzzled. "You must not ride without a groom, dear."

"I want William."

"They're all replaceable."

"No one else knows my ways."

"As long as you observe the proprieties, what can it matter?"

James, the first footman, appeared, and Lady

Searle entrusted Pet to him with instructions for the animal's outing.

Ophelia was left with the friezes. They formed a tight border around the entire upper edge of the room. There was no escape, they said. The lofty dignity of the house of Searle would be preserved. None of Ophelia's tricks would let her escape marriage.

Lord Searle's London stables were built along palatial lines and run like a minor kingdom. In addition to sixteen stalls, there were four coach houses for the two chaises, barouche, curricle, and phaeton, separate shoeing facilities, and a room for livery. Straw was abundant, the routine smooth, the equipment clean. Neither drunkenness nor mistreatment of the animals was permitted, and every man had his job. Alexander liked the place.

At least, he had until he'd become Miss Brinsby's groom. Riding with her awakened him to the curious doubleness of his position. There wasn't much deception in working directly with the horses, but as her groom he was actively pretending to be something he was not.

Late afternoon shadows covered the stableyard when he spread a final layer of sweet straw in Shadow's stall and stabled the mare. He still had chores to do for Clagg, and he wanted time to work with Raj.

He had thought of little besides Miss Brinsby for most of the day, and he'd had plenty of time to think. She was not precisely a beauty, except for the eyes and the skin. If he had to describe her, he would say she was as full of tricks as one of the night fairies that the hill people loved to tell tales about, and just as likely to tweak a man's nose or knock the stool from under him and send him tumbling. When she'd failed to get away from him at first with the trick in the square, she'd reversed her tactics, slowing their pace, prolonging their ride.

It was clear she'd had some objective other than a ride in the park. He had expected to see a suitor approach and signal the girl for a clandestine tryst, but they'd met few riders and she'd been indifferent to them all. When she'd stopped to linger by the water, he'd had a new feeling about her. Her whole person expressed yearning for something just out of her reach beyond the park, and he had had to wrench his gaze away.

Those moments apart from her had allowed him to regain his composure. Something about her made him bold, and her tricks had brought them uncomfortably close. Each time he got near her, his body reacted with cunning greed, extending the moment, and he waited to swing her down so that he might enjoy her touch on his shoulders and the feel of her slim waist in his hands. Twice the scent of her, subtle but sweet under the scents of leather and horse and dust, had made him forget to move. She felt the pull between them, too, he was sure, but she was the hardheaded sort of woman who resisted temptation stoutly. He wondered again what her hair was like under the blue velvet bonnet.

At Lady Talhurst's unremarkable gathering, Ophelia found that her gaze followed certain golden-brown heads. She was inevitably disappointed when the man turned and revealed a familiar face. She decided she was looking about in such an idiotic way because the ball was so dull and the prospects of good company so remote. Her mother stayed at her side long enough to ensure that Ophelia dutifully accepted several partners and headed for the card tables as soon as Charles, Lord Dent appeared to lead Ophelia into a set.

Ophelia believed she had been dancing with Dent forever. His thick, fair curls, his constant smile, and the perfect half circles of his brows above his pale, guileless eyes reminded her of a child's drawing of a face.

"Remarkable ball, eh?" he said, as the pattern of the dance brought them together.

"Mmmm," said Ophelia.

"Lady Talhurst must have invited everyone in town."

"I think she did."

"She's my uncle's cousin, you know."

"Really." Ophelia was hardly surprised. Dent's family tree was extensive, and his connections were his favorite subject.

"That is to say, Uncle Aldous, Aunt Pamela's husband—actually, Pamela's second husband. Her first, the Comte de Frossert, was guillotined." The dance separated them.

"In France, you know. Naturally, the family expected Pamela to remarry," he said, as they crossed the center of the set.

They were reunited a few steps later. "Aldous seems to have been a good choice for her, although I wonder sometimes if John Minor might not have been a better choice. He's my cousin, on my mother's side . . ."

Ophelia lost the thread of Dent's family history somewhere among the second cousins once removed and recovered her attention only as the dance came to an end.

"Dent, I feel quite faint. Could you procure me a glass of wine?" She smiled.

"Right. Dancing and all. Very fatiguing. Get you a negus."

Ophelia nodded. She hoped he would meet one of his relations and forget all about her.

She turned back to the crowd and saw her brothers approaching. With a little wave she caught Jasper's eye, and he steered Sebastian her way.

The two made a striking entrance, as they were fond of doing. Sebastian was thin and straight in every line—thin brows, thin nose, lean length, thin brown hair. Jasper had an indolent, athletic ease, quick smile, and hair as dark and thick as Ophelia's.

"Who were you dancing with, Ophelia?" Sebastian asked, frowning at Dent's retreating back.

Ophelia made a wry face at Jasper. Their oldest brother seemed to think his nearsightedness contributed to a lofty air. "Dent."

Sebastian nodded. "Most well-connected fellow in the *ton*."

"So he was just telling me."

Sebastian peered at her, checking for irony. A man's ancestry was no light matter to him. "He's worthy of you."

"Give it up, Sebastian. Dent's got nothing between his ears," Jasper said.

"He's sharp enough."

"Not for Ophelia. She wants to be able to talk to her husband."

Ophelia grinned at Jasper. At least he understood she valued intelligence. Suddenly, she wanted to tell him about her dismal marriage prospects and her new groom.

"Worst thing's happened," he said before she had a chance to speak.

"What?"

"I've been assigned the Trevigna situation."

"With your reputation, what could you expect?" Sebastian said.

"What's Trevigna, and why is it such a disastrous assignment for you, Jasper?" Ophelia asked.

"Trevigna," Jasper began, "is—"

"A fly speck of a nation," finished Sebastian.

"With a major port on the Adriatic," retorted Jasper.

"What makes it of consequence now?"

"The Congress simply forgot it at Vienna. They'd got things pretty well sorted out and then Bonaparte escaped. After Waterloo, they lost sight of some of the smaller nations."

"Can't Trevigna stay forgotten?"

"Absolutely not. If a small nation doesn't line up with one of the great powers, it will be without any protection in a fight."

Sebastian snorted. "Ophelia, who's that with the Candover heiress?"

Ophelia followed Sebastian's myopic gaze. "Trevor Nash."

"Hmmm. Good enough family. Younger son, though."

Ophelia nodded and turned to Jasper. "I take it Trevigna must offer something to England in return for our protection?"

"Access to the harbor. Otherwise there'll be no holding back the Turks and the Russians."

"Seems little enough to ask. What's the problem?" Ophelia never knew Jasper to be particularly concerned about his work for the Foreign Office.

Sebastian laughed. "The prince isn't cooperating. Castlereagh's been courting him for months."

Jasper looked glum. "He's disappeared."

"And Jasper's supposed to find him." Sebastian smirked.

Ophelia turned to her middle brother. "That doesn't sound like a disaster; that sounds like a compliment to you, Jasper."

"Hardly," said Sebastian. "Prince Mirandola's one of those vain, ornamental monarchs. The secretary picked Jasper to find him because he figures a frippery fellow like Jasper knows just the places to look."

Ophelia tried not to smile.

"It's true. Castlereagh told me I was hopeless in the office, so I might as well mingle in society."

"Castlereagh expects you to find this man at the Talhurst ball?"

Jasper flushed. "Mirandola was educated in England. Winchester and Oxford. He has dozens of friends among the *ton*. And he's out of cash. Castlereagh thinks he's bound to turn to his friends or the gaming tables, so I'm to keep an eye on them."

"Check with the man's tailor," said Sebastian. "He's famous for his coats." Sebastian tapped Ophelia's arm. "Who's Sally Candover with now?"

"Her mother."

"Excuse me, I think I will claim my dance."

Ophelia and Jasper exchanged amused glances as Sebastian made his way across the ballroom. "Do you suppose he ever knows who his partner is?"

Jasper's grin faded. He looked genuinely disheartened. "Do you think I'm such a worthless fellow, Ophelia?"

"Of course not. You have dozens of virtues." She saw that she had been too quick with her reassurance, and she couldn't think of anything more to say.

Jasper gave her hand a squeeze, but his eyes followed a ringletted blonde in a pale blue dress. "Thanks, you're a good sister, Sprite. I think I'll go make sure Sebastian can identify his partners."

Ophelia stared after him. She hadn't had a chance to say anything about her troubles. Her brothers, as always, were absorbed in their own. Not that she expected anything different. People were generally selfish. She was herself. Of the people Ophelia knew well only Hetty was genuinely selfless, and that made her rare . . . and made Ophelia's new groom terribly inconvenient.

*   *   *

At midnight Alexander let himself in the back door of the tailor's shop on Maddox Street. Hours of raking had worn blisters on his hands and made his shoulders ache. His stomach growled.

"Majesty, you're back." Lucca Gavinana dropped the ribbon he was tying around a single red rose and rushed to Alexander's side. "I forgive you. You've not been yourself."

"I beg your pardon, Lucca, but I am more myself than I have been in months."

Lucca shook his dark head sadly. "It was the terrible strain. And the news from that witch." He snatched Alexander's right hand, gave it a hasty kiss, and pulled, drawing Alexander into the fitting room of the little shop and jerking the heavy curtains closed. He turned to look Alexander up and down and slapped the palm of his hand against the side of his head. "*Madre della Virgine*, your clothes!"

"I've been working in them."

Lucca pressed his hand to his heart. "You smell like . . ."

"Horses." Alexander dropped into a leather chair and began to tug at his left boot.

In an instant Lucca was on his knees at Alexander's feet. Alexander glared. "I am capable of removing my own boots." Lucca's face fell, and Alexander softened his tone. "You don't want the muck of London on your hands."

Lucca stood and moved the rose discreetly out of sight. "You have been sleeping in a stable?"

"I know you've been worried," Alexander said. "But I think by now you can trust me to take care of myself. We are not in the mountains of Turin or on the coast of Greece."

Lucca gave an affronted sniff. "I know where we are, majesty, but you disappear, leaving me only a few words on a scrap of paper. How am I to think or work or be at peace in my mind?" He threw his hands up. "A week you are gone! I will spend fewer decades in purgatory for this week, you may be sure."

"You were so worried you bought a rose?" Alexander dropped his boot. "Who is she?"

With a veiled gaze, Lucca turned away. "A girl in the perfumer's shop across the street. *Com'è bella, com'è . . .*"

Alexander removed his other boot. "You don't have to describe her. I can imagine."

Tall and dark, and with deep, soulful eyes, Lucca found sweet, willing women wherever they went. Even when they'd been in school and Lucca'd had but a few words of English, he had coaxed kisses and embraces from barefoot village girls. Alexander's fate was smart, willful women, hardheaded women whose sweetness was so deep, so hidden, a man crossed deserts of longing to taste it. This time he meant to resist. "Any more letters from Aunt Francesca?"

"Two."

"You read them?"

Lucca shrugged. "You must not let that witch upset you. Who is Donna Francesca to pick a bride for the Prince of Trevigna?"

"Whom has she picked?"

"The daughter of Federico Tesio."

One of the noblest families of Trevigna. "She may be right; marrying Tesio's daughter may be the only way to appease the nobles." The idea that in this most personal of choices he would have no say had been one cause for his running away.

"If you get the money from the committee, you will not need to appease the nobles."

"If." He stretched, his aching muscles protesting the move. His body had been idle too long. "Any action from the committee since they put Hume and Tollworthy in charge?"

"A card came." Lucca disappeared through the curtain and returned with a heavy square of creamy paper.

Alexander broke the seal and read the enclosed invitation and a small accompanying piece of paper. It was an instant reminder of the tangled affairs of Trevigna, affairs that needed a firm hand and a clear mind. The nobles wanted the old order. The republicans wanted a constitution. The bandit Ferruci wanted the factions to remain at odds so that he could terrorize the countryside at will. Alexander needed to sort it out and bring the factions together.

He looked up to find Lucca watching him. "They're having a banquet to announce the Fund for the Restoration of the Italian Republics. If I'm there, the fund will likely succeed and I'll have the management of the monies."

"When is this banquet?"

"May."

"If you go to the banquet before you make a treaty with England . . ."

"Castlereagh will see that I can't return to Trevigna."

"Then the money will be in Ferruci's hands inside of a month."

Alexander shook his head. "Never."

His stomach growled. "Did you sell anything?"

"Two coats." Lucca pressed a glass of wine into Alexander's hand.

He took a sip. "Paid for?"

"Yes."

"Good. We won't starve. I have a job." He was surprised at how much it pleased him to say it.

"Majesty!" Lucca crossed himself. "May your father rest in peace."

"I am no longer a useless ornament."

"You make too much of a fool's remark. What job?"

"As a groom in a respectable household. Magnificent horses, Lucca. A big chestnut fellow that likes the stall no more than I do, and a black mare, sweet and smart."

"Where is this fine stable?"

Alexander stood, ignoring the cunning look in Lucca's eyes. "Did you spend all our profits on roses, or did you buy any food?"

"Majesty, I am not an idiot." Lucca bowed.

"Good, I will eat; then I've some work to do."

"Of course." Lucca wrinkled his nose. "But perhaps, first, a bath."

Chapter 3

On Thursday, as the first streaks of a red dawn lit the undersides of the clouds, Miss Brinsby came directly to Shadow's stall. The mare leaned her head over the gate, whickering softly, and allowed her ears to be scratched. Alexander's grip tightened on the feed pails he carried. There might be nothing in it except a girl's fondness for her horse, or it might be Miss Brinsby's way of asserting her mastery of the situation between them. She could come and go freely, step in and out of his realm as her whim moved her. He could only stand and serve.

Alexander gathered the tack and opened the stall, moving in a smooth, automatic sequence he knew by heart. Miss Brinsby stepped in after him and the stall enclosed them in warm, hay-scented air in which there was some indefinable influence of her presence. He paused for an instant, forgetting what came next. She took the bridle from his unmoving hands and turned to Shadow, murmuring softly and rubbing the mare's neck and ears.

Alexander blinked, recovering the faculty of

motion, and laid the blanket on the mare's back.

A tiny "mmm" from Miss Brinsby made him glance her way.

"Are you sure she has no bruises or tender spots?"

Their eyes held, hers testing not his competence, but his patience. She knew he'd checked. From the other end of the stable came the clang of someone collecting the empty feed pails.

"You may see, miss, whether I've overlooked anything." He stepped aside, and she took his place and began an expert examination of Shadow's back and shoulders. It was a mistake to watch. A helpless stillness took hold of him, narrowing his attention to her hands. Incongruously he wanted those hands skimming his body. The erotic thought evoked an image of Miss Brinsby in his narrow bed above the tailor shop. When she shrugged and stepped away, he had to force himself to move toward the horse, to return to saddling the mare.

His hands seemed detached, part of a machine separate from himself, doing the familiar work while he tried to bring his mind to order. As he hefted the saddle, she stopped him with a touch on his arm, as feather-light as air, but the sensation of it sank through him like a stone settling in the unresisting waters of a pond, and he paused, letting the shock ripples dissipate.

"Make sure the cinch doesn't slap her side."

He gritted his teeth. "I know my business." With exaggerated care he settled the saddle in place.

As he leaned down to do the cinch, their shoulders brushed, sending another current of awareness swirling through him. He sucked in a deep breath that filled his senses with her fragrance, a sweet contrast to leather and horse and dust.

"You'll cinch slowly, won't you? It must not pinch her."

He let out his breath, incapable of reply.

While she watched, he slid the flat of his unsteady hand along the mare's belly under the cinch. His hand grew hot, his pulse pounded. He straightened and stepped back, gaining some distance from her, and murmured his need to saddle Raj.

When he'd got the horses to the mounting block, she paused with one hand in his, the other on Shadow's saddle.

"It's going to rain," she observed, looking not at him but at the clouds.

He hardly heard her, his mind absorbed in memorizing the feel of her small palm in his. "Yes, miss."

"I don't think I'll ride this morning, after all. Thank you, Alexander."

She slipped her hand free and walked off without a backward glance, as if he were a stair rail, a fence post, a stile. He stood fighting anger, humiliation, and most of all, desire.

In an hour she was back.

"It's going to hold off. I think I should like to ride after all."

Silently, he invoked the Virgin of Laruggia, Queen of Patience. "Begging your pardon, Miss Brinsby, but are these false starts fair to the horses?"

She tilted her head, the curve of her cheek soft

and pink against the deep blue of her bonnet, her expression conscious of another victory. "I hope you're equal to the demands of the position, Alexander."

They rode out in a light rain.

He clamped his jaw shut, his gaze locked on her small form, his grievances against her bottled up inside him. No one else, not Clagg, not the duke, made him feel the humility of his position. On Tuesday she had appeared at the stables so early that he went without breakfast. He swore that she had been prepared to turn back until she heard his stomach growl. Instead, they rode for two hours, stopping and starting more times than a hackney cab plying Fleet Street.

On Wednesday she had come so late he'd despaired of her coming and been irked with himself for waiting. They did not stir above a walk. He'd gone to Clagg, acknowledging Miss Brinsby's pointed dislike, offering to do some other service, and been treated to a sermon on the virtues of order. Neither Miss Brinsby's displeasure with her groom nor his reluctance to serve her would alter Clagg's arrangements. Jasper Brinsby's purchase of a difficult horse and the abrupt dismissal of Miss Brinsby's former groom had unsettled Clagg's kingdom. In Clagg's not too flexible mind Alexander solved both problems neatly.

In truth, Alexander admitted to himself he might not like Miss Brinsby, but his body craved her presence. It was his peculiar misfortune to respond most eagerly to women who were utterly indifferent to him . . . unlike Lucca, who seemed to smell a responsive woman.

By the time they entered the park, he had worked out an explanation for her singular effect on him. His mind was empty. For weeks he had filled his head with Trevigna's problems; now there was room for other thoughts to come crowding in. And as she was the first female he'd encountered, inevitably thoughts of her obsessed him.

There certainly wasn't any other female in his life. He wasn't a monk, but he'd never kept a regular mistress in England. Kings' mistresses were notorious for intrigues and favorites, two ills of government he wished to avoid.

He was pleased to understand his condition; now he would master the feelings she stirred in him and be able to regard her with calm indifference.

Inside the park gates they set off at a decorous, rolling canter down a stretch of deserted track. It was the most ordinary thing his troublesome mistress had done. Then Miss Brinsby leaned into Shadow's neck and the mare shot forward, a black arrow of a horse. Alexander, a length and half behind, holding Raj's reins lightly, was caught off guard. But Raj reacted instantly, answering the mare's challenge, reaching out with his forelegs, hooves striking the ground, consuming it. The wind whipped tears from Alexander's eyes, but he kept his gaze on the girl.

When Raj came abreast of Shadow, the brief blazing mile came to an end in a spray of gravel and a dance of hooves. The horses blew, tossing their heads. As they settled to a cooling walk, Alexander wiped his eyes.

"Is there some criticism you wish to make?

Some rule of ladylike behavior you'd care to remind me of?'' she asked.

He wanted to shout. She was beautiful. She was mad. He made his dry throat work. "No."

"Good, because then I'd have to remind you that a lady's groom stays a length and half behind.'' She said it seriously, but an impish delight sparkled in her dark eyes.

They continued at a walking pace along the drive toward the Serpentine. Where the path curved to follow the edge of the little lake, she wanted to dismount. There was a brief awkward moment when her hands were on his shoulders, his at her waist, but he mastered himself and let her go. Then they were walking side by side, leading the horses. She looked about the park, apparently undisturbed, while he attempted to slow the heated rush of his blood.

At the end of the lake where the ground fell away to a dell, a flock of ducks and moorhens bobbed in the water. She halted to watch the birds, the yearning look back in her eyes.

"I think I'll bring bread for the ducks tomorrow."

Alexander looked away. If he let himself feel any sympathy for her, she'd get the better of him for sure.

Ophelia had accepted Haddington's invitation to ride in the park as a matter of policy. He was the least tedious of her supposed suitors, and if she wished to avoid marriage to Wyatt or Dent, she had to have some alternative. All she required was a man sensible enough to manage his estate and her inheritance. That was if the man were not cow-fisted or a poor rider. At the moment, she had her doubts about Haddington.

He was insisting upon the merits of his horses and his equipment as they headed for the afternoon crawl through the park. Though he lashed his team of showy bays, they moved sluggishly.

"My pair doesn't really show to advantage in town," he said. "Real goers need the open road."

"London is always difficult for horses," Ophelia said mildly, as a smart curricle passed them briskly, going in the opposite direction. The park lay ahead, the drive already clogged with low, open carriages, ladies waving to one another, plumed hats nodding. Ophelia put her hand on Haddington's arm as he was about to lash the horses again. "Why don't you take them out of town a ways, just to show me their paces?"

"Certainly, Lady Ophelia." He turned his pair, and with a smart crack of his whip, sent them into a trot. As they headed north, leaving the city behind, Ophelia discovered that Haddington had not exaggerated the horses' speed, after all, but he had failed to mention their jouncing, bone-jarring gait.

When they slowed at last and Ophelia could release her grip on the seat, she looked about at the landscape with its first hints of spring, green spears of grass poking up along the banks and puffy balls on the catkins in the ditches. The sun, descending on their left, bathed the fields in soft golden light

Suddenly Ophelia sat up straight.

"What is it?" Haddington asked.

"That's my brother's horse," she said. Raj stood in the middle of a close-cropped field, his ears pricked alertly. He was without a bridle or lead of any sort. Ophelia twisted on the carriage seat. "Stop, Haddington."

He reined in his pair.

"I wonder how he got away?" Ophelia said, gathering her skirts to descend from the carriage. "Haddington, do you have something I could use as a lead?" She had no idea how to recover the beast, but she had to try.

Across the field Raj lowered his head and took a few slow steps forward. He poked his nose into a clump of grass, and in a fluid streak of motion Alexander came to his feet, grasped a handful of mane, and leapt to Raj's back. For a moment Raj danced with a springy step, as if neither his rider nor gravity had a hold on him, then he checked and stood perfectly still. Instantly, Alexander slid from his back, offering the stallion something from his pocket, stroking the beautiful proud curve of the horse's neck. After a minute he turned and walked away.

A very unladylike term came to Ophelia's mind. Of all the cocksure, irresponsible idiots who went by the name of man, Alexander had to be one of most conceited. She pressed her lips together. She couldn't shout or she'd startle the horse, but she couldn't allow Jasper's prize to get away.

Then, like a puppy or a duckling following its mother, the stallion trotted after Alexander.

Ophelia could not prevent the little "O" of surprise her mouth made.

"Now, that's a tame horse," said Haddington. "Thought your brother bought that beast of Plimpton's that smashed his rig to bits."

"You must be thinking of a different horse," said Ophelia, smiling sweetly. "Will you take me home now, Haddington? You know what a stickler my mother is."

"Of course, Lady Ophelia." He slapped the reins against his team's rumps.

Ophelia caught one last glance of her groom and the chestnut stallion, walking side by side through the quiet evening, like friends.

Friday morning Miss Brinsby stalked into the stableyard, clutching a paper bag he thought must contain bread for the ducks. He'd dreamed of her hands on him and wakened taut and aching.

"Do you know how much my brother paid for that beast?" she asked, as he led Raj out into the yard.

"He's worth every guinea, miss."

"Then explain to me what you were doing with him yesterday afternoon in an open field without a lead."

Alexander could not help smiling at her. "Teaching him to like being caught."

Her mouth puckered, and Alexander found himself staring at her lips, pink and soft looking. She spun away.

He saddled the horses, watching with a wary eye as a footman entered the stableyard dragging a short, fat dog on a leash. The magnificent, liveried footman clearly regarded the dog as an encumbrance beneath his dignity. He stopped inside the gate and pulled a pipe from one of his pockets. Draping the dog's leash over his arm, he cupped the pipe in his palms and nursed the tobacco to light with a bit of burning straw.

The dog looked around fiercely, saw Miss Brinsby, and bristled just as her idle glance turned his way.

"Good morning, Pet, you vile creature," she said.

As if he understood the insult, the dog started a furious high-pitched yapping. Shadow's head came up and Raj snorted, rising instantly to his hind legs, pawing the air. Alexander pulled Raj down and the footman aimed a kick at the dog.

The kick missed, and the dog threw itself at the end of the slack leash, erupting from the startled footman's hold and barreling for Miss Brinsby.

"Stand!" Alexander commanded Raj. He dropped the stallion's rein, lunging for Miss Brinsby and spinning her out of the charging dog's path.

Having missed his target, the dog plopped his hindquarters down, skidding to a stop under the stallion's nose. The stallion's nostrils flared, his teeth showed.

"Raj, stand!" Alexander shouted.

Stallion and dog regarded each other a long moment, breathing in sharp bursts, before the careless footman scrambled for the loose leash and tugged the dog back.

"Beg pardon, miss," said the footman.

"Archaic functionary," she muttered.

Alexander looked down at the girl in his arms and knew why he had been in such a turmoil for days. Her face tilted up to his revealed the hidden sweetness he had sensed from the first moment he looked on her.

"A rescue? How gallant!" she said. Her eyes refused to meet his. "Pet hates me."

"Pet?"

"My mother's dog. He had a name once, but mother never calls him anything but 'Pet.'"

"What did you do to make him hate you?" He was whispering, conscious of holding her close.

"I suggested that he earn his keep."

Under his scrutiny, the hint of dawn in her cheeks deepened against the blue of her bonnet. Dark curls peeked from under the brim.

He let her go, moving resolutely to put Raj between them. The few seconds he'd held her had heated his blood. He was likely to unsettle the stallion with his own state of excitement.

She gave him a puzzled look over Raj's back. When he came around the stallion to assist her, he was careful to avoid any contact except where their gloved hands met.

Ophelia refused to alter her plans because her groom had rescued her from the demon dog.

They had a good gallop, making a circuit of the park that brought them near the water's edge north of the Serpentine. She accepted his aid in dismounting, smiling and leaning on him, so that his face assumed a deliberate blankness, as if he were unconscious of her presence. He didn't want the charge of her, and as soon as she put her plan into action, he would be free. He maneuvered so that Shadow was between them as they walked, but after a moment she crossed in front of the horse to walk at his side. By now she could read the stiffening of his countenance.

"You like horses better than people, don't you?" she said.

He looked straight ahead. "They're easier to manage than people. They live simply. They work hard. They trust you."

"And they don't make contrary demands on those who serve them."

"They aren't very good at independence, though. They need the bit, bridle, and reins." He turned toward her, his remarkable blue eyes the only color in the acres of park around them.

And she tried to remember that they were talking about horses. "They'd do very well with independence if we let them be free as nature intended."

"Would you give up your morning ride so your horse could be free?"

She saw the trap he laid. "Perhaps when the steam engine is perfected, our horses will be free."

"What sort of freedom is it to be useless?"

She looked at him sharply. "You'd rather be in service than free?"

"I would rather be your horse than your mother's dog."

"I don't think being my groom suits you, however."

She was glad he made no reply. To hear him speak that way of horses would make her like him, but it had taken days to come up with an escape plan, and she wouldn't falter in resolution now merely because her groom had some interesting ideas. Still, it was harder than she'd expected to end their conversation.

She gave him Shadow's reins and strolled away from the bridle path down the dell toward the east end of the water, picking her way over the soggy ground. Ducks quacked and waddled toward her, anticipating bread, the flock folding over itself to get close to her. She glanced over her shoulder. Alexander was watching, but she was sure she had lulled his suspicions with two mornings of good behavior. She began tossing crumbs to the noisy birds, turning a little bit at a time until the flock was between her and the horses at the top of the rise.

After a few minutes of her lazy scattering of crumbs, he seemed to lose interest in her. He turned to the horses, talking and stroking, as was his way. She flung the last of the bread at the ducks in a wide arc, gathered her skirts in one hand and darted behind a cover of reeds and bushes, resisting the temptation to look back in triumph. He was stuck on his side of the milling flock with Shadow and Raj.

His responsibilities trapped him, for he could not leave the horses untended, and he would never get Raj through the milling ducks.

She dashed around the end of the lake, slipping just once on the wet grass, up the dell, and across the Row. Once she gained level ground, she felt she could run forever. There was no one to notice her. A lone rider cantered west, and a detachment of Horse Guards trotted out of sight in the trees at the other end of the Row. She had only to reach the Kensington Road to find a cab or a cart to catch a ride to Hetty's.

The duck quacking increased in frenzy and Alexander glanced over his shoulder. What he saw was a flash of blue disappearing behind the shrubbery around the end of the lake. He swore. He should have known he couldn't trust her. He looped the horses reins together, told the stallion firmly to stand, and plunged down the hill. The milling ducks flapped upward around him in an explosion of squawks and feathers. At the top of the rise he spotted the blue of her riding habit through the early spring foliage. A month later and she'd have had perfect cover. He doubled his speed, angling across the Row and up a slight rise.

She must have heard him then, for she glanced over her shoulder and increased her pace, but her direction didn't change. She had some destination in mind, her escape planned from the moment she'd mentioned the bread. All the frustrations of his week in her service coalesced in a furious energy that drove him forward. *Damn*, she would explain herself.

She pressed her free hand to her side, and he knew he had her. Her harsh breathing rasped above the flapping of her skirts, and the thud of his pursuing footsteps on the grass. He reached out, grabbing the flared gathers at the waist of her jacket. With a cry she tried to wrench free, stepping on her skirts and tumbling down a short incline. He clung to the jacket, stumbling after, hitting the ground with a sharp impact that took his breath and sent his hat rolling ahead of them down the dewy grass to the base of a hedge.

She pushed herself up at once, scrambling to get to her feet, but Alexander lunged, pinning her legs.

"Let me go!" Her bonnet had come off. Unconventional short dark waves, thick and shiny, fell away from her face, her cheeks pink from her exertions. Her eyes glittered with tears of frustration, her lips parted with her gasping breaths, her chest rose and fell.

He couldn't speak. He pulled himself up her body until he covered her and trapped her wrists against the ground. There he held himself above her on his elbows, waiting for the breath to question her.

But as he waited, suspended above her, her scent rose to fill his nostrils, her ribs met his, their breaths mingled. A tremor passed through him, signaling his body's inevitable response to her nearness. She must have seen or sensed the change in him, because her eyes grew wide and wary. He knew that look. She was not as indifferent to him as he'd imagined. The longing that had been building in him all week sharpened. He moved one hand to brush a soft curl back from her hot cheek.

Then he pressed closer, sinking down against her, closing his arms to frame her body, lifting his fingertips to her silky hair. Girl and grass filled his senses.

Her mouth drew his. He wanted it, lowered himself to touch her lips until a gasp from her made him check. He was forgetting who he was and who he pretended to be. In her eyes he was a servant, about to insult a lady. If the truth was different, he still had no freedom to kiss a pretty girl simply because he wanted to.

He shoved himself to his feet and turned his back. The desire he'd allowed himself to feel, now thwarted, made him shake.

He heard her rise and slap her skirts. When he thought he had himself under some control, he glanced over his shoulder at her. She was brushing tears from her eyes with the backs of her knuckles.

His hands closed in fists. "Are you all right?"

"My maidenly sensibilities are not offended."

"I was asking about your limbs. No broken bones or twisted ankle?"

"No." Her voice was small.

He risked turning to look at her. "Where were you going?"

Her chin came up, and the expression in her eyes grew haughty. "To see a friend."

"Your friend couldn't meet you in the park?" He had no good opinion of a lover who would expect a girl to come to him.

"She doesn't ride."

His resentment evaporated. He grinned stupidly. "Can't you call on your friend in a more conventional way?"

"A mere tradesman's daughter," she said, mimicking a deep, rumbling voice obviously not her own. She was brushing the grass from her skirts.

"A friend from the lower orders?"

"My dearest friend."

"Your family's disapproval must be pointed if you are driven to such ruses to meet."

"They have an excessive regard for rank and breeding."

"You don't?" He retrieved his hat from the hedge.

"I believe in democratic principles."

"All men are created equal?"

"And women."

He laughed. "You practice these principles by ordering your groom about?"

"It's nearly impossible to practice any sort of rational principles in my family, but among clever, well-informed people with a liberality of ideas, there can be real, easy, and equal fellowship in spite of differences in rank."

"Is this what you find at your friend's house?"

She nodded, looking up at him almost shyly. "You could take me there."

"As your last groom did? The one who sacrificed his position for your egalitarian principles?"

"You think I was unjust to him?"

"He lost his livelihood for your freedom."

"His situation not his livelihood, and he was well compensated."

"Bribed."

"Yes, bribed. I did not say I believed all men were created good."

"Plainly, you don't think a groom might be a man of integrity."

"That's not the point."

Alexander raised a brow. "Enlighten me."

"Oh, how can I make you understand the need for escape? People in society have fixed ideas. Their heads are like oak."

"Even your family?"

"Especially my family. Talking to my mother is like trying to take a deep breath with stays on."

Alexander had to laugh.

"I just want a very little freedom, the freedom to choose my friends without regard for rank or birth. Believe me, my friend Hetty has more merit than a dozen 'gently bred' ladies of society."

Alexander reached down and retrieved her bonnet. "Are you still willing to offer me a bribe?"

Her eyes changed instantly. He recognized disappointment and wariness in them. "How much do you want?"

"It's not money I want." He stepped up to her, turning the soft velvet bonnet in his hands.

"What then?" Her mouth was a cynical line, her eyes cold, focused on the horizon.

He closed the gap between them. "I want your name and the freedom to use it whenever I like."

Color flooded her face. Her gaze swung back to him. "That's impossible."

"So much for your egalitarian principles."

"This isn't France, you know. Ladies and grooms don't mix as social equals."

"Do you want to see your friend? Without your parents knowing?"

He knew she did. He held his breath so long he thought she'd changed her mind.

"My name's Ophelia," she whispered.

"Ophelia," he said. He pulled a thin blade of dry grass from the curls at the side of her face and stuck it between his teeth. He made the gesture appear careless, but his hand shook. "Let me take you to your friend."

It took a moment for his willingness to register. Then she smiled, a tentative smile. "Thank you."

They turned back toward the dell when she stopped abruptly. "But what's become of the horses? I never thought you'd leave them."

"They're waiting for us."

She cast him an incredulous glance. "You think we'll find Shadow and Raj in the dell?"

"I know it."

"What on earth will keep them there?"

"I told Raj to stand, Ophelia."

Chapter 4

Ophelia slipped into the breakfast room of the Grays' Kensington townhouse unnoticed. The room smelled of coffee, apricot preserves, and hyacinth—every comfort familiar to Ophelia, from the print of berries and flower clusters on the walls to the clutter of jam pots and open books on the table, and her friends bent over their newspapers.

The select and restricted world of Miss Weston's Academy had been unintentionally kind to Lady Ophelia Brinsby and Miss Henrietta Gray when it had brought them together. At twelve years old, Hetty, the new girl, had been plump, pretty, and unprepared for the snobbery and cruelty of her classmates. Ophelia, though younger, knew the haughty ploys of her privileged schoolmates and set out to teach her friend survival. Hetty, for her part, offered Ophelia books, books Ophelia had never dreamed existed.

They read the novels of Mrs. Smith, Mrs. Radcliffe, and Mrs. Brunton, following their heroines into ruined abbeys and down American rivers. They followed Samuel Richardson's Clarissa

Harlowe from the priggish confines of her family
home through all her encounters with her seducer Lovelace to her inevitable death. They read
Voltaire and Rousseau, Tom Paine and the
French Encyclopedists and Wollstonecraft. At
sixteen they wrote *A Treatise on the Ideal State of
Man*, which Solomon Gray, Hetty's father,
printed for them. Some five hundred copies were
out when Ophelia's parents discovered the book.
The duke purchased or reclaimed all of the copies and threatened Solomon's publishing business. Ophelia was removed from Miss Weston's
Academy and forbidden to continue her friendship with Hetty.

Ophelia had a clear recollection of that day.
Her father had taken her aside after he'd de-
stroyed the copies of their treatise to tell her
about the duties of her station in life and what
she should do to please him. "You are to be
lovely and proper and quiet. Call no notice to
yourself while your mother and I make every
provision for you." He had made repeated allusions to the disgrace Lady Caroline Lamb had
brought upon herself, and had urged Ophelia
never to make her family look ridiculous. After
that episode she'd developed her strategy of
compliance. She would willingly keep most of
the rules, in order to break the one that kept her
from Hetty.

Ophelia looked down at her friends, absorbed
in their newspapers. Solomon Gray was entirely
bald, but his lack of hair contributed to the fierce
vigor of his face with its dark, sharply peaked
brows, intense eyes, and strong, straight nose.
Hetty's pale golden curls framed a delicate coun-

tenance in which a pair of intelligent blue eyes seemed at odds with her soft beauty.

"What a solemn pair!"

Hetty's head came up instantly. "Ophelia! Where have you been? We've been very dull, as you plainly see. We've needed you." She rose and came to Ophelia, giving her a quick hug and drawing her to the table.

"And I you. You don't know how much."

Solomon Gray smiled broadly. "Miss Ophelia, come, sit," he invited. "Let me tell Mrs. Pendares you'll be wanting some coffee."

Ophelia took a chair beside Hetty, peeking at an open book. "What's this?" She scanned the title. "*Celia in Search of a Husband.*"

"It's for review," said Hetty, pushing the book aside.

"May I help?" Ophelia opened the volume.

"Of course. Where have you been? I didn't know what to think," Hetty said, "or whether I should risk a letter."

"Father sacked William, and I've had to contend with a new groom this week."

"You must have brought the new man around to your side."

Ophelia kept her gaze on the little book. "By a lady," the title page read. "We've achieved a sort of truce."

"Has it been war?"

A little commotion outside the breakfast room made them both turn. Mrs. Pendares, the Grays' housekeeper, opened the door for Solomon, who carried a tray laden with coffee and a plate of biscuits.

"Now, Mr. Gray, you oughtn't to be taking my

business upon yerself in this way," Mrs. Pendares protested, blocking the door. She was slim and cheerful, with silver strands in her dark hair, and Ophelia could not remember a time when she had not been with the Grays.

"Step aside now, ma'am," said Solomon. "I don't want to drop your biscuits in Miss Ophelia's lap." He winked at Ophelia, who grinned in return. Poor Mrs. Pendares struggled constantly to hold onto her duties in the face of the two Grays, who besides being very self-sufficient, were fond of their widowed housekeeper. Indeed, Ophelia saw with sudden insight that Solomon and Mrs. Pendares felt rather more than fondness for each other. Their glances met and danced away, and Mrs. Pendares's cheeks brightened. It was so like the way Alexander moved in relation to Ophelia that unaccountably she felt her color rise and caught Hetty's intelligent gaze on her.

"Good morning, Mrs. Pendares," she said.

"Good morning, dear. It's good to have you back at the Gray table. My biscuits have been ignored this week."

"Outright slander!" Solomon set the tray on the table and lifted a biscuit, taking a defiant bite. Mrs. Pendares laughed and retreated, and Hetty invited Ophelia to pour herself some coffee, dark and rich in a perfect white china rim, one of the ceremonies of their friendship.

"Tell me what's new," Ophelia said.

Hetty cast a glance at her father. "Father has a poem for you to look at, and so do I. And we had a noted personage join us for Tuesday night supper. Amelia Hart."

''The novelist?''

Hetty nodded, and Solomon disappeared behind his paper.

''Is she as radical as we've always heard?'' Ophelia broke open one of the biscuits and reached for the preserves.

''More so. Sensual, charming, daring.'' Hetty paused, her face taking on a careful air. ''It's a performance, but an engaging one. Forthright, fierce, very sure of herself, but surprisingly conventional in dress and appearance, a classic oval face, large blue eyes, delicate features, not what I expected.''

''And did she speak well?''

Hetty's gaze strayed to her father behind his newspaper and returned. ''Oh, yes. A great deal about what is permitted a woman in this world. She firmly believes women are allowed to exercise power only by guile or charm, never by right.''

''My life precisely. Did any gentlemen challenge her?''

''Berwick.'' Hetty made a face.

Ophelia watched her friend closely. Hetty had been talking about Berwick for weeks. ''I suppose Mrs. Hart ate him alive.''

''Yes. He mentioned that Princess Charlotte would someday rule vast numbers of men as queen, but Mrs. Hart was quick to remind him of the likelihood that Charlotte, if she does rule, will be governed first by her own sober husband.''

''She calls herself 'Mrs.'?''

''She says she's as entitled to it as any widow, having once bound herself to a man. I can tell you, she stirred up discussion all night."

Solomon put down his paper abruptly and stood. "Work to do. I'll leave you girls to your talk." He turned at the door. "Miss Ophelia, Berwick, who fancies himself the next Byron, has offered me a new poem. Take a look, will you?"

"Of course, Mr. Gray." Ophelia smiled. Just like that she had a commission. Her opinion mattered in the Grays' house as it never did in her own.

When the door closed behind Solomon, Ophelia turned to Hetty. "I take it your father doesn't admire Mrs. Hart as much as you do."

Hetty frowned, a little white crease between her brows. "He's published all her books, but they always fight about the money. She refused to call here before now."

Ophelia spread jam on her biscuit. Solomon Gray was a self-made man, with an entirely unaristocratic air of confidence, the air of a man who'd achieved something, the sort of air Wellington had. To see him shrink from girlish talk was curious.

"You think your father's dislike of Mrs. Hart is something besides the money?"

Hetty poured fresh coffee. "I suppose he finds her fame irksome. We live far from your sort of society, Ophelia. One doesn't meet luminaries in Hetty Gray's drawing room."

Ophelia pondered it. The Grays did live in obscurity, though Solomon's success as a publisher was equal to that of John Murray, who published Byron. There were far more literary addresses in London, and the Grays could easily afford a grander style of living in one of the newer squares.

After a little lapse, Hetty spoke again. "In some ways Mrs. Hart disturbs me, but she is exciting. There was definitely more energy in the room for her being there."

"I'd like to meet her." Ophelia sipped her coffee. It was an escape she'd yet to work out. To get away in the evening when the social whirl of London was at its peak, was more difficult than in the morning, when only servants and vendors were stirring.

Hetty said, "You must come some evening soon, no matter what tricks it takes to escape. It would be so much easier to make up my mind about Mrs. Hart if we could compare observations. But tell me about your week."

"Danced with Dent everywhere. Offended mother's demon hound. Hems will be deeper this spring. Princess Charlotte's wedding dress will be silver and has metal thread enough to circle the globe. My mother, by the way, has triumphed over her fellow hostesses. She's to give a ball for Charlotte and her prince, at which she hopes I'll announce my betrothal. Dent or Wyatt will do."

"Not Wyatt!" Hetty looked sympathetic. "He hasn't bothered you this season, has he?"

"No." Ophelia had seen him dancing attendance on a new girl, giving her that flattering sensation of being important to someone's happiness. She had no way of knowing whether the new girl was destined to be disillusioned, as Ophelia had been. Her pride wanted to believe it, but she didn't wish that suffering on anyone.

It had been mortifying to discover her vanity and frailty, flaws that were not even original, just the faults laid at every woman's door since Eve. She saw herself as she'd been last season, weak and trusting, allowing intimacies and touches, thinking that because Wyatt let her talk, he was actually interested in what she said.

He had been the cruelest mirror into which she'd ever looked. On a bench in Vauxhall Gardens, her breasts spilling out of her stays, her skirts hiked up about her thighs, showing the tops of her stockings, Wyatt's hand on her knee, she learned Wyatt's true estimation of her. *You're one of the hot ones, Ophelia.* To think of it again sent an immediate wave of shame through her, hot and then cold.

Hetty's expression was quite sober. "Should you expose him?"

"How can I?" She couldn't, of course.

"Poor Ophelia."

Ophelia drew a breath and straightened. "I mean to ignore Wyatt, make him feel he has no power over me. But it's difficult. My new groom has more wit than my dance partners."

"Do you talk to him? I mean, have conversations with him?"

"Only minor philosophical discourses on the nature of man and beast."

Hetty laughed. "Be serious, Ophelia. You move in the best circles. There must be a man, men, of your acquaintance who are clever, amiable, and principled."

"All married, I'm sure." She picked up the little volume of *Celia in Search of a Husband.* "I suppose this heroine has her pick of eligible gentlemen, but will meet the man of her dreams only when she has been reduced by every vicissitude of fortune to living in a hovel with her dying grandfather in some foreign land."

Hetty laughed. "After their canoe goes over a steep waterfall and capsizes, flinging them ashore on the edge of the darkest, most extensive forest in America."

"You see, it's easy for Celia. Now, if she were a duke's daughter, trapped in London society, there would only be a score of men to consider."

"And your parents have fixed on Dent and Wyatt?"

"The right lineage, sufficient income, connections." Ophelia split another biscuit and regarded its sweet, warm center.

"There must be others."

"Last night I told Ayres that I made it a rule to sleep in a hair shirt. Do you know what he said?"

"Ophelia, you didn't."

"It was a test. I wanted to see whether he was listening."

"What did he say?"

" 'Interesting!' Handsome men are the worst. A man who catches his own eye in a glass and smiles approvingly! Spare me."

"Is there no one you might love?" Hetty asked, suddenly quite serious.

"Love," Ophelia spread preserves on her biscuit, "feeling, seems an untrustworthy basis for a marriage. What one wants is someone sensible enough to manage twenty thousand pounds. I should advertise."

"I don't think you should judge love by your experience with Wyatt."

"Oh, I agree. There was certainly no love in that."

"But you do believe in love," Hetty insisted.

"It's a bit like believing in the moon. One can see it, but one hardly knows how to get there from here."

Ophelia stirred her cooling coffee. It was true. Love was as remote as the moon. "Hetty, show me your poem."

Alexander put aside the clutter of papers on his desk, his latest attempt to create a parliamentary framework for Trevigna. His Sunday holiday was nearly done, and he'd made little progress on his declaration of the principles of a democratic state.

He closed his eyes and rubbed them with his thumb and forefinger. As long as he stayed at his desk, Lucca would not bother him, but if he ventured below, they'd quarrel again about his job, a pointless conflict, since Alexander knew he'd be going back to see Ophelia.

Getting her name had given him the upper hand only briefly. She'd come from her friend's house, cheerful and blithely indifferent to him, and at the end of their ride had vanished into her pampered existence without a backward glance at her groom, without even one excessive, petty demand to show that he was on her mind.

He wished he knew what she thought of him. He wished that she did think of him, but his disguise made it unreasonable to hope that he meant any more to her than an inconvenience.

He wished he'd paid more attention to the feminine mind over the years, but there had been so many other subjects to master.

First, he'd done the work of two in school until Francesca had come and treated the masters of Winchester to an explosive display of Italian temper, explaining which of their charges was the servant and which the prince. Then he had had to learn history, politics, economics—everything that might serve Trevigna and rescue his father. And still later in the mountains, among the rebels who resisted Napoleon, he had had to learn it all over again with Trevigna as his schoolroom.

Of course, he had heard his friends speak of women. At Oxford, over wine, few topics had been as enduring. But the boasts, the crude humor, the veiled allusions had hardly enlightened him. All the talk seemed to be about casual liaisons and had more to do with men than with women. His few successes had been due to indifference. Women remained elusive creatures, their natures hidden in the silences of men's conversations.

He opened his eyes and took up Aunt Francesca's latest letter. If he could persuade Francesca to accept his republican ideals, he could persuade the rest of his countrymen.

Mirandola,

You have, apparently, taken leave of your senses. In that at least you show signs of your Italian heritage, but not your royal descent. What is that idiot Gavinana about, to permit a prince of the blood to live above a shop?

You must act now to restore confidence in the monarchy. If you cannot come home to marry, I will undertake to persuade Tesio's daughter to come to London. You must produce an heir.

Have you forgotten why your father sent you to England? Do you imagine that base men who have been following sheep, or gathering grapes, or throwing their nets into the sea, are prepared to decide the fate of Trevigna? Do you think the merchants of Laruggia counting their sovereigns are prepared to put the common good before self-interest? I am beginning to think your education wasted on you.

You and you alone have been prepared by birth, education, and training to rule Trevigna. You have been bred to put Trevigna before any of the common desires of ordinary men. Your commission comes not from some committee of the greedy and self-important but from God. Would you refuse the title of king with all its dignity? To be called citizen? To be called a common man?

> *Francesca di Piovasco Mirandola*

The common desires of ordinary men. When had he been allowed such desires? He had been putting Trevigna first all his life. The first duty of a king was to sacrifice for the people. And he rarely minded, but he wanted to forge a Trevigna worthy of the sacrifice of even one life. He wanted Trevigna to be a better state than others in Europe, to be an example of freedom, justice, and harmony. And if Trevigna was to move forward in this new century, not seventeen years old and already excessively bloody, she had to accept new ideas.

Alexander mended his pen and put out a fresh sheet of paper. How was he to persuade Francesca that there was no indignity in the title *man*? Send her Voltaire? The equality of man was an utterly unfamiliar concept in Trevigna. To think the simple fishermen of Trevigna's coast were equal to the nobles of the great houses required a new mind, a nineteenth-century mind. Then there were the fruit thieves in the orchards and the soot-coated colliers and tinkers in the woods. The inequalities were obvious while the equality lay hidden.

And if he were to persuade his fellow Trevignans of the equality of men, how then would they act toward one another? They would still be separated by circumstances, the fishermen and peasants in huts, the nobles in *palazzios*.

Maybe he could experiment. Ophelia Brinsby had a lifetime of privilege and training in the finer points of English class distinctions, yet she claimed to believe all men were equal. Could Alexander persuade her to treat him as an equal?

"Majesty?" Lucca stuck his head in the door of the small upper room where Alexander worked. "Supper, Majesty."

"In a minute," he answered. He looked at the letter he'd begun to his aunt and discovered half a line ending in a large ink stain. He threw down the pen. Ophelia Brinsby ruled his brain.

In the chilly, inadequate dining room, he found one place set with the royal plate of Trevigna, carted to the tailor's shop when Alexander had abandoned his costly manor outside of Windsor. Lucca, in Trevigna's blue and gold livery, stood stiff and silent at the door, ready to serve his prince.

"Only one place, Lucca?"

"Your majesty has no guests tonight." The frostiness in Lucca's tone hadn't warmed at all.

"I'd hoped to dine with a friend."

There was a silence while Lucca, his haughty nose tilted at the ceiling, decided whether to pretend incomprehension. "It would not be seemly, Your Majesty."

Lucca was repaying him for working in a stable and undermining the dignity of the Crown.

Alexander took his place at the table and lifted the lid of a silver tureen. A mingled aroma of wine and bay and garlic swirled up from a rich fish soup. The familiar smell of Trevigna's kitchens held him for a moment, a smell from childhood, from before England and school and duty and sacrifice, when he and Lucca had wandered the port of Laruggia barefoot, always glad to accept a bowl of soup in one of the huts along the shore.

He could command Lucca to dine with him and receive instant obedience, but that would not put the dinner on the footing of equality or friendship. He didn't want to be a potentate. He stirred the soup, letting the rich smell do its work. Lucca sighed, homesickness warring with notions of dignity. Abruptly he released a string of curses and stomped off. Alexander lowered the tureen lid.

In minutes Lucca was back with another setting and without his livery. "A priest's trick," he muttered, as he slapped silver and plate on the table.

They ate in silence until Lucca's abrupt, jerky movements subsided into a smooth flow of the spoon from bowl to lips.

"I know you don't like our circumstances, Lucca, but we've seen worse. And a few more months should see us back home."

Lucca put down his spoon and lifted his great dark eyes to Alexander. "Why don't you stay here and do your work? Why must you lower yourself to a stable? Who is giving orders to the Prince of Trevigna?"

Alexander traced the pattern of the damask with the tips of his fingers. "I feel free there. I can joke with my fellow grooms, drink with them if I want to, and no one will think I've undermined my princely dignity."

Lucca shuddered.

"I can flirt with—"

"There's a woman?" Lucca froze. "What sort of woman is in a stable?"

"A duke's daughter," said Alexander. It was comic to see Lucca's face change.

"Ah," he said. "A sweet and proper young lady, who rides."

Alexander laughed. "An imperious, hard-headed miss with more tricks than the devil. You must tell me how you always find women who are soft and yielding, while I always find those who have been to Aunt Francesca's School of Independence."

"It's the nose," said Lucca, lifting his handsome, substantial Roman protruberance into the air and giving a sniff. "You have too much the brain working."

Alexander studied the tablecloth. His brain hardly functioned at all in Ophelia's presence.

Lucca left him for a moment and returned with coffee in cups that had once belonged to Alexander's mother, sent to him by Francesca—a reminder, like the livery, of Alexander's royal heritage. Lucca asked about his progress on a constitution for Trevigna.

"I am not writing a constitution, you understand, but a declaration of the principles that need to underlie it, like the American declaration."

"And what principles are these? Liberty, I suppose?"

"And equality," said Alexander carefully.

"You are trying to straighten the dog's legs, you know."

Alexander regarded Lucca through the steam rising from their cups. "Perhaps, but if I am going to give up every choice a man has in life for Trevigna, I want her to be better than other nations." He was afraid when he'd said it. He'd put the dream and the sacrifice into words.

Lucca bowed his head. "Do you have anything for me to do?"

"I have letters for Hume and Tollworthy about the committee's loan scheme. Will you deliver them?"

The Grays had two stalls in a common mews across the lane behind their garden. In practice the shared stable arrangement meant the place was often neglected, so Ophelia couldn't help

noting the change Alexander had made. The
floor was raked clean, buckets and tools had
been put away, and tack hung on the walls in
neat array. He sat on a bench, leaning against the
wall, his muscled legs stretched out, a book in
hand, the picture of idleness, as if he'd had nothing whatever to do with the improved state of
the stable. She peeked at the book but couldn't
make out the title.

She'd brought him biscuits again, and now
shifted them to one hand, tucking under her
other arm the latest bundle of Berwick's manuscript.

"You're free, you know, while I visit Hetty."
She refused to blush over her past behavior toward him. She had treated him fairly from the
day he'd agreed to bring her to Hetty's. "You
don't have to clean stables, especially not for
someone else."

He slipped the little book into his pocket and
came to his feet, taking the offered biscuits.

"For me? Thank you, Ophelia."

Her name again. He wouldn't stop using it. A
tiny ripple of warmth passed through her as if
they'd touched.

She remembered her bare hands and began
pulling on her gloves. "You needn't wait for me
here. I daresay you'd find company if you ex-
plored the neighborhood. William used to visit a
cookshop nearby."

"You didn't bring him biscuits, did you." He
stated it as a fact that she couldn't deny.

He set the biscuits on the bench.

It was an invitation to conversation, and she
ought to resist. "You prefer books to company?"

"I'd prefer to come inside and meet your friend."

The stunning boldness of such a wish stated so simply made Ophelia speechless. He wasn't moving, wasn't gathering tack or following orders, but waiting for her reply—testing her, of course. She glanced at the stalls, giving him a hint of his duties.

What did she believe about equality? All men were equal in theory, but in practice, a lady's groom didn't accompany the lady beyond the pavement when she made her calls. Any ease or comfort in their connection would disappear in a drawing room, where he would not know the first thing about how to conduct himself.

It would not make them more equal but rather less. Here with the horses was the only sphere in which there could be some equality. "I doubt you'd enjoy our conversation."

"Too deep for me?"

She knew that wasn't true. Whatever the limits of his education, his mind was not like William's. "No." What could she say? He could not come into Hetty's dining room because . . .

"I'd like to meet the friend who changes your face each morning."

Ophelia concentrated on her gloves. He had a habit of noting minute details about her and then revealing them. "Changes my face?" She looked up, determined to watch him as closely as he watched her.

"When you leave home, your face is tight and closed." He was looking at her intently. "Especially around the mouth."

She ought to do something—laugh, shrug, turn away—but she stood frozen.

"When we leave Miss Gray's, I can tell you've been laughing. Your face has lost its ... pinched look." He took a step closer, his head tilted to one side, his gaze on her mouth.

"Pinched!"

He drew his lips together.

She had to laugh. "A lady does not look pinched." His brows went up. She certainly hadn't convinced him. "Weary, perhaps. Dancing all night, rising to greet the dawn."

"Your face starts to close up as we approach Grosvenor Street."

It was dangerously thrilling to listen to him, to hear how minutely he'd observed her. No one in her household noticed her much, certainly not enough to read her mood.

"It's because I must wear a hair shirt to bed."

He laughed a pleasant laugh of shared amusement, and it sent a wave of deeper warmth through her. But she would not let her vanity lead her down that path again. She would be tougher and less transparent. She hardened her expression.

"I must ask a favor of you."

He was instantly alert. He would probably insist on some bargain or other.

She held out the bundle of sheets of Berwick's poem, wrapped in crackling brown paper and string. "I need to smuggle this package into the house."

"Smuggle?"

She nodded.

"What is it? Seditious speeches?" He was looking at her, not the package.

"Of course, calling for the rights of women."

"Or a novel your mother could not approve?"

"In which a woman's groom is tortured to death for teasing her." She felt silly offering it to him while his hands remained at his side, but she couldn't quite order him with the same capriciousness she had shown days ago.

"Or is it a packet of letters from your many importunate suitors?"

"You're expecting a bribe?"

"You offered one first."

"What do you want, then?" He was asking just to put her off balance, and he had something in mind. She could see it in his eyes.

"Nothing." His expression changed, became veiled. "I was teasing. I'll smuggle for you without repayment."

At last he took the bundle and began unbuttoning his brown silk waistcoat from the bottom. The sight of his fingers freeing the buttons caught her attention. Helplessly she watched the growing patch of white cambric. Then, as if he felt her gaze, he paused, looked up. A carriage rattled past as they regarded each other. His fingers resumed their task, deliberate now. When his unbuttoning had reached halfway, he sucked in a breath and shoved the manuscript under the open sides of the waistcoat.

Ophelia heard the paper crackle as she turned away, cheeks flaming.

Chapter 5

Waltzing with Charles, Lord Dent temporarily exhausted Ophelia's store of ballroom chatter. Apparently Lady Searle had given Dent a hint that Ophelia favored his suit, and it was difficult to dislodge an idea once it became fixed in Dent's brain. So she had labored to steer his mind from his family and found that he could be reasonably engaged in a discussion of the weather.

Beside the column where they stood between sets, she plied her fan steadily, resting the smile muscles in her cheeks, nodding at her companion whenever he seemed to expect it. With the orchestra silent, babble and heat filled the crowded room. Ophelia's curls were damp and wilted, and a decidedly unladylike drop of perspiration trickled down her back while decorum constrained her to stand still and straight.

Since she'd left Alexander, she'd been unable to sit or read or think—in short, unable to occupy herself in any rational manner. Dancing seemed her best hope for relieving the odd sensation of bottled energies swirling inside her.

She'd smiled and flirted and accepted partners for every set. Still, she could not shake Dent, and her cousin Cecile glared at her each time they passed.

"Poor Ophelia," said a voice in her ear. "Looking so forlorn."

She stiffened, but didn't turn. "Go away, Wyatt."

"I don't think so, Sprite," he whispered, taking an intimate, conversational stand beside her, as if he, not Dent, had been her partner. He greeted Dent, who with little encouragement was led back to the subject of his family. It was a deliberate sabotage of the conversation, as Wyatt let her know with a sly, mocking glance.

It was a look they would have shared last season, one that made a joke of Dent. Seeing it in Wyatt's eyes, Ophelia could not recall how she'd once found him so handsome. The dark curling hair, straight brows, and perfect symmetrical features were the same, but his countenance now struck her as smug and cruel.

"But Dent, is that everyone?" Wyatt asked. "I thought Frederick Holdsworth was a connection of yours."

Dent looked alert. "Well, yes. He's a cousin to my mother's brother-in-law, Cornelius, the one who went to India. Frederick himself—"

"The one who's here tonight?"

"Frederick, here? I didn't know." Dent looked around eagerly.

"I believe I saw him in the card room just now," said Wyatt.

Dent glanced toward the door and back at Ophelia. "I beg your pardon, Lady Ophelia. If you'll excuse me, I must pay my respects." To Wyatt he said, "Do you mind keeping Lady Ophelia company?"

"I'll come with you, Dent," Ophelia offered. "I could meet your cousin."

"Not necessary, Lady Ophelia, not necessary at all. I'll just be a minute." He gave her an abashed look, as if he might be conscious of his own tediousness, and hurried off.

Ophelia turned to Wyatt. "Don't you have some other victim to pursue?"

"Not when I see an old friend so in need of rescue. You look quite—wilted—by Dent's ardor."

"Hardly."

Wyatt shook his head. "Dent won't do the job, Ophelia." He took her fan and studied the names of her partners written on the sticks. "But there's a man or two here who might."

Dozens of eyes were watching their exchange. Ophelia snatched her fan back. She managed a smile. "You're despicable, Wyatt. Go away."

"Ophelia, you wound me. As a friend, I can't let you play Princess Charlotte to Dent's Saxe-Coburg." He ran his hand up her arm. "You lack the fat."

She shook him off. "I certainly won't play Caro Lamb to your Byron."

"Ah, that's what I like about you, Sprite, the wit."

"Don't call me that. What you liked about me, Wyatt, was the trusting innocence, and now that it's gone, there's no reason for you to pretend interest in me."

He laughed, leaning very close, his breath ruffling her curls. "What I liked about you was the sweet way your heart fluttered at the sight of me, the way you trembled in my arms." His gaze lingered on her bodice. "And best of all those tiny buds, so charmingly concealed tonight by thin silk, puckering in my hands."

Ophelia felt her color drain away. *You're one of the hot ones, Ophelia.* He knew just how to evoke her humiliating weakness. That he still had any power to embarrass her with past folly made her insides quiver with sick anger. A new set was starting, the crowd shifted around them. Her next partner approached. She gave Wyatt a swift, hard parting look. "You've the soul of a toad."

Her new partner had less conversation than Dent. Uncalled, words of Wyatt's came back to her. It was he who had pointed out the lovers in society, making her aware of the looks exchanged, the carefully timed arrivals and departures. He made her world, which had seemed merely frivolous, seem wicked indeed.

Then, when she had gone into his embrace, he had mocked her for imagining that he loved her, told her she must not expect love or fidelity in marriage, and offered to be her first lover once she had married.

She had discovered then that her heart had not been thoroughly engaged by him. Rather she had been his dupe, as she had often been the dupe of her older brothers. Whenever as a child she'd succumbed to some prank, they had teased her with the old saw *more hair than wit*. After Wyatt, she'd cut her hair.

But there was no mistaking what she'd learned about herself. She had a passionate nature.

Maybe it made sense to marry someone like Dent, who would never stir her desire. He was complacent and easily managed and would not notice her trips to Hetty's. She could work on a manuscript under his very nose without arousing his suspicions in the least.

She dismissed the idea. Life had to offer more than the prospect of deceiving a dull-witted husband. Surely somewhere in society there was a sensible, reasonably self-restrained gentleman to whom she could entrust her fortune and her person. Perhaps she should launch a canoe on the Thames and see who came to the rescue.

Hours later it seemed, she was dancing with Dent again when Jasper caught her eye across the room. She smiled, and at the end of the set, he claimed her from her Dent. "You look fagged, Sprite. Too much dancing?"

"Too much Dent."

Jasper laughed. "There must be someone who's more your style, Sprite."

"I haven't found him."

"Come to the Candovers' with me tomorrow. You'll find a livelier set, and no Dent."

"Sounds appealing." She looked at him. "Are you going to pursue Miss Candover?"

"I'll leave that to Sebastian. I'm following Prince Mirandola's set about."

"How is the search going?"

"Badly. I can't seem to find any friends who've seen or heard from him recently. They love to tell school stories about him, but nothing that really helps. He's apparently got his own tailor and more coats than you'll find on Bond Street. He sold all his horses at Tatt's a couple months back.

He must not have a feather to fly with, but we already knew that." Jasper looked glum. He was staring at the dancers, and she followed his gaze.

"Why do you suppose fellows like Trevor Nash get the plum Foreign Office assignments?" he asked.

"Jasper, there's no mystery in that."

He looked at her in surprise.

"His late mother had tremendous influence with the foreign secretary, the prince, everybody."

"You don't think he's actually good at diplomacy?"

"Not at all."

"Devil take it, I will find Mirandola, then they'll have to take me seriously."

A heavy rain woke Ophelia, drumming on the window and making the solid mass of gray mansions across the square disappear behind veils of gloom. She hugged a shawl around her nightdress, wishing the rain away like a child. No doubt Alexander would be pleased not to have her ordering him about. He would tend the horses and likely have the day free. She tried without success to picture him loitering about the Running Footman Tavern the way other grooms did. The idea did not seem to fit him.

She moved to the hearth, letting the fire warm her nightdress. Where would he go? What would he do with his free hours? The questions made her restless and discontent, overcome by a wretched impatience to inquire of her groom how he meant to spend his day, as if he could charm away the dullness of the rain. Then she remembered the manuscript Solomon Gray had asked her to read, Berwick's new poem, "The Prince of Balat." Bless Solomon Gray for rescuing her from idleness again.

The brown paper wrapping around the loose sheets crackled as she removed the manuscript from its hiding place under her shifts. It was just like the sound of the paper as Alexander had slipped the package under his shirt. She clutched the bundle to her chest, closed her eyes, and willed her mind to think about . . . Berwick.

He was the only young man in the Grays' set that Hetty talked about with interest. Hetty's prospects were no more exciting than Ophelia's, except that Hetty believed in love. Berwick was apparently a regular at the Tuesday night dinners. Though he was a poet and had no certain income, his family had a small estate in Hertfordshire that would eventually belong to him as the only son. By marrying Berwick, Hetty would rise in the world. However, Ophelia wasn't sure their minds were equal. Berwick's talent was for a vein of popular, satiric verse, while Hetty's was deeper, more lasting, truer poetry in the end. Once again Ophelia imagined attending one of the Grays' dinners, where she could judge Berwick's character for herself.

She wrapped a quilt around her shoulders and settled in a chair with her morning chocolate and Berwick's poem. It would require hours of close attention. He had a diffuse, unvaried style and could not resist embellishment to save his life. It was the kind of thing she was good at, seeing the merits of a work in spite of flaws in the writing.

Though few his years, all ancient Balat knows
Young Azim's fame;—beyond the
    emerald shores,
'Ere manhood darken'd o'er his downy cheek,
He fought where liberty was lost and weak,
There felt those godlike breathings in the air
Which mutely told her spirit had been there.
Betrayed by foes, his ship to rocks consigned,
He 'scaped cruel fate, his life for
    fame designed.
And now, returning to his own dear land,
Full of those dreams of good that,
    vainly grand,
Haunt the young heart, Azim sets out to free
His fettered land from ministers too vain,
And bring its rightful glories back again!

Ophelia read on as the shipwrecked prince, abandoned by evil counselors who meant to take over his realm, made his way from the shores of southern India to his capital along the banks of the great Ganges. Disguised as a beggar, the prince first met and befriended a beardless young lad fleeing the port city. Ophelia strongly suspected the delicate boy, Kamala, was a maiden.

Soon Azim and Kamala saw the road darkened by a moving line of black and discovered a great army of spiders advancing to the capital. As they watched, the spiders broke into small companies and swiftly spun their webs in the trees, catching flies and insects as a fisherman fills his net with herrings. The spiders were dividing this spoil when a very grand spider came through the ranks, drawing salutes along the way. Azim resolved to approach him and know the reason for the army's march toward the capital.

The spider king, for so he was, told them the sad tale of how the great lords and merchants in the capital, for their own profit, had developed mechanical looms to weave cheap webs. Now not even the humblest houses in the kingdom would welcome a spider in the corner, for all had machine-made webs in which to trap annoying insects.

Azim declared it a crime against nature to deprive the spiders of their weaving livelihood and offered to help them make their plight known in the capital.

The story charmed Ophelia as much as the excesses of Berwick's style irritated her. She would tell Solomon that "The Prince of Balat" was definitely publishable and much in need of editing. A review began to take shape in her mind, and she was puzzling over some obscure lines when her mother summoned her. Reluctantly, she shoved the manuscript back into her drawer.

Dinner at Searle House was an excruciating affair of multiple courses and as many removes and the dullest exchanges between her parents, each idea leading nowhere, like a stone dropped in a well. The duke listened to his lady's plans for the ball, his perpetually sad face troubled.

Ophelia had heard the plans already. The rain had altered her mother's schedule, and Ophelia had spent most of the day assisting her mother in such considerations as the number of violinists, the relative merits of crab cakes or lobster, and the color of the icing on the cakes. The smell of damp dog, the obsessiveness of her mother's concern for detail, and the dreariness outside had fretted her nerves. She'd had no chance to return to the manuscript, no chance to walk or move or stretch her limbs. No word came from Jasper about his offer to take her to the Candovers'. At the end of an interminable day, she was left with the prospect of a musical evening with her mother.

She had tried to take herself in hand as she dressed, reminding herself that such an evening was nothing more than she was used to. She would not encounter Wyatt or Dent, and she could plead a headache and go home early. The rain would go away, and tomorrow morning she would ride. At her window she had seen patches of fading light as the clouds broke up.

A serious note in her father's voice made her aware that the topic had changed. "A disturbing event occurred today which I take as emblematic of the state of society," he said. "A Mr. Johnson stopped me outside the club this afternoon."

"No, truly?"

"You may imagine my surprise. The fellow makes porter."

"And is like to be lord mayor," Ophelia pointed out.

Her father shot her a quelling glance.

"Ah well, Searle," said the duchess. "I daresay the man's rich. Money will go to people's heads."

The duke jabbed an unoffending piece of the poached turbot with particular vehemence. "He put his hand on my sleeve."

The duchess stiffened, her fork poised above a bit of potato. "You set him down, I hope."

"Instantly, but I think we will soon drown in the tide of presumption sweeping the town." It was the sort of apocalyptic metaphor that made stocks fluctuate when her father spoke in the House of Lords.

The duchess nodded, and the duke laid aside his fork and patted his lips with his napkin. He was plainly preparing to enlarge upon his favorite topic. Ophelia saw the footmen escaping by the simple expedient of carrying off the empty platters. She glanced at the door longingly, and by a miracle Jasper strode in.

"Sir, Your Grace," he said with a quick bow. Ophelia flashed him a grateful smile, and his brows went up, acknowledging her situation. There was a little stir as Jasper inquired about their plans for the evening and the duke sent a footman scurrying to bring a glass of wine.

As the duke described Lady Egerton's musicale, Jasper's gaze met Ophelia's. She gave him a pleading glance.

"But Ophelia must join me at the Candovers'," he said, taking the hint. "Surely you can spare her tonight, Mother?" He appealed to the duchess.

The duchess smiled at Jasper and shrugged. "Of course."

"I'm to dine with Hatherly first, but I'll call for Ophelia at ten and see her home later."

Ophelia demurely kept her eyes on her plate while Jasper remained in easy conversation with her parents. As soon as he'd announced his plans, a scheme had popped into her head. There was no reason to go to Candovers' when she could go to Hetty's instead.

Ophelia had to admit that Jasper had a knack for distracting their parents from their own injuries. Jasper had them laughing about an encounter between Sebastian and an importunate old soldier outside his lodgings. The man had asked for a farthing, and Sebastian had given him a shilling, claiming to be unacquainted with the lesser coin.

When the duke and duchess retired to prepare for their evening, Ophelia walked Jasper to the door.

"See you at the Candovers'," she said.

Jasper turned away from the footman holding his hat and gloves. "Sprite, I told them I'd call for you here."

"Did you never tell them you were going one place, when they thought you somewhere else?"

"Thank you," Jasper said to the footman, dismissing the man with a nod. He regarded Ophelia speculatively, as if she were a puzzle he couldn't quite make out. "Where are you going?"

Ophelia raised her brows. "Never mind. It's entirely respectable, and I'll be perfectly safe. I'll take my groom with me."

"You'd jolly well better."

"I will. Meet you at Candover's." Ophelia gave him a light kiss on the cheek and retreated before he could change his mind. Her slippers had sprouted wings. She sent a hasty note to the stables.

*   *   *

Alexander heard her light, quick steps before he turned and saw her. He could see the shimmer of her dress where the silken cloak opened in the front, and under the hood he caught a glimpse of something shiny coiled on her dark curls. She stopped when she saw him. A deep rose gown warmed her skin. Ropes of pearls at her throat, gathered with gold filigreed clasps, echoed the delicate ivory lacework of her narrow, dipping bodice. He was muddy and tired and too pleased to see her.

When he'd first wakened to rain on the stable roof, he had told himself a day without her was a relief, yet every hour he'd wondered if she would come, if she'd make some excuse to leave the house. When his work was done, he'd occupied himself with a few extra chores better left to the stableboys, even though it was folly to hope she might come down to see her horse. He should have gone back to the tailor's shop to work on his plans for Trevigna.

Then her note had come, asking him to wait for her and prompting all sorts of improbable speculation. Her name was on the tip of his tongue. In the dim and drowsing stable, she was like a bright, flickering flame.

"Am I keeping you from your fellows at some tavern?" she asked. Her breath came out in a bright vapor.

"What do you want?" He lowered his gaze to her feet, too tempted by her in her finery. He realized the riding habit, while elegant and fashionable, was a heavy garment. In silks, she was a winged creature—firefly, moth, night fairy.

"I want you to take me to Hetty's."

"Not a good idea."

"No one will know I've gone. My parents believe Jasper's calling for me at ten, but I'm meeting him later. I'm free." High spirits and raw energy radiated from her. She seemed to have lost all sense of caution.

He raised a practical objection. "I can't put horses to a carriage for you."

She glanced along the stalls. "Take me on Raj. No one will care if you take Raj out."

He had an instant image of the intimacies riding her in front of him would allow and a wave of heat swept through him. "No."

"No?" She stiffened, looking puzzled and annoyed.

He had to make her think about what she was doing. "How did you get out? Who knows where you are?"

"No one knows, that's the beauty of it. Jasper trusts me. He told me to take my groom wherever I was going."

"I won't take you, Ophelia."

She stared at him, frowning in concentration. "Why are you doing this? You're not my father or my brother. You know there's no true impropriety in my going to Hetty's."

The desire to take hold of her was very strong. He shoved his hands in his pockets. He wasn't prepared to explain his reluctance. "I let you go in the mornings because you bribe me, Ophelia."

"So much for ideals, then. Must you have another bribe?"

She asked the question carelessly, expecting some demand on her purse or her friendship. He couldn't answer. He suddenly knew exactly what he wanted from her. Her reckless mood infected him. He craved the chance to hold her against him as they rode through the dark, his arms about her ribs, his face in her hair.

The air around them pulsed with unseen energy.

"If you won't escort me, I'll go on my own." She spun toward Shadow's stall and whistled softly. The mare stuck her head over the stall door and whickered.

Alexander reached out and snagged Ophelia's elbow.

She looked at him over her shoulder. "You can't stop me."

He didn't want to; fool that he was, he wanted to go with her.

Chapter 6

❧❧

Rain dripped from the eaves, horses blew softly in the row of stalls. Slow footsteps sounded from the grooms' quarters above them. The late hour, the silence, altered things between them. They were two ends of a rope that must snap, impatience and restraint.

Now, she wanted to shout. *Go, now, before anyone comes.* Only the expression in his eyes held her, a serious, measuring look. He was cautious, patient, thorough, always moving with the horses in mind.

She would not persuade him. Then his eyes lighted with a reckless glitter that made her giddy. He released her elbow. "Wait here," he said through his teeth.

His footsteps on the stairs sounded with exaggerated loudness in her ears. She was glad for the moment apart. A shiver of strange exhilaration passed through her, the excitement of escaping, the shock of getting her way. She had stepped outside the boundaries that defined them as servant and mistress, and he had followed her. Not that she could not ask him to accompany her. To be in service was to be subject to the jingle of a bell at any hour. But to aid in her escape without a bribe—it made them almost friends. She ran a shaking hand up and down Shadow's nose, promising the mare a good run in the morning.

He returned, wearing a coachman's greatcoat that made her stare.

"I don't want you to get muddied riding in front of me."

He saddled Raj with quick, tight motions, and no more speech, not even as he lifted her to an awkward perch across the lip of the saddle and Raj's withers.

She tried to settle herself, grabbing hold of Raj's mane, but Alexander swung up behind her, his weight tipping her body into his. It was a subtle alteration of the balance of wills. His will, not hers, would move them through the night.

His breath brushed across her cheek, a teasing gust of warmth. His arms closed around her, his hold on the reins tight.

In the yard Raj broke into a skittish prance, a clatter of hooves that roused an answering whinny from Shadow. Ophelia's left shoulder bumped against Alexander's chest with each jerky step. At the contact his muscles tensed.

"You're making Raj uneasy," she said.

"You make me uneasy," he answered in a tight voice.

She twisted a bit so she could look up at him and felt him suck in a breath. Raj tossed his head, sidling and fighting the bit, drawing Alexander's attention. Ophelia felt the play of muscle in his thigh as he relaxed to the movement of the horse.

He brought Raj to a steady walk in the alley along the high wall at the back of the Searle House garden. "Do you ever follow the rules?"

Ophelia sat up straight, opening a gap between her shoulders and his chest. She wouldn't be corrected by him again. "There's no real impropriety in going to Hetty's."

"What about riding through the streets of London like this?"

His meaning was unmistakable. He meant this closeness between them that made her exquisitely conscious of every place their bodies touched. The friction of it spread a melting heat through her limbs.

"It's dark. No one will notice us."

Unexpectedly a cat hissed and leapt from the wall above to a shed roof and to the ground, a gray blur bounding across their path. Raj shied, and Ophelia clutched Alexander's arm for balance. The muscle bunched under her hand.

She tapped his arm as if she could ease his taut hold on the reins.

"Don't," he said in a choked voice.

"Then please, loosen up on Raj."

They came out of the dim lane into the lights of the street where a row of carriages lined the sidewalk approaching Marchmont House. Link boys stood about with torches, horses blew steamy breaths into the night air, and glittering passengers descended with the assistance of liveried footmen. In the darkness the muddy puddles became shimmering pools of light reflecting the gaiety of the scene. When they got beyond the crush and noise, Ophelia spoke again.

"I keep the little rules regularly, so I can break

the big ones when I need to." She wanted him to understand her. Society exercised its subtle tyranny over you, and you broke the rules when you could. Society didn't want you to be free or different. Society didn't want you to acknowledge anyone outside the inner circle.

"You don't care what happens if you're caught tonight?" he asked.

"I won't be."

"Won't someone at Miss Gray's recognize you as Lord Searle's daughter?"

"I'll be plain Miss Brinsby there, a school friend of Hetty's. No one will notice."

A short syllable of derision was his answer. "In that dress?"

Ophelia fell silent.

A stiff breeze blew, scattering the last of the clouds, exposing the cold, bright stars. The chill air washed over Ophelia, and she couldn't help pressing closer to Alexander. He made a low noise in his throat. His body tensed, then yielded a hollow for her to nestle in.

After a while his voice broke their silence. "I'm surprised your parents sent you to school."

"My mother didn't want the inconvenience of a governess and dancing master underfoot." Ophelia had no idea how to explain her mother's lack of interest in her children. One by one Sebastian, Jasper, and Ophelia had gained her notice as they'd entered society. Even then, Ophelia was most interesting to her mother as an object to dress. Acquiring sufficient bosom for décolletage had been the best thing Ophelia had ever done, in her mother's eyes, and could she manage to grow another two or three inches, she would please her mother even more.

"At school your parents couldn't keep you from the humble Miss Grays of the world." Alexander sounded perplexed.

"They didn't know about Hetty until Solomon published our book."

"You wrote a book?" His amazement was hardly complimentary.

"Hetty and I did." It had been a long time since she'd thought about their book and the dreams that had gone with it. "Is that so difficult to believe?"

He laughed. "When did you sit still to write it?"

"I can sit quite still when my mind's engaged."

He shifted in the saddle, and she realized that her left hip was wedged against his loins. To squirm or wiggle or attempt to defy force of gravity would probably only call attention to their intimate situation. Ophelia held still.

"What was the book about?" he asked.

She waited. It was important that he not laugh. She didn't tell these things to Ayres or Haddington or Dent. "The ideal state of man."

"What did you say that was?"

She tried to see him in the dark. He didn't sound mocking, only interested. "Free and equal, like horses."

"Not a view your parents could accept."

"Oh, they never read the book. They merely disliked the notoriety of a young woman of rank putting her name to any work that circulated generally among the public."

He was silent a moment. They were beyond

Mayfair now, beyond the dark expanse of the park. Raj's hooves clopped steadily on the paving stones. Carriages rattled by in the opposite direction.

"How old were you then?"

"Sixteen. They took me out of school, issued ultimatums."

"Fobidding you to see Miss Gray?"

"Forever. So you see why I break the rules."

"She must be a good friend."

Ophelia caught herself. In this whole exchange she had been more open than she was with anyone except Hetty. She shrugged, twisting her hands in Raj's mane, seeking her own hold on the horse. "Hetty laughs at my humor," she said lightly.

The lantern in the Gray stable seemed bright after the darkness outside. Alexander swung down and led Raj to a stall. A pair of stableboys looked up from their dicing, but paid no more attention. Alexander lifted Ophelia down.

Her feet touched the ground, but his hands clung to her waist. His eyes seemed to ask something of her, but that was likely a deception wrought by going from the dark to light.

"I should be back by midnight," she said. He still held her waist. "Thank you," she added. "I'll slip in through the garden."

"You can't go alone." He held her with his gaze. "I'll walk you to the door." His hands dropped away from her waist.

The Grays' Tuesday suppers had started by accident after a particular publishing success of one of Solomon's authors and had become a habit.

At the door of the book-lined rose drawing room, Ophelia hesitated. The arrangement of the chairs, the turn of the guests' heads, suggested not conversation, but a queen holding court. A woman with golden curls around a fine-boned oval face had drawn everyone's notice, and Ophelia guessed she must be Mrs. Amelia Hart. If her beauty was the first impression, a closer look showed a porcelain coolness of the skin, a detachment, a calculating gleam in the eyes, and absolute assurance.

When Mrs. Hart looked up, the others turned to Ophelia. She had entered salons, grand ballrooms, and the court, but always preceded by some functionary announcing her title to people too self-absorbed to look twice. In the eyes of Hetty's guests Ophelia saw that her evening gown was wrong, overstated. She was a wren in a peacock's plumage.

"Ophelia, you came, after all," said Hetty, rising with unimpaired cordiality to welcome her, as if her coming had been agreed upon between them. "You must meet everyone."

On round tables at the ends of a long sofa, coffee, wine, and cakes had been laid out. Hetty gave Ophelia a glance that said she expected an explanation and took Ophelia's arm to lead her around the room, introducing writers and scientists, a bookseller and an attorney. Ophelia nodded and smiled in a kind of daze. Hetty's friends were as warm and unceremonious as the Grays.

Mrs. Fenton, a slim woman whose wispy brown hair was escaping its pins, enlisted Ophelia's support at once. "Miss Brinsby, can you help me? I'm defending our poets against all detractors."

Ophelia looked at a trio of cheerful faces, unable to see where an attack was coming from.

"Come, Edie," said a Mr. Archer. "You can't defend Wordsworth!"

"Not all his work, but there are some poems— help me, Miss Brinsby," she said.

Ophelia laughed. "The sonnets are good. The one on sleep?"

"There you are." Mrs. Fenton beamed. "He's never really good about politics, but then . . ." Mrs. Fenton looked around at her audience. "What man really is? They must seize the dais and proclaim."

"Now, Edie . . ."

Hetty pulled Ophelia along.

"Which one is Berwick?" Ophelia whispered, and Hetty's glance shifted to a short young man with fair curls and self-conscious good looks. Ophelia smiled to herself as she realized he had modeled Azim after himself. He and Mrs. Hart stood apart at a side table, apparently conscious of a shared importance that the other guests lacked, Berwick speaking earnestly. Mrs. Hart, bored and not bothering to conceal it, toyed with the blooms in a tall silver epergne. Hetty made the introductions and drew Berwick aside with a question about his poem.

Mrs. Hart turned her scrutiny on Ophelia with a glance Ophelia knew, the glance of one rival measuring the other, though in what arena they could be competing Ophelia could not guess.

"It's a pleasure to meet a school friend of Hetty's, Miss Brinsby," she said, smiling as if to encourage an awkward child. "Are you long out of school?"

Ophelia kept her countenance. "My school days do seem long ago, ma'am."

Mrs. Hart laughed a husky laugh. "I suppose last week seems long ago when one is young."

"Not so very young. I've been in society some time."

"And how do you find society, Miss Brinsby?"

"Necessary."

Solomon Gray passed them at that moment, carrying a decanter, and Mrs. Hart held out a glass for him to fill with amber liquid. Their eyes met with the familiarity of long acquaintance, Mrs. Hart's gaze mocking, Solomon's chagrined. Ophelia watched openly. She had never seen Solomon Gray bested in an exchange or embarrassed as he was in his famous guest's company. Mrs. Hart detained him with a light remark about the party.

When she could, Ophelia excused herself and pulled Hetty aside to the refreshment table. "Your father seems uncomfortable with Mrs. Hart. Is something wrong?"

Hetty followed Ophelia's glance and quickly looked away from her father and the novelist. Their intimacy seemed to bother her. "I don't know," she confessed. "How did you get here?" she asked, abruptly changing the topic.

"Alexander brought me."

Hetty's eyes widened at the daring of it. "How? Not in a carriage?"

"No, on Raj. I'm free."

Hetty frowned. "Can you trust him? How will you get back?"

"He's waiting for me in your stable."

"Who's waiting?" Mrs. Hart had moved to their corner, and there was no way of knowing how much of their conversation she had heard.

"The . . . friend who accompanied me, ma'am," said Ophelia.

"A friend?" Mrs. Hart's lazy cat gaze said she scented some deception. "Do invite him in, Miss Gray."

Ophelia's stomach did a strange flip at the thought. "Here?"

"Of course. It won't do to have a friend languishing in the stable while we talk. It could be hours." Ophelia didn't dare look at Hetty.

"I don't mind," said Hetty.

Ophelia's brain refused to work, to think of the necessary evasion.

"I'll speak to your father, Miss Gray. He can send his man to the stable. We'll make your friend quite welcome, I assure you, Miss Brinsby."

Ophelia stood helpless as Mrs. Hart approached Solomon. The woman would use civility as a weapon. Ophelia turned to Hetty. "What are we going to do? My *friend* is covered in mud from grooming horses all day."

"He won't come in, will he?" Hetty asked.

Ophelia suddenly knew he would. She had supposed he would join the other grooms in their dicing game, but she knew as soon as she had the thought that he wouldn't. It was difficult to assign him a place in society. He seemed outside of it, somehow. If he didn't fit in Hetty's drawing room, he certainly didn't fit among low men gambling for shillings.

Hetty squeezed Ophelia's hand. "Drink your coffee. He'll be welcome. Didn't you say he had more wit than your dance partners? I'll slip out and make sure he looks like a 'friend' and not a servant."

Ophelia turned blindly to find the bookseller, Mr. Archer, at her side. He was a large man with a calm, contemplative countenance. He seemed aware of Ophelia's distraction without being offended by it. After a few weak remarks from her, he took up the burden of the conversation. She could follow him without effort while her glance kept straying to the door.

As if a signal had been given, the guests returned to seats around the room, laughing, adjusting the chairs to form a loose circle. Mrs. Hart took a green velvet chair next to the attorney. Ophelia's companion invited her to join him on one of the couches covered with bright chintz in a pattern of roses.

The conversation passed from poets to engines to politics. Ophelia wanted her whole mind on the talk, but she kept looking at the door. Just as it occurred to her that Alexander might have left the stable, might not be found, the door opened and he entered with Hetty.

Ophelia had to adjust her thinking about him instantly. He fit in her father's stable, with his quiet confidence and competence, his easy way with the horses, but he fit here, too, strikingly. The candlelight favored him, lighting the gold strands in his hair. The mud had been scraped from his boots and brushed from his breeches, and he wore a borrowed brown coat—respectable, but, she realized, inferior to his usual coats.

Even so, he outshone the other men in the room. His pride of bearing drew the guests' notice as Mrs. Hart's beauty had.

His gaze met Ophelia's, and he halted as if he'd forgotten other eyes were on him. The look he gave her burned a path from her toes to the dipping "V" of her bodice, halted indiscreetly there, and rose to her face. Ophelia found herself rising with the others. There was some polite ritual to be observed, but she'd forgotten what it was, her heart beating wildly, her breath trapped in her throat.

Hetty was going to present him, to name him. Ophelia leaned forward, impatient to hear his name. She had never asked, and now strangers were going to hear it first.

"I beg your pardon," Hetty said. "Our friend, Mr. Alexander."

The moment passed. He had kept his secrets, after all. There was no time to wonder at it. Berwick was urging them back to the conversation. Hetty and Solomon found a chair for Alexander, and there was a brief shuffle as Mrs. Fenton shifted places, and Alexander settled next to Mrs. Hart and opposite Ophelia.

Mrs. Hart swirled the brandy in her glass and asked about the Prince Regent.

Mr. Archer turned the talk away from direct criticism of the regent with a theory that government evolved in an organic way out of a nation's character and history.

"No need to criticize the Regent," he declared. "The right form of government is inevitable."

Berwick leaned forward in his chair, his shoulders squared as if he were ready to lunge at an opponent. He seemed to be waiting to interrupt, determined to assert himself.

"Your theory won't hold, Archer," he said. "Or a nation of such industrious, practical people as the English could not have produced such fat leeches as the royal dukes have become."

Ophelia saw Hetty flinch. She did not appreciate Berwick's clubbing kindly Mr. Archer with his opinion, and felt she must apply some conversational balm to soothe the irritation that Berwick had created. While the guests cleared their throats and shifted uneasily, Mrs. Hart turned her smile on Berwick, asking him to explain himself.

Berwick's posture relaxed at once, his ego apparently soothed. The grateful look Hetty sent Mrs. Hart made Ophelia oddly jealous. It was another sign of the intimate control Mrs. Hart seemed to exercise over the Grays.

Berwick declared the royal princes the dregs of their race.

Ophelia thought it a mean-spirited attack. "In his defense, the Regent has taste," she said. "And he has undertaken great building projects."

Alexander watched her with his intense blue gaze, and her glance settled on him almost against her will.

"What is taste," said Berwick, "when Prinny doesn't know what the humblest cottager knows—how to live within his means?"

"Alas," said Mrs. Hart, "the poor Regent can't even manage to live within his waistband."

General laughter relieved the tension of the moment. Mrs. Hart raised her glass and sipped delicately. Berwick looked bewildered at the suddenness with which the confrontation evaporated. Ophelia wondered again at Mrs. Hart's assurance and glanced at Solomon to see how he took the woman's lofty manner. Mrs. Hart acted as if she were the lady of the house, not Hetty. She lowered her glass and turned to Alexander with a snowy bosom, a throaty voice, and a languid air.

"We haven't heard from you, Mr. Alexander," she said.

Ophelia was instantly alert. There was something in Mrs. Hart's voice that disturbed her. Alexander had remained quiet intentionally, she supposed. She clutched the delicate cup in her hand. She had become used to his speech and saw no uncouthness in it. She knew he read books, but how would he sound in the midst of people of deep education?

"You've heard all sides of the issue, ma'am," he said.

"Then you must tell us which side you take," Mrs. Hart insisted. Her mouth curved in a slow, inviting smile, her body leaned toward his. "Has the Regent hurt the monarchy?"

"The idea of monarchy has been in question for fifty years at least," he said. "No man can blame the Regent for that."

Ophelia could see he was evading Mrs. Hart's efforts to make him speak against the Prince, but she seemed more intrigued with him than ever.

Berwick broke in. "The Regent's making everything worse. The monarchy won't have any power when he's crowned."

"If that's so, it must be because he's forgotten how to serve," said Alexander quietly.

"A prince serves the nation?" asked Mrs. Hart. "What a quaint idea!"

Ophelia could see it was no joke with Alexander.

He looked about at the others in his bold way. "A man in power, surrounded by servants who rush to do his bidding, forgets that he is subject to power. A man waiting to be king, with none of the duties and responsibilities of the king, but with all the ceremony, forgets that he is a man."

There was a change in the atmosphere of the group. Ophelia could sense the others' interest in his perspective.

"If a prince is a mere man," she asked him, "how is he to win his people's esteem?"

He smiled at her, a slow, satisfied smile, and she had the feeling the question had made talk easy for him.

"Nothing makes a prince more esteemed than great undertakings and examples of his unusual talents." He said it as if he were reciting a familiar lesson. "Then it helps a prince to display examples of his skill in dealing with internal affairs."

The ideas sounded like a book. She knew what he would say next.

"A prince should also demonstrate that he is a lover of talent." He was quoting someone, she was sure.

He stopped and dropped his teasing gaze from hers, speaking quietly and earnestly. "The work of the prince is to serve the people, protect them, put all self-interest aside for their good, and die if he must. His readiness to do that is what gives him power."

The room went quiet, no stir, no clatter of cups. Without pretension he spoke of an ideal of kingship that lifted it above a joke. They were so used to the Regent's failings, his fat person, the print shop caricatures, they couldn't see any majesty in kingship any longer, but Alexander made them see it.

"Surely no one expects a prince to die these days." Mrs. Hart broke the spell, her eyes teasing.

Alexander's serious gaze turned to her. "It's the readiness to sacrifice all for the people that marks a true prince. Without it, he's too apt to think they serve him." He said it easily, but refused to make light of it.

Mrs. Hart merely watched him more openly, a keen sparkle in her eyes, the brandy glass in her languid hand.

Somewhere a clock chimed the hour, and Mrs. Hart asked Hetty for the tea tray. A flushed Hetty rang, and Mrs. Pendares appeared with another tray of cakes and pots of fresh coffee. Ophelia was surprised to see Mrs. Pendares go about her business without a glance at Hetty or Solomon, a strange silence around her, as if she were invisible.

Berwick backed Ophelia into a corner by the refreshments. She smiled grimly at him, intending to be civil, but not to cater to the man's pride. He had energy and wit, but he was sharply critical and ungenerous in his opinions. Listening to him, she was amazed his poem was as good as it was, and she realized he would never do for Hetty.

Across the room Mrs. Hart found Alexander's

side and rested her hand lightly on his sleeve. Their golden heads inclined toward each other, their conversation plainly private.

Ophelia could no longer make sense of Berwick's words. She couldn't remember where she'd set out to go this evening. Alexander astonished her. He was not the man she'd thought he was a fortnight earlier.

She left Berwick spouting something about the number of farms that had failed under the current government, and went to extricate Alexander from Mrs. Hart.

Chapter 7

The fragrance of the Grays' rain-soaked garden sweetened the air, and Alexander halted, filling his lungs with a deep cleansing breath. Beside him at the top of the stairs, Ophelia whirled in a brief dance. "You see why I had to come tonight."

"No." He was being perverse.

"Because there is no artificial nonsense, no gossip. People talk of engines, poetry, and princes. They lose themselves in ideas."

"Berwick hardly lost himself. He waved his opinions about as if he were leading a charge at Waterloo."

She sighed. "I grant you Berwick's egotism, but you have to admit Mr. Archer and the others were splendid, especially about poetry."

He could admit it as long as she dismissed Berwick. She'd spent half an hour tête-à-tête with Berwick, nodding gravely at whatever the blond idiot said.

Now Alexander wanted the breeze to sweep away his deceptions. He needed to recall who and where he was, to sort out the lies. It was one thing to play a groom in a stable, another to involve Ophelia publicly in a masquerade before the Grays' guests. In an impulsive moment he'd taken his plan to make her treat him as an equal far beyond his original intention.

But the temptations of the evening had come rapidly, one after the other, like breakers when one tried to launch a boat. First, he could not refuse to take her to Hetty's when he understood the tyranny of a social calendar that herded London society in and out of ballrooms like sheep. Then he had been unable to refuse Hetty's invitation when he might see Ophelia in company for hours. And once there he had been unable to sit silent and cautious while Berwick spouted idiocy about princes. His will had been unequal to such restraint, and he'd been rewarded for his fall the moment he'd entered the Grays' drawing room.

Seeing Ophelia in her evening dress, he had forgotten everything but her brilliance. Excitement lit her from inside, her delicate skin flushed like a clear dawn sky. Her throat bared to his gaze had left him standing stupidly in the midst of strangers, all his habits of caution abandoned in the singular desire to touch her. His gaze had been drawn to her irresistibly, and the disposition of the chairs had allowed him to continue his folly.

Whatever the others made of him as an uninvited guest, Mrs. Hart obviously recognized his secret desire for Ophelia. When the conversation broke up, Mrs. Hart sought him out. His senses, already quickened by Ophelia's radiance, had lain open to Mrs. Hart's assault. She pressed her soft bosom against his arm, murmured in his ear with her warm voice, and tangled him in her rich scent. He had wanted Ophelia's nearness, and reaching for it was like straining to catch a faint, sweet melody over the swelling sounds of a street band.

He stretched, trying to shake off the lingering effects of Mrs. Hart. At least he had his own coat back again, felt more himself.

Ophelia ran lightly down the steps into the garden, a fairy tale creature in a gossamer cape, flitting through the darkness, while he stood transfixed, watching her.

Abruptly, she stopped and cast him an impatient glance over her shoulder. "What are you waiting for?"

"I need to clear my head."

"I can imagine." She strolled back to the foot of the steps. "The scent of flattery can be very strong."

Alexander laughed. So she thought him under Mrs. Hart's spell. He came down the steps, stopping just in front of her, taken with the bright glitter of her eyes.

She challenged him with her stance. "You made a fine impression on Mrs. Hart. What did she want?"

"She invited me to return."

"Tonight?"

The question came and went so quickly he could not make out the tone. "Next Tuesday."

"Oh." She shrugged. "That's perfect. We can come again."

"I'd rather not." He tried to think of an excuse

she would accept. "I don't much relish performing on cue like a pet dog."

"Really? I thought you rather enjoyed yourself."

He made himself look away. "You don't know what I enjoy or don't enjoy, Ophelia."

"It seemed clear enough to me with Mrs. Hart's generous bosom under your nose."

Alexander said nothing. He was not going to speak of bosoms when just an arm's reach away, concealed by Ophelia's cloak, were the high, small, uptilted breasts of his restless dreams. A nearby churchbell rang the quarter hour. He'd forgotten time entirely. Now he remembered that she was supposed to meet her brother somewhere. He stepped around her and indicated the garden path. "Let's go."

"Wait," she said, putting out a gloved hand to stop him, close but not touching. "Promise you'll bring me to Hetty's again."

He kept his gaze on her hand. "It's not wise."

"How can you say so? What impropriety is there in coffee and ideas and interesting people?" Her voice had risen.

"You don't know what the dangers are," he said quietly.

"I didn't get caught."

"You're not safely home yet." He started down the path.

An instant later he heard her quick steps behind him. "Are you afraid Berwick will reveal a plot to overthrow the Regent? Or Mr. Archer will offer me some insult?"

"No."

"Well, then, you don't want me here because you want to come on your own."

"No." He was forgetting his role as groom. He stopped where the stone path turned and ran along the back wall of the garden to the gate. She came up behind him, a little breathless.

"One of your brothers should bring you," he said quietly without turning.

"Coward."

He was. He walked on. It was only a few yards to the gate. He was afraid he was going to do something rash if she kept goading him this way. "You will cost me my situation." He spoke without conviction, too conscious of the lie.

"I will see that you get another."

He stopped, the crunch of gravel under his boots an echo of the anger he felt. She had reminded him that he was not quite a person in her eyes, that she forgot him daily when she left the stable.

"There are other reasons," he said coldly. "You don't need the scandal Mrs. Hart would be happy to embroil you in. You don't need to present . . . me as your equal when I'm not."

"You don't believe that. You spoke as if you . . ."

He tried one more argument. "There's too great a chance of . . . intimacy in riding together." He held his breath. Truth and lies blended strangely in his words.

"Fine democratic principles you have," she said, disgust evident in her tone. "You're a snob."

She brushed past him, and the light sweep of her cloak against his leg jolted him. Before he could steady himself, she spun, facing him, backing away, holding his gaze helpless.

"Why worry about intimacy with me when you spent the better part of an hour gazing at Mrs. Hart's chest?"

He reached for her, but she retreated, colliding with a low hanging branch that sent a shower of cold drops over them. With a little cry, she stepped forward, shivering and shaking the water from her mantle. Its hood slipped from her curls, and raindrops sparkled in her hair, a tiny diadem. His will broke and he caught her shoulders, pushing her against the rough wall of the garden, trapping her, silk against stone.

In the dark, her eyes grew big with awareness. She pushed against his ribs, and his breath caught at her touch. For a moment their breathing filled the garden—irregular, mingled, charged with longing.

He couldn't believe he'd done it, trapped her there. He'd never been driven enough by a woman just to take what he wanted, but he was ruled by a hunger which weeks of watching Ophelia had fed. By now he knew the delicacy of her skin, the sweet scent that clung to her, the temptation of her uptilted breasts, the vulnerability of her narrow waist.

"I'm not interested in Mrs. Hart's chest," he said, the words clipped by his uneven breath. The surge of boldness crested in him. Whatever happened afterward when he regained sanity and restraint, he was not going to let this moment pass without kissing her.

He shifted his weight, lifting one hand from the wall, tracing a line across the softness under her chin. "The collar of your riding habit comes to here."

A small incoherent sound came from her throat, drawing his attention down to where he rested the "V" of his hand against the flutter of her pulse. With a slow, reverent move, he brushed the mantle over her shoulder. "All this," he gazed at the white glimmer of her flesh, "was hidden from me until tonight."

He bent and kissed the base of her throat, drinking in the scent of her. Her fingers opened and closed, bunching the cloth over his ribs. The motion tugged at his shirt ends, sending flashes of desire down through the roots of his nerves. He kissed his way up her neck to her ear, her cheek, and paused, his face pressed to hers. She was resisting him, avoiding his mouth, and it occurred to him that he should stop now, that he should not kiss her while she believed him a lowly groom, but his whole body beat with longing. He was greedy with it.

"Ophelia." He didn't recognize the low rasp of his own voice.

She kept her face averted, but her hands still clutched his waistcoat. "It's not me you want."

"It is." He pried one of her hands from his ribs and pressed the palm flat over the rapid beating of his heart. She turned then, trembling, her mouth inches from his.

He lifted his hand and traced the outline of her lips with his fingertips. "One kiss."

"You make me weak."

"No more than me." That, at least, was a true thing in all his lies.

She went still, her hands flat against his ribs.

He lowered his face and touched his mouth to hers. Her kiss was hesitant, untrusting, dry, admitting nothing. He offered more, breathed his desire into her. He was a fool to let her see how completely he wanted her. She would gain more power over him, but he wanted to convince her that he thought of her only, and no one else. He coaxed and teased and knew the moment she yielded and acquiesced to his kisses, opening sweetly, letting him taste.

Ophelia tasted need, frank and demanding. It was there in the thrust of his tongue and in the press of his hot, hard body against hers. And it made her frantic to open, to give, to soothe. But against his melting heat pressed the cold, wet stones at her back.

Alexander felt caution and reason vanish. There was only Ophelia. He put his hand to her waist and slid upwards, up the fan of her ribs to cup the soft swell of her breast, drawing his thumb once across the nipple.

She wrenched her mouth from his, struggling to free herself from his hold. "Don't."

"Please." The plea came raw and impassioned from somewhere deep within him.

She tried to slide away along the wall, but he pressed his body to hers, pinning one of her hands between them. At the contact he froze, giving in to the pleasure of her hand accidentally cupping his hot, swollen male flesh. Her eyes widened and he shoved away from the wall, freeing her.

She pulled her mantle closed and hugged herself tight, her arms crossed over her chest.

He turned away, balling his hands into fists

and tucking them under his arms. He threw his head back, looking up at the distant stars, willing the riot in his body to calm. "You see why I can't bring you to Miss Gray's again."

"Yes."

"I apologize for any offense I gave. I will leave your father's stable if you wish."

The stars glittered coldly while he waited for her reply.

"No."

"Wait here," he said. "I'll bring Raj to the gate."

Alexander wrapped her in the greatcoat and kept Raj moving briskly. They rode in silence. It was too early for the traffic of carriages returning from the evening amusements of society. She burrowed into the folds of the heavy garment and tried to think how she had come to stand helpless and trembling, accepting the kisses of her groom.

After Wyatt, she had vowed never to be weak again. She had been determined to prove that her nature was cool, not passionate. She had carefully cultivated men who did not stir her senses. Yet her weakness had appeared where she least expected it, with her groom, with Alexander, who had done nothing to seduce her, offered no flattery, no attempts to get her alone, no soulful gazes.

She had yielded however briefly to a man who had spent the evening absorbed by another woman. His carnal appetite had been stirred, and she had been the available female. That might explain his actions, but not hers. Why had she been so weak-willed as to permit his advances? Because it had seemed for a few minutes as if he truly did want her? Vanity. But she had felt the rapid beating of his heart and for one startled moment the pulsing heat of his most male part.

Then she had had to break away. Just the flick of his thumb across her breast had sent a bolt of sensation through her. She had been humiliated again by her body's response to a man. Alexander was knowing and clever. He would sense, as Wyatt had, that Ophelia's nature was passionate and weak. She had as much resistance as a brandy-soaked pudding that went up in flame at the first touch of a taper.

Her character was worse than she'd thought. She was a woman who accepted the embraces of a servant, a man dependent on her for his livelihood. She could not ride again.

When Alexander let himself into the tailor shop sometime after one, he found Lucca in the sitting room with a lamp lit, lying on a couch by the fire, a glass of wine in hand.

He was dressed in evening finery, with only his cravat loosened.

"Majesty!" He jumped to his feet, offering Alexander the couch.

Alexander waved him back down and went to a side table to pour himself some wine. "You look very fine."

"I went to the opera," Lucca said, "and had a long ride home." A sly grin hovered in his expression. His limbs seemed loose and heavy.

Alexander had no trouble reading the signs of an amorous encounter. "In a hackney?"

Lucca had the grace to look abashed. "I could not bring her here," he pointed out. He yawned and stretched, rising and moving to the hearth, poking at the fire with the lazy repleteness of sexual satisfaction.

Alexander had a brief vision of embracing Ophelia in a hackney and rejected the unworthy image with disgust.

Lucca put the poker aside and looked at him more sharply. "What brings you here tonight, Majesty? Your quarters at the stable no longer suit you?"

Alexander sank into a chair.

"The hardheaded lady refused you!" Lucca slapped his thighs with his palms and went off in the coast dialect of Trevigna about the vagaries of women.

"Lucca, you can't blame the girl for refusing the attentions of a groom in her father's stable."

"Majesty, you must drop this base disguise." The look in Lucca's eyes was anguished. "Come back. Let Lucca take care of you. Soon we will go home. Forget these English who do not know how to treat a prince of the blood."

Alexander stared at his wine. He was too tired to fight Lucca tonight. He certainly should not return to Lord Searle's stable. "I'll stay the night. I have work to do."

"Good." Lucca assumed his best servant manner. "First, I will prepare your bath."

Alexander knew better than to refuse. Better a bath than questions. But once he lay soaking in the copper tub, he realized a bath was a bad idea. His mind, empty of other thoughts, was open to visions of his encounter with Ophelia in the garden.

She had been jealous of Mrs. Hart's attentions toward him, of that he was sure, but she had been fearful of his attentions to her. As much as her hands clung to his sides, she'd held her face averted, frightened and longing at once, and he didn't think his low rank bothered her. If anything, she might kiss him to defy convention. No, he thought something in her experience of men had made her break away.

He allowed himself to relive those moments in the garden even though his thoughts roused his aching flesh once more. What had she said? *You make me weak.* He knew the precise moment she'd broken away. He had stroked with his thumb across her breast, one stroke only, too fleeting to gauge her response. Then she'd crossed her arms over her chest. If her body had responded to his touch, she did not want him to know. And she had been horrified to discover the state of his arousal.

He had recognized his own need the moment he'd backed her against the wall. But in spite of his pressing his attentions on her, she had not insisted on his dismissal and she had not run from him. Only she had wanted to keep something of herself back.

He suspected Ophelia was like his aunt Francesca, unwilling to show a weakness to anyone. She had not wanted him to know she attached any importance to seeing Hetty Gray, and now she did not want him to know she had any vulnerability.

Meanwhile, his experience with Blanca could

not guide him with Ophelia. Blanca's sexuality was open and frank; her weakness was also her power over men, a strength she used in the service of her country.

He had met her in a mountain inn in Segonzano, where she was seducing a French officer. She moved from table to table, apparently serving wine, but all the time concentrating her energy on the officer, her hands touching, lingering, making him believe her eager for his flesh. Their awareness of each other had filled the room. Alexander, seated at a table in the shadows, had been unable to look away. By the time the officer abruptly snagged Blanca's arm and told her he would have her, Alexander's loins were aching, his knees pressed up against the table to keep from shaking.

The officer, suddenly called to his regiment, went without hesitation and Blanca turning away, caught a glimpse of Alexander's face, in which he knew there was an open confession of his lust. Their eyes met and he discovered that Blanca needed to complete what she'd begun. There had been no falseness in her sexual interest in the officer. She had wanted him. She might take back to her father and others in the independence movement whatever she gained in the unguarded moments of the Frenchman's passion, but she needed release. Slowly, she had crossed the room to Alexander, her hands on her hips, her breasts straining against the cotton blouse.

He had gripped his wineglass tightly, certain the table would quake with his effort to control his trembling limbs. The scent of her made his head swim. He wanted her touch and feared it.

"You want me," she said.

"But you don't want me. I have not the experience of your officer."

She cocked her head to one side, apparently intrigued by his frankness. "A virgin?"

He had nodded, his throat too dry for further speech.

He had refused her that night, but the next time they met, they began an affair that lasted until he left the hill country. Blanca made it clear from the start that love could not be part of their liaison. Whatever sex did to her body, it left her head clear and cold.

Their connection had ended at the seige of Godolfo, where Blanca had been sent into the town to seduce valuable information from the defending French. Alexander had had to watch strangers receive gestures as familiar to him as his name, touches that he had wished to believe were for him alone. Blanca used her sexuality as a man used a sword or a rifle. Her desire for her victim was real; that was the secret of her success. She wanted the man, whoever he was, that she set out to win. Alexander left the hills.

Since then he'd been more or less content with abstinence. But abstinence was one thing when there was no woman who caught one's fancy and quite another when one could see and hear and touch daily the object of one's desire and not have her.

The bath water was cold when he stepped out of the tub and toweled off. There was another, more sobering cause for regret in his advances. Ophelia had been happy at the Grays', and he had made it impossible for him to take her back there again, which meant he had cost himself the chance to see her happy, to see her glowing with excitement.

He would mortify his sexual appetite as he should have done earlier. He would do penance. He would read all of Francesca's letters and work on the dullest section of his principles. And if he went back to Lord Searle's stables, he would keep his mind on horses.

Chapter 8

~~~⌒⌒~~~

Ophelia sat in the windowseat of her mother's green sitting room, reading a book, pretending nothing was out of the ordinary. Lady Searle, who spent very little time out of doors, had conceived the green room as a controlled encounter with nature. In fact, she used it for the meetings with her secretary and housekeeper that preceded a ball. To Ophelia the walls, covered in a print of vivid vegetation, seemed to close in on her, rather as if she were picnicking in a grove of giant celery stalks.

She had sent a note to the stables to say that she would not ride. She had no choice in the matter. What had happened between her and Alexander could not be repeated.

Ophelia was not entirely ignorant of sex. She had been around stables enough to pick up some very obvious lessons. The breeding instrument of a stallion and when in season the eagerness of a mare for her mate were rather more instructive than her mother's veiled allusions to such matters. At eleven she'd received a further lesson when she'd come across Cyril Weston, one of Sebastian's classmates, pressing a housemaid up against a wall.

Cyril had later apologized to Ophelia for offending her sensibilities.

"Shouldn't you apologize to Jenny?" Ophelia had asked.

Cyril had laughed. "Oh, she's the sort that likes a good tumble," he'd replied.

Then Mrs. Pendares had tried to enlighten Ophelia and Hetty on the nature of sexual congress between men and women. She had explained that a man's breeding instrument swelled and stiffened and that a woman's place grew moist and warm before their joining could be accomplished.

Now the facts were plain to Ophelia. Alexander had pressed her against a wall. Her protests had been feeble. Her heart had beat wildly. Her breath had come in quick, shallow pants. That most male part of him had been warm and stiff, and she had wanted to touch him. Apparently, like Jenny, Ophelia was the sort of girl who liked it. Wyatt had said as much.

It must be true. Even now, thinking about Alexander, she grew edgy and restless, and to allow herself to recall those moments against the garden wall brought a betraying consciousness of her breasts.

"Ophelia!" The note of irritation and urgency in her mother's tone was a clear warning that Ophelia's inattention had violated the sacrosanct ritual of preparing Lady Searle's guest list.

Her mother frowned at her, a piece of paper clutched in one hand, as she stroked Pet's white belly with the other. At a small work table, Lady

Searle's secretary, Mr. Graves, made notes on several loose sheets of paper.

"What are you reading?" her mother demanded.

"Nothing, a little story from Jasper's shelf." Ophelia slipped a bookmark in Sismond's *History of the Italian Republics*.

"Well, put it aside. You could develop a squint."

"Yes, Mother." Ophelia had tried to keep her mind occupied every waking moment since the episode in Hetty's garden, no small feat in her family's company. The convoluted politics of Italian history in Sismond's book required just the intensity of concentration that kept her from unwelcome thoughts. The background she gained might be of some use to Jasper.

Under her mother's severe gaze, Ophelia surrendered the windowseat. She squeezed into the space at the end of the sofa on the other side of Pet and slipped the book between her hip and the arm.

Her mother turned to Graves. "Next page, please." A piece of paper changed hands, and her mother studied it silently.

Graves smirked. No doubt he'd pointed out the omissions to Ophelia's portion of the list.

Lady Searle stroked Pet in long, mildly agitated strokes. "Your list of suitors is too brief, Ophelia. We must add Atherton, Clermont, Dent . . ." She glanced at Graves.

"Haddington, Wyatt?" he asked.

"Mother, last season I declined the addresses of three of those gentlemen." Ophelia had no regrets. Her former suitors had been prompt and dutiful in a way that had hardly been flattering. She had been a duke's daughter, a prize, nothing more.

"All the more reason to include them now. Everyone will see that you are inclined to think seriously about this marriage business. You will be forgiven for being particular in your first season."

Ophelia shrugged. It was surprising how firm her parents were about her marrying. Her mother exerted so little energy as a rule that Ophelia had expected to escape another season at least without being pressed to accept anyone. "Invite them, then."

Her mother stared at her, uncertain, as always, what to make of her compliance. "It's unnatural for a lady to take so little interest in her future. You will embarrass the family if you end like Augustine. And you will, if you do not concern yourself with gaining an establishment suitable to your taste and rank."

Graves handed Lady Searle another sheet of paper, and they began a consideration of more names. Ophelia stopped listening. She had appeased her mother for the moment. Marriage, while it lay on the distant horizon of her life, had seemed neither reasonable nor unreasonable. But as she'd approached it more closely, she'd found it had a definite shape and dimensions. One ended up being married to this man or that and only to him. It was very like nearing a cottage nestled in some distant hills. One could imagine all sorts of romantic possibilities, until one crossed the threshold and found the ceilings too low, the windows too small, and a pervasive odor of dampness throughout.

Her mother's voice intruded once more. "Must we have Colonel Cooke?"

Ophelia sensed this remark was directed at her. "Lady Cardigan's brother?"

"The Duke of York's *secretary*." Her mother crumbled a biscuit into a saucer on the tea table at her side. Pet lay still, watching her hands intently.

Graves cleared his throat. At Lady Searle's nod, he suggested, "If you invite him, you'll have to invite Colonel Armstrong as well."

"Colonel Cooke goes everywhere, Mother, in the best company," Ophelia pointed out. She liked him. He was amusing, one of the few people she felt easy with in society.

The duchess put a weary hand to her brow. "Yes, but once one abandons rank as a principle, persons of obscure birth receive undue notice." She let the papers slip from her lap.

Graves retrieved them instantly. "Perhaps the solution is to exclude everyone beneath the rank of baron."

Lady Searle nodded, and Graves shot Ophelia a triumphant glance.

So much for an enjoyable evening. Hetty's parties were different. With Hetty there was never any question of a guest list, and it was never trouble to include one more. Even a groom from the stable.

Ophelia offered Graves a thin smile. He was possibly the worst snob on her mother's staff, gaunt and pursed and severely elegant. "May I see the list, Mother?"

Pet growled as Ophelia reached across him for the handful of sheets. Ophelia scanned the list. Her mother had questioned most of the names Ophelia added. "Mother, how large do you want the party to be?"

Her mother was scratching Pet's ears. "Grand, but intimate. Only the best society."

"I think," said Ophelia with a glance at Graves, "that you can keep all these names."

"All? You don't think some of these persons too obscure for the Prince's company?"

Ophelia shook her head. "Mother, a crowd will be more flattering to their royal highnesses."

Her mother appeared to consider the idea, handing Pet a large piece of the broken biscuit. Her fingers scattered crumbs over Pet's fur.

"Have you invited the foreign ambassadors?" Lady Searle shot her secretary a glance. "Graves? Did you think of that?"

He fumbled with the papers on the table. "I did, Your Grace. I've a list of them for your consideration right here."

Graves rose to offer the duchess another sheet of paper just as a footman entered. Pet tensed, and Ophelia had a moment's hope that it was time for the beast's walk. But the footman carried a silver tray with a single missive on it.

"For Lady Ophelia, Your Grace," he said with a bow.

"Set it down here, James," said the duchess. Her tone said the letter would have to wait.

The footman placed the small folded bit of pressed paper on the tea table at the duchess's elbow, next to the crumbled biscuit. Lady Searle's head was bowed over her lists. Ophelia shifted and slipped the book from its hiding place to her lap, disturbing Pet, who dug his sharp little nails into her thigh.

"You malevolent walking cream puff," she whispered.

"Where were we?" said the duchess, her hand automatically soothing the dog.

"The foreign ambassadors, Your Grace," said Graves.

Ophelia opened her book, tried to read, and failed. She twisted and stretched, straining to see the letter. It was not the regular post, but it could not be from Alexander. Ophelia could not believe she'd even had the thought. Her treacherous mind was determined to think of him when she willed otherwise. Perhaps if she saw the handwriting, she could rid herself of the ridiculous expectation that her groom had something to say to her. The sofa cushion dipped under her as she leaned toward the tea table, and Pet growled.

"Ophelia, do sit still. You're disturbing Pet," her mother said.

Ophelia clutched her book and turned resolutely from the letter. Her curiosity about it was all out of proportion to any possibility of its being something unusual. It was most likely an obligatory invitation to a dull party from someone who felt she could not snub a duke's daughter. She tried to recall the last chapter she'd read. The treaties by which Napoleon had taken over more and more of Venice. Monte Bello, Bergamo, Campo Formio, Presburg. The states of Venice that had fallen. Pechiera, Verona, Bassano, Vicenza, Padua, Friceli, Palma Nova.

Her mother, reaching another bite of biscuit for Pet, scattered crumbs on the little letter. In old Venice, Pet would have been the doge's dog, Ophelia decided, and poison would have been his inevitable end. Or maybe exile to one of Venice's island holdings. She wondered if she could smuggle him into a carriage and drop him off somewhere in the East End of London, where he might have to make his way in the world without a velvet cushion to sit on and crumbs handfed to him.

She recognized this fantasy as a bit of malice, and the obvious explanation for her ill humor was that she missed her morning rides. She had sent her note to the stables before she could change her mind, saying she would not be riding Shadow any longer and asking Alexander to exercise the mare daily. It had been the only sensible course. She could not go near Alexander if she was so weak.

She refused to think she missed seeing him, as often as the thought nagged at her. She missed Shadow and Hetty and her freedom, but her days were no duller than they had been before Alexander had become her groom. The trouble was that she couldn't quite convince herself of that.

If she could be attracted to a man with such a low position in society, Wyatt was right about her. She could not count on her morals ever. "Get thee to a nunnery," Hamlet had said to his Ophelia. Sound advice. What sort of life did nuns lead in the nineteenth century? No doubt they devoted themselves to prayer and charitable works. When had Ophelia ever had a charitable impulse?

She forced her mind back to the present. Her mother handed the lists to Graves. "That will do for now, I think, Graves."

The secretary stood and bowed. "Yes, Your Grace. Do you wish me to begin addressing the invitations?"

Lady Searle nodded. "Come, Pet." She stood, and the dog rolled to his feet on the sofa, looking at the few broken bits of biscuit still on the tea table. With a sharp bark, he tried to call Lady Searle back, but she didn't turn. He took two waddling steps across the cushions and bounded up on the sofa arm, his feet on the tea table. With a quick swipe of his tongue he cleared the saucer of crumbs, nudging the dish across the table. Ophelia gasped as Pet's enthusiastic slurping overturned her mother's cup of cold chocolate.

Lady Searle glanced over her shoulder. "Pet, naughty dog. Ophelia, ring for a maid, and remember you've a fitting with Madame Rondeau at one."

Ophelia mumbled an acknowledgment, her gaze on the spreading pool of chocolate.

"Pet." Lady Searle snapped her fingers and the dog leapt down from the sofa. Ophelia snatched her soggy letter from the chocolate. The fine paper had absorbed most of the dark brew, blurring the writing on the cover. Ophelia blotted it with her mother's discarded napkin. Carefully, she opened the cover. Several lines were lost in the dark, sweet dregs of the cocoa. Only the salutation and the closing had survived the spill, but that was enough.

Dear Ophelia,

No sign of you for three mornings. Should I worry? Has anything bad come of your visit on Tuesday night? I would hate to think . . .

. . . today at Hatchard's. I'll wait for you as long as I can.

As ever,
Hetty

Ophelia smiled. Hetty offered just the escape she needed.

Ophelia tried three floors of Hatchard's before she found Hetty in the poetry section, examining a collection of Mr. Coleridge's poems. She had the arrested look she got in the presence of poetry, an absolute stillness of inner attention, undistracted by anything around her. Ophelia chose a book of her own and waited, rewarded after a time by Hetty's looking up and smiling.

"You made it home safely," she cried. "I'm so relieved. I didn't know what to imagine when you didn't come these past few mornings."

"I'm sorry to worry you. I should have sent a message."

"I feared you'd been caught by your father and locked in your room."

"With irons on my legs and thin gruel to eat?"

"Yes, while you carved your dying message in the plaster with a spoon."

They put aside their books and arm in arm made their way out of the store to Piccadilly. With a little coaxing, Ophelia persuaded Hetty to try Gunter's, society's favorite sweet shop. They strolled along Piccadilly and up Berkeley Street to the confectioner's, enjoying the mild day. The budding trees of the square seemed to rain down sunshine. Most of the patrons of the famous shop sat in open carriages around the square, while white-jacketed waiters scurried back and forth with trays of ices and pastries.

Ophelia returned waves and greetings, but kept moving.

"Do you know all these people?" asked Hetty.

Ophelia looked about the crowd. "No. There's a gentleman and a lady just below that plane tree, there," she indicated them with a glance, "whom I've never seen before."

"It's like a holiday. Is this what the rich do?"

"Yes, as little as possible." Ophelia realized the scene was strange to Hetty, who did not often come to Mayfair, and who imagined that most people had some duties with which to occupy themselves during the day.

"Even the gentlemen?"

"Especially the gentlemen," said Ophelia.

"You're teasing me," Hetty protested.

"Hardly. You should know the idleness of society is no joke. Ask Berwick."

They found a quiet table inside, among other parties of ladies, and gave their order to a prompt waiter.

"I was glad to meet your friends at last," Ophelia said. "How spoiled you are!"

"Me?" Hetty looked up from unbuttoning her gloves.

"By good conversation. I like talking with people whose interests take over, who forget themselves in talk."

"Did you like everyone?"

"Most everyone." Ophelia wouldn't lie. "Especially Mr. Archer and Mrs. Fenton and the Gardiners."

The waiter brought them coffee and slices of yellow cake with creamy frosting.

"But you didn't like Berwick?" Hetty asked, her fork poised above the cake, as if she didn't quite know how to attack it.

"Well," said Ophelia. "He . . . was witty . . . and . . . confident."

Hetty laughed. "You didn't like him at all. Why not?"

Ophelia finished a bite of cake. "Berwick is the sort of young man who thinks it is the duty of women to be unfailingly polite and patient while he talks on whatever subjects he knows best."

"Ophelia, you are too severe on him."

"Am I? He never once took a woman up on any remark. Mrs. Fenton had a wonderful insight into Byron, but it would have led the conversation in quite a different direction, so Berwick simply repeated his point and went on."

Hetty made a series of precisely equal little cuts in her cake. "I confess I was disappointed in him, too, but he was not so . . . strident until your Mr. Alexander appeared. That somehow brought out the worst in Berwick."

It was Ophelia's turn to concentrate on her cake. This was the part of the conversation she dreaded. She feared Hetty would have no trouble connecting Alexander to Ophelia's recent absence from the Grays' breakfast table. She wanted to tell Hetty about the kiss in the garden, but her feelings about Alexander were too confused for her to speak them. She hated the way he made her weak, but the worst of it was that she *was* weak, and that she wanted to hear his confession of weakness again. She pushed a dollop of frosting over the edge and spread it down the exposed slope of the cake.

"You did not tell me he was so very handsome and so assured. He seemed to know just how to conduct himself. When he came in from the stable, I thought I would have to prompt him, you know, but I didn't at all."

Ophelia could not meet Hetty's eye. "He told me once that his father was an educated man."

Hetty tilted her head to one side, taking in the information, weighing it. "That may explain his speech, but there was something unusual in his manner, I thought. He felt very strongly about the Regent, I'm sure."

"He felt strongly about Mrs. Hart."

Hetty looked surprised. "I thought it was just the other way around. I thought Mrs. Hart was drawn to him."

Ophelia frowned, trying to recall the picture in her mind. She could see the two golden heads bent together, but at whose instigation she could not say.

"What did you think of her?" Hetty asked.

Ophelia saw that the question mattered to her friend. "What puzzles me is your father's reaction to her. He seems disturbed by her, and he lets her manage things."

"That's what Mrs. Pendares says. I'm afraid she disapproves of Mrs. Hart entirely." Hetty sighed. "It's an . . . uncomfortable situation."

"But she's so lovely, isn't she?" Ophelia said quietly.

"And so strong." Hetty smashed the perfect little cake bites under her fork. "You just feel her strength. She won't let anyone stop her from doing what she means to do."

Ophelia wondered why she didn't admire Mrs. Hart for her strength, why she admired Hetty more. Mrs. Hart had published her work to the world, while Hetty's poems collected in drawers, seen by no one except Ophelia.

"Sprite," said a familiar voice. Ophelia looked up to find Jasper standing beside them, looking elegant in a blue coat and buff breeches and staring at Hetty with an entire lack of discretion.

"Hello," he said, a dry-throated, unpolished greeting.

Hetty sent Ophelia an uncertain glance. Ophelia did some quick thinking. Jasper would not recognize Hetty's name or connect her to the scandal of their book. He would probably assume Hetty was some ordinary friend of Ophelia's.

The stunned concentration of his gaze made Hetty blush.

"Miss Gray, my brother, Lord Jasper Brinsby," said Ophelia.

"I'll get a chair," said Jasper. He was back before Ophelia and Hetty could exchange a word. "May I treat you to ices?" he asked.

"Of course," said Ophelia, drawing his gaze to her.

"I missed you at Candover's the other night," Jasper said in an ordinary voice.

Ophelia shrugged. "Well, I was quite safe. Miss Gray and I were at a perfectly respectable party."

"I hope so, Sprite." He turned to Hetty too easily, with a confiding air. "Our parents are sticklers."

Ophelia tried to draw her brother's too interested gaze back her way. "Yet Jasper has managed dozens of exploits."

"Don't embarrass me in Miss Gray's eyes before I've had a chance to prove my worth to her."

"You won't prove it with ices," said Ophelia. "You're not at work."

"Ah, but I am. I'm in hot pursuit of the missing prince."

"Like a Bow Street Runner?" Hetty asked.

A waiter appeared to take their order.

"What is this pursuit?" Hetty was daring to look at Jasper now.

"An important diplomatic mission," said Jasper, turning the full force of his smile on her. "The Foreign Office believes Prince Mirandola of Trevigna is hiding somewhere in London. He disappeared in the midst of delicate negotiations that would secure an important port for the British navy as well as an alliance in a difficult and dangerous part of the world."

"I've never heard of Trevigna. Where is it?"

Jasper seemed to forget Ophelia's presence, his gaze focused on Hetty's mouth, shiny with a trace of icing. "It's a tiny triangle of land north of Venice, sloping from the foothills of the Dolomites to the coast."

"You've been there?" Hetty asked.

"No." Jasper's gaze had moved to a golden

curl, lying across Hetty's collarbone. Hetty's bare hand fluttered up to the strand uneasily.

"How does a prince disappear?"

Jasper appeared to understand the question through some delayed process that required staring at Hetty's mouth, as if he were reading her lips. "Well. He gave up his villa outside Windsor and his lodgings in town."

"But a prince could not conceal himself easily. He has a retinue and trappings, surely?"

"This prince has only one servant that we know of."

"Why did he disappear?"

Again the long pause while Jasper's apparently sluggish brain made sense of the question. "He wasn't satisfied with the terms we were offering."

The waiter returned and set their ices in front of them. Ophelia picked up her spoon, but Jasper and Hetty had fallen into a daze of mutual admiration while the ices melted.

After a moment, Ophelia judged it time to interrupt. "Have you made any progress in your search, Jasper?"

"No. That's the devil of it. Apparently Mirandola is sending letters to the London Committee for the Restoration of the Italian Republics, but they can't or won't work with us to discover how he does it."

"Sounds unBritish to me," said Ophelia.

"The sapskulls want a Republic of Trevigna, which would be an invitation to French intervention again."

"I don't understand," said Hetty. "Why does this prince write to them, but hide from you?"

The word *you* seemed to mean Jasper, not England, and there was a little silence. If her brother wished to impress Hetty, he was doing a poor job by appearing so slow to comprehend her.

"Money must be his motive." He rallied. "The committee is trying to raise money for the treasury of Trevigna."

"Jasper, that still makes no sense," said Ophelia. "Why would the committee for a republic give funds to a prince?"

"I agree. Another reason I've got to find him."

"You've talked with his friends?"

"Some of them. Apparently, the last person to see him is a fellow named Burke, who was with the Prince at Tatt's about a month ago when he sold off his horses. No one's seen him since. They think he's living on the proceeds, and Burke might know."

"Where's this Burke now?" Ophelia asked. Her brother had no difficulty answering her questions, and even managed a few bites of his dessert.

"He's been out of town. His uncle died, and he inherited. But he should be at Ingram's tonight. Will you be there, Miss Gray?"

The question caught Ophelia off guard. Hetty directed an imploring glance her way. She should have expected her brother's pointed interest in her friend. She knew his weakness for a certain kind of beauty, but once he knew Hetty's real position in the world, he would withdraw his attentions abruptly.

"No." Hetty lowered her gaze. "I have another engagement for this evening." Jasper's disappointment was plain. Hetty temporized. "Perhaps another time we'll be going to the same party."

Jasper smiled, a blinding joyful smile. Ophelia put down her spoon and gathered up her gloves, giving Hetty a swift glance. "We've got to be going," she said.

"Let me take you up in my curricle," Jasper offered.

"Thanks, Jasper, but we're just going round the corner to a fitting." Hetty stood, following Ophelia's lead with mechanical gestures, gathering gloves and parcels.

They exchanged parting words, and Ophelia resolutely turned Hetty away. She could sense Jasper standing just where they had left him. She linked her arm with Hetty's and kept them moving until they'd turned the corner.

"You think I'm an idiot to be so affected by a first meeting with your brother." Hetty's eyes were lowered.

"No."

"He has an extraordinary smile. It makes one feel light, as if one had swallowed bubbles."

Ophelia glanced at her friend.

"I know nothing can come of it, Ophelia," Hetty said firmly. "I would have admitted who I am at once, but I thought maybe you didn't want him to know we were meeting."

After their encounter at Gunter's, Ophelia avoided Jasper at the Ingrams', gravitating toward the small crowd around the outspoken Miss Mercer-Elphinstone. They were an elite group, the inner circle. The ladies changed a feather or a hem and found themselves instantly copied. Their talk, all private allusion and slang, could not be comprehended by an outsider. In their snobbery they were something like the hydra, a shared body from which the multiple heads dispensed venom. They could be counted on to outdo one another in malicious witticisms, but Dent never went near them.

Eventually Jasper found her. He scanned her companions as he approached.

"Miss Gray didn't come, did she?"

"As she said."

"What are you doing in this crowd, Sprite? You despise them," he whispered.

"So does Dent," Ophelia confided.

Jasper gave a brief laugh. "Well come with me. I can keep you from Dent and Miss Mercer-Elphinstone. I've got someone I want to show you."

Ophelia gave him a questioning look but allowed him to lead her away, suffering only a few quips from the crowd as they departed. Jasper's energy told her he'd had some luck in his search. "You found Burke?"

"Yes, and he was most helpful, but he told me something strange, too. I don't know what to make of it." Jasper steered her through the crowded ballroom, across the grand entry, and into a long salon set up for cards. Ladies and gentlemen gathered around a dozen tables for everything from whist and loo to more serious games of hazard and faro.

"See that fellow?"

Ophelia followed his gaze to a tall, raven-haired gentleman in an extremely elegant evening coat.

"Revelstoke." Jasper leaned close and whispered, "Burke swears the fellow is wearing one of Prince's Mirandola's coats."

"What?"

Jasper started to repeat himself, but Ophelia interrupted.

"Why would he be wearing another man's coat, and how would he come by it?" Jasper plainly had not thought through Burke's information. "Did you understand Burke?"

"Of course I did."

"Revelstoke must be wearing a coat *like* the Prince's—he must have the same tailor."

Jasper frowned; obviously he hadn't considered that. "I've got to talk to Revelstoke," he said, his brow furrowed. "But I can't just ask him his tailor's name."

Ophelia laughed. "Get me a glass of champagne."

No one could say later precisely how the accident occurred. Lord Revelstoke turned from the table, just as Lady Ophelia Brinsby moved to elude her disapproving brother, who was about to snatch away her champagne. Her glass held high, Lady Ophelia whirled into Revelstoke and showered his coat from the lapels to the waist with bright, bubbly wine.

"Miss!" Revelstoke jumped back too late.

"Look what you've done, Jasper," Ophelia told her brother. Jasper stepped forward to offer his handkerchief. "I beg your pardon, Revelstoke."

He raised his quizzing glass as if Ophelia were a species of insect.

"I'm so sorry," Ophelia murmured contritely. "You must let us take care of your coat."

"It's nothing," said Revelstoke, dabbing his coat with Jasper's linen.

"*Oooh nooo*," said Ophelia, with the intensity of the very foxed. She swayed toward him and put a light hand on Revelstoke's arm. "You must let us replace the ruined coat. Who is your tailor?"

"Really, miss."

"I insist. We'll take care of it tomorrow." She tried to look devastated. She was aware of the stares of others and knew her victim wanted to be let off the hook.

"Very well," said Revelstoke. "Lucca of Maddox Street."

Ophelia smiled sweetly. "We'll be there in the morning to see to your new coat," she promised. Then her brother whisked her away, leaning close to speak in her ear, apparently chiding her for her high spirits.

"Sprite, you're a genius," he whispered.

Chapter 9

Alexander kept Raj to a steady walk through the gray streets. The stallion had nearly overcome his tendency to shy at the city's frequent offenses to a horse's dignity and sensibility. Rumbling coal carts, bell-ringing hawkers, absurd clattering phaetons brought barely a flinch. But Jasper Brinsby seemed to have forgotten Raj. His curricle was his favorite toy, the one he called for whenever he came to the stables. Like his sister, he moved with impatient energy from one idle pursuit to the next.

Alexander liked to imagine that he would offer for Raj as soon as he returned to himself, got Trevigna's affairs settled, and had sufficient guineas in his purse . . . if that day ever came.

Raj tossed his head as the final turning brought the scent of the park, fresh from a rain. At the gate Alexander had to rein in for two gentlemen who rode past, serene in their assumption of privilege. When they passed, Alexander urged Raj to a canter along the north ride.

His trips to the park had become like the practice he'd abandoned in his adolescence of examining his conscience. No point in recalling one's sins, if in the recollection, one sinned by wanting to repeat them. And he did want to repeat them.

Along the north ride he could recall the teasing touches of the first day, which led as inevitably as the path itself to the hollow where Ophelia had escaped through the ducks. Beyond the Serpentine were the ridges over which he'd pursued her until they'd tumbled to the grass. In the distance was the road that led to the Grays' garden.

His experience with Ophelia was unlike any he'd had before. With Blanca in the hills there had been an immediate and fierce consummation. Later, in Venice, when he had gone at Lucca's insistence to Magdelena, the famous courtesan, he had experienced in a single night an erotic progression from innuendo through a catalogue of pleasure to repletion, like saying an alphabet. But with Ophelia desire was not an episode; it was a territory he had entered where eyes and hands and voices spoke in unguarded ways.

Every morning her eyes met his with a little shock, a quick look away that acknowledged awareness. Their hands met through gloves and clung beyond his duty to assist her. He steadied her horse while she mounted, brushing past him in a swift surge of movement that awakened a beat in his loins. When their ride ended, there came a moment more intimate than the most scandalous waltz, when he put his hands to her waist and she slid down into his arms, her scent around him, her weight in his hands.

It was like launching his boat for the point of

Laruggia against the afternoon breeze, a constant wind in his face, the boat rocking over waves, and every other minute turning his hand, his body, the stick, so as not to spill a breath of that wind from his taut sail. And when he reached the point, he would come about and let the wind swell the big-bellied sail and blow him home.

The real park—the trees coming into leaf, the twittering birds, the reviving green of the grass—held almost no interest for him, except as a map of his strange unacknowledged flirtation with his mistress. What did he see in her? A blithe realist without illusions, not a dreamer like himself. She would not attempt to reform society, did not imagine it could be reformed. Society enclosed young women of privilege in a maze of restrictions. Ophelia Brinsby simply tucked clippers in her pocket and cut her way through the hedge.

He wanted her to want him. Her confession of weakness in the garden puzzled and inflamed him. So he rode, unconscious of his surroundings, inventing conversations and other meetings in that garden in which she did not pull away and he went on caressing her sweet breasts.

She had been the wise one, sending him word that she would not come to the stables again. The church had a phrase for frail virtue like his. They called it avoiding the near occasion of sin. He wondered how long she would avoid him.

Jasper knocked on Ophelia's door early the morning after the Ingram ball.

"What are your plans for the day?" he asked.

"I'm free." Ophelia pulled the counterpane

over Berwick's manuscript. "Did you want me to come with you to Revelstoke's tailor?"

Jasper nodded. "But if you have plans, well . . ."

"I don't." Ophelia watched her brother move restlessly about her room.

"Well, then, some other day," he said, as if he hadn't heard her at all. He strode for the door.

"Jasper?"

He paused.

"Did you want to include Miss Gray in our adventure?"

"Yes." The single fervent syllable seemed wrenched from him.

They passed the tailor's shop three times before they were sure of the spot. Nothing so obvious as a sign marked the establishment, but Jasper, peering in the grimy bow window, insisted that all the accoutrements of a tailor's shop were there—weighing chair, cheval glass, sporting magazines.

A little bell tinkled as they entered, and from behind a brown velvet curtain came an indistinguishable muttering. A moment later a tall, elegant man stepped through the curtain. His features—great dark eyes, an imposing brow, and a full, sensuous mouth—were not at all English.

The man bowed. "I am Lucca," he said in a lightly accented voice. "Please sit and tell me how may I help you."

Ophelia glanced at Jasper, wondering if they hadn't stumbled upon the missing prince himself.

The thought must have crossed Jasper's mind,

because he met her look with a warning nod and
began introducing their errand.

He steered Hetty to a low chaise, offering his
arm as if she might stumble on the threadbare
carpet. Ophelia gazed about the shop, noting the
bare walls, their paper faded around several rec-
tangles of darker hue where pictures must have
hung once. Only one remained. She did not recognize the subject, but the painter's style looked
familiar. The name eluded her, but she suspected
the artist's work was too fine for the walls of a
small, unprosperous shop.

"We've come to see if you can replace a coat,"
said Jasper. "For Lord Revelstoke. You made one
for him recently, and quite by accident the coat's
been damaged."

Lucca's face remained impassive.

"We're entirely to blame for Lord Revelstoke's
loss," said Ophelia.

"Naturally, we would like to replace the coat,"
Jasper concluded. He might as well have addressed the wall. The only response from the
haughty Lucca was a slight raising of the
straight, black brows.

"You do remember Lord Revelstoke?" Ophelia
asked.

"Yes, certainly," said Lucca. The dark eyes
were not as imperturbable as the face. Lucca
looked like a man who was thinking furiously.
"A black coat, evening wear."

"Yes," said Jasper.

"And you would like another, just like it?"

"Yes," Jasper agreed, looking at Hetty as if the
investigation were making great strides.

"I'm afraid I cannot be of assistance in this

matter," said Lucca. He made a small bow and muttered something.

Jasper's head turned sharply. "I beg your pardon."

"*Cavoli riscaldati*. Reheated cabbage." An impatient sweep of his arm accompanied the phrase.

Ophelia exchanged a glance with Hetty. Lucca's connection with the missing prince seemed more probable by the minute. Jasper leaned forward as if to catch the man's meaning. "I don't understand."

Lucca threw his hands up in the air. "I do not repeat myself," he said. "One jacket is a work of art. I do not make two of the same." He crossed his arms over his chest, a sullen curve to his mouth.

Jasper frowned. "Look here," he said. "You will be well compensated for your work."

Lucca shrugged. "I tell you, it's not possible. One time, one coat."

"What kind of tailor are you?" Jasper demanded. "Surely you have forms, patterns. How do you expect to maintain an establishment?"

Lucca drew himself up. "Lucca's is not the holy water font for every passerby to dip his hand in."

Jasper reddened with uncharacteristic temper. Ophelia saw that he did not like being put off in front of Hetty.

"Excuse me," said Ophelia. She smiled as sweetly as she could. "Jasper, perhaps you could have a coat made for yourself. You admired Revelstoke's coat, didn't you?"

"Yes," said Jasper, whirling on Lucca with a

challenging glint in his eye. "What can you do for me? Can you create an original for me?"

There was a long pause. Ophelia caught a glare from Lucca.

"Of course," he said to Jasper. "What sort of coat interests you, my lord?"

Jasper ran a hand through his hair. "A green one."

"Oh, a green one." Lucca's full mouth curved in disdain. He looked Jasper up and down, and gestured for him to turn.

Jasper did as the tailor bade him.

"Walk," Lucca urged.

An impatient breath escaped Jasper, but he took a turn about the room. Hetty's glance followed him until he turned and caught her gaze. Their eyes met and held while Ophelia and the supercilious Lucca were forgotten.

"No," said Lucca. "I can do nothing for you."

Jasper swung to face the tailor. "Why not?" he demanded.

"You do not know what you want." Lucca's voice rose. "Look at you." Lucca stepped forward and pulled up the seams at Jasper's shoulders. "Excellent shoulders hidden with this slope. And here." Lucca indicated the bottom of Jasper's waistcoat. "Too long, two inches too long, hides the waist. And here." Lucca gave a tug to Jasper's cravat, untying it. With swift fingers, he redid the knot. Then he turned Jasper toward the cheval glass.

"Now see here," Jasper protested. "My tailor is—"

"—Poole. I know. I recognize the work."

Jasper stared at himself in the glass. The careless new folds of the cravat changed his appearance, slightly perhaps, but definitely. He turned to Hetty with a surprised look.

"You see, my lord. Not this English stiffness. You want . . . *sprezzatura*."

Ophelia regarded the change in her brother. There was something familiar in the new fall of his cravat, but she couldn't place it and she needed to get Jasper's mind back on his investigation.

"What cloth do you suggest for him?" she asked Lucca.

"Cloth?" Lucca lapsed into his uncomprehending state. This time Ophelia was sure there was furious thinking going on behind the blank expression. "I will show you a coat I just finished. That will give you an idea. Excuse me."

He disappeared through the velvet curtain, and they could hear his footsteps on stairs. Ophelia walked over to examine the painting. Even with a closer look she did not recognize the building, or the setting, which did not seem English at all. But the painter's name in the corner was Canaletto, certainly an artist fit for a royal commission.

"What an odd fellow," said Jasper. "I thought for a moment he might be Mirandola, lofty enough for it."

"What does Prince Mirandola look like?" asked Hetty

Ophelia turned. She hadn't thought to ask the question. Hetty was looking up at Jasper, who seemed to forget how to speak. "Well, he's tall and dark and . . ." Jasper stopped and stared. "I have no idea what he looks like."

It was an astonishing admission. Ophelia couldn't remember either of her brothers ever admitting ignorance. "You don't know what he looks like?"

Jasper laughed an odd, dry laugh, without enjoyment.

"Oh, dear," said Hetty, looking stricken, as if she'd wounded her idol. "Forgive me. I shouldn't have asked."

Jasper took a deep breath. "No, it's exactly what you should ask. How can I hope to find the man without knowing what he looks like?" He stared at Hetty with a kind of rueful reverence. "I suppose you think I'm an idiot to go racing about, not knowing what I'm looking for, dragging you along to this second-rate shop where the tailor doesn't know how to win a client."

Hetty shook her head.

"He may not have to win many clients if his sole client is the prince," said Ophelia. "He's certainly familiar with Italian."

"If he *is* the prince's tailor, how does that help us? The prince won't be dropping in for new coats now."

At the sound of footsteps on the stairs, Ophelia put her finger to her lips to quiet her brother.

Lucca returned with three coats. Hetty stood, and Lucca spread them lovingly across the chaise. "Green," he said.

The shades were subtle, the cloth fine. Ophelia could not resist touching the soft, smooth wool. The styles differed, but there was an obvious sameness to the three coats. She lay one down on top of another, noting the length of the sleeves and breadth of shoulders. Lucca watched her with a narrowed gaze.

He turned to Jasper. "Does my lord wish a coat, then?"

Jasper nodded. "One like that," he said, pointing to a double-breasted jacket in a deep forest green.

A pained look crossed Lucca's face. "Of course," he said. He began to gather up the coats. "One moment. We measure, then you go." He took the coats through the velvet curtain and returned with his measuring tape. He turned Jasper this way and that, stretching the tape across his shoulders and down his arm, making note of each length.

"A week then, my lord. Thank you." He clearly wanted them gone.

On the pavement outside the shop, Jasper laughed. "I hope you're pleased with yourself, Ophelia, now that I'm buying a coat from the fellow. I don't know when I've been so insulted by a tradesman. You'd think the man was royalty himself."

Ophelia winced at her brother's careless snobbery, but she thought it good for Hetty to see it and not be blinded by Jasper's charm. "Actually, I think he's selling Prince Mirandola's coats."

"Don't be absurd, Ophelia. Princes don't sell their coats, and nobody buys secondhand coats. Certainly Revelstoke wouldn't."

"Nobody knows they're buying them," she said. "The coats are cleverly altered by the artist, who claims to make only one coat."

Jasper stared at her.

"You said Mirandola was desperate. He's sold

his horses, now he's selling his coats."

"Rubbish."

Ophelia shook her head. "I think you just agreed to buy a secondhand coat, brother dear. Come on, Hetty, let's go."

"Wait," Jasper called after them. "I'll take you home in my curricle."

"It's not necessary, Jasper. We're not going home."

He caught up with them. "But Miss Gray."

"I'll see her home, Jasper. Besides, you should watch the shop to see who appears."

"Will I see you tonight, Miss Gray?"

Hetty cast Ophelia a hesitant glance. "We're bound to be going to the same party sometime." She smiled wanly at Jasper.

"I'll look for you then," he said.

"You don't have to tell me how foolish I'm being," Hetty said a few minutes later. A chill breeze ruffled their skirts and tugged at their bonnets.

Ophelia looked at her friend directly. "Do you truly like him?"

"Are you going to tell me he's vain, idle, frivolous?"

"Apparently I don't have to," Ophelia said dryly. "I was going to say that Jasper's interest in ladies has been inconstant, but—"

"Oh, I know his interest won't last." Hetty clutched her reticule. "I just want to enjoy his regard while I can. I promise to return to being sensible, as soon as he . . . looks elsewhere."

Ophelia stopped. "You should promise no such thing. You should . . ."

"It's silly to think of anything else. He's a snob, isn't he?" Hetty's voice was gentle.

"Like all my family." Ophelia recalled Jasper's story about Sebastian and the beggar.

"I wrote a poem about him."

Ophelia said nothing. If Hetty had written poetry about Jasper, she was smitten indeed.

"You'll laugh at me. It's a sonnet."

Ophelia made an effort at lightness, but her throat ached. "Shakespearean?"

"Yes, and I've made your brother 'my sun' that shines with sovereign eye, 'kissing with golden face the meadows green and gilding pale streams with heavenly alchemy.' So you see, my case is hopeless."

"He wants to impress you," Ophelia said carefully. "He wouldn't go to Lucca's without you. He wanted you there to witness his success when he found the missing prince. That's something new, Hetty. I don't know when Jasper has tried to impress a woman. Charm them, yes—but impress one? I've never seen that."

It was the most hope Ophelia could offer. She procured Hetty a hackney in Piccadilly, and they parted. Her friend's view of Jasper made Ophelia think differently about her brother. It was as if she had to reinvent Jasper to see what Hetty saw, but she could not imagine her brother going to the house in Kensington, shaking hands with Solomon Gray, treating Hetty's father with respect. And no blindness to Jasper's faults would lead Hetty to permit her father to be treated with contempt.

Weighed down by her thoughts, Ophelia turned the corner of Moreton Street and saw a liveried Searle footman walking Pet in front of Madame Rondeau's elegant shop. Pet looked decidedly unhappy to be on the pavement in the care of a servant. He waddled impatiently as far as the footman would allow, then turned the other way. Ophelia could see that there was a definite struggle going on over who was truly at the leading end of the leash. Pet moved in jerks, trying to anticipate the footman's actions so that he did not suffer the indignity of being dragged by the collar. As soon as he saw Ophelia, he stopped and barked all his frustration at her.

"Pet, you walking bolster," she crooned. "Discovering what it means to be a dog?"

He lunged for her, forgetful of the collar and leash until he reached its length and fell heavily onto his forefeet, panting.

Ophelia smiled, allowing her mother's second footman to open the shop door, and with a little wave, passed inside.

Madame Rondeau's was the one place where Lady Searle's air of indolence fell away. The duchess and her modiste discussed every aspect of the creation of a gown. Watching this intense collaboration usually put Ophelia in charity with her mother. There was no doubt of Lady Searle's talent for costume, her unerring eye for style and fashion.

The dress they were creating for the royal ball was a blue Spitalfields silk, brocaded with silver threads. The color was ethereal, but not so pale as to make Ophelia look like a debutante. The dress had virtually no bodice; two narrow wedges of silk barely skimmed her breasts. A thin silver cord spanned Ophelia's chest below her breasts and fell to her hemline, giving the illusion of height. A silver clasp gathered soft blue gauze across her bosom and shoulders. Ophelia thought an Amazonian breastplate would be more appropriate, considering the nature of society, but refrained from saying so.

Today they were deciding on the headpiece. Her mother favored feathers, while Madame Rondeau favored a coiled band of the blue silk and silver thread.

Ophelia stood for an hour, the line of pins up her side under her arm pricking as she breathed. Then her mother asked Madame to make an adjustment to the feathered version of the headpiece so that they could consider that. The modiste and her assistant disappeared, conferring in rapid French.

Ophelia lowered herself gingerly to a velvet-cushioned bench, and regarded her mother silently.

Lady Searle looked up from her pattern book. "Don't sit, Ophelia, you'll wrinkle."

Ophelia considered disobeying and decided against it. She circled the fitting room, trailing her fingertips across bolts of silk and coils of trim. She needed to know whether her mother was truly set on any of her suitors. Her mother, focused on the trimmings and details of a costume, was likely to answer Ophelia's questions without considering them too deeply; still, it was best to approach the topic of marriage obliquely. "Mother, do you think Princess Charlotte is marrying well?"

"Saxe-Coburg will suit the princess nicely."

"But suppose he likes wet, muddy dogs and

she likes delicate, fastidious cats? Or he likes farce and she tragedy?"

Her mother looked mildly uncomprehending, her gaze on a sketch from the modiste. "A wife is hardly constrained by her husband's interests. She has her sphere, her resources, and he has his."

Ophelia considered that. It summed up her parents' marriage precisely. "But what happens when the spheres collide? When husband and wife come together in intimacy?"

Lady Searle lifted her gaze from the dress and gave Ophelia a hard scrutiny, as if she'd said something truly offensive.

"You are not yourself this week, are you?"

"Me? I'm as I've always been." Surely her mother didn't see past the blue gown to the real person.

Her mother continued to study her.

"Clagg told me just the other day that you've not been riding. You must ride, dear, keep up your routine. You don't want to develop odd notions." Without appreciating the activities that gave her children pleasure, Lady Searle insisted that they do whatever kept tempers even.

"No, of course not."

Her mother continued to study her. "I will speak with Clagg. I want to see you behaving sensibly this season." Her mother looked down at the pattern book. "If only you were two inches taller, Ophelia, we wouldn't have this difficulty."

Chapter 10

❦

The sky outside Ophelia's window grayed. In the stable the grooms would be readying horses for the day's work. Below stairs, the servants were at work, shoulders bent under the first duties of the day, hauling buckets of coal and water.

A mist obscured her view of the stable roof, but Alexander must be there, talking to Shadow and Raj, preparing to accompany her to the park. Sleep had been impossible with her mind inventing a thousand ways this first meeting would go. Could she see Alexander and not kiss him? The question had consumed her through the opera, a long supper party, and the quiet hours of the night. She turned from the window, stepping over the glittering debris of silk, jewels, and feathers from her evening dress that lay in a heap by her wardrobe, waiting for her maid's attention.

With a yawn she reached for her riding habit. Colonel Cooke had told her once that it was the raw recruit that wasted hours of thought pondering that which could be determined only by the battle itself—whether one would stand and fight or crack and run.

She gathered the heavy velvet riding habit in her arms and headed for her dressing room. With her short curls, she had no need of a maid in the morning. She could think her own thoughts as she dressed for the day's battles.

She frowned at herself in the glass. The rules of society forbade ladies' stooping to the embraces of their servants. Yet the offense in such a liaison was not in the adultery as much as in the woman's giving of her favors to a man beneath her in rank and breeding. Society dictated whom you would wed and even whom you could take as a lover.

Ladies like her mother and the patronesses of Almack's guarded their lists of guests. Like the defenders of ancient castles, willing to pour boiling oil on the heads of would-be invaders, the ladies ruthlessly preserved the inner circle of society. Ophelia was to find a husband among the privileged or nowhere.

The rules kept the elite together in a pattern as elaborate as a dance, where one moved up or down the set in a prescribed series of steps. Alone you were nothing. As part of the pattern, you had power.

The rules were a reminder that you could be cast out by scandal or misfortune. Not even your family could save you then. If Ophelia caused her family embarrassment, they would lock her up on the smallest, most remote manor in her father's dukedom or marry her off by special license to whoever would have her, most likely Dent.

*　*　*

The mist enveloped the stable in a deep hush. Shadow and Raj, standing ready at the mounting block, nudged her, demanding to have soft noses stroked. Raj snorted uneasily, tossing his head as she reached out to him. Instinctively she glanced around for Alexander, but saw no sign of him.

She reminded herself not to blush or shrink. There was no need for talk, really, and above all, she would not look into his eyes. She could manage a morning ride without succumbing to inappropriate feelings for her groom.

Then he came across the yard, something like eagerness in his stride, and her pulse fluttered. Her riding habit covered her from her chin to her toes, yet she felt he must see the heated flush of her skin. She dropped her gaze, gripping the leather crop, steadying herself until he halted a few feet away.

"The usual ride this morning, Alexander," she told his boots, unable to risk a direct look into those blue eyes.

He murmured some assent.

Just that, not her name. She felt bereft.

He wiped the damp saddle dry and held Shadow for her to mount. She was careful that their hands didn't meet.

Once she was settled, he pivoted abruptly, startling Raj, and the stallion reared, circling back on his hind legs, his nostrils streaming vapor, his eyes wild. Ophelia's breath caught at the display of power and her hands froze on Shadow's reins. Alexander slapped the mare's hindquarters. Shadow leapt aside. Another groom came running with ropes, but Alexander waved him off. He moved toward Raj smoothly, apparently indifferent to the pawing hooves above him.

Fog swirled around them. Raj raked the air with slashing hooves, and Alexander spoke, his voice coaxing the stallion gently down again until Raj descended, his hooves touching the earth without a sound. When he stood quivering and still, letting Alexander stroke his neck and whisper in his ear, Ophelia knew she would kiss her groom.

In the park he rode behind her in proper fashion. Pockets of cloud bound them in a cool, silent awareness. Sensations startled her, a bird cry unnaturally loud to her ears, or a sudden overwhelming fragrance of grass and earth. They were headed for Hetty's almost before she noticed.

When they reached the Gray stable, she had either to throw herself into his arms or run. She lifted her knee from the saddle, kicked loose, and slid to the ground with only a slight stumble.

"Ophelia," he called.

And she fled into the house.

In the hall, Ophelia paused to catch her breath. Outside the morning room she saw Mrs. Pendares stop with a tray in one hand, reaching for the knob. Just then Solomon came from the other end of the hall, and Ophelia caught the expression of longing on his face as he saw the housekeeper struggling with her burdens.

Ophelia fell back against the wall, waiting for the moment between them to pass before she made her way to Hetty.

"I didn't expect you," Hetty said.

Ophelia pulled off her gloves, avoiding Hetty's

gaze. "My mother insisted I go back to riding in the mornings." She managed a wry smile at the irony of it.

"You look burnt to a cinder." Hetty poured coffee and set a cup in front of Ophelia.

"Thanks," Ophelia said. "I've always striven for that haggard look."

Ophelia sipped her coffee, conscious of Hetty's thoughtful gaze.

"Is it something you want to tell me about?"

Ophelia shook her head. "I'd rather hear about you, hear your poems."

"Not my poems, this morning, unless you want to hear your brother praised in poor meter."

"If you found any way to praise Jasper in rhyme, I'm impressed. My love is like a red, red—what rhymes with 'Jasper'?"

"Casper?"

"You didn't."

"No," said Hetty, "but I tried." Hetty hung her head.

"I can imagine. *Sweet Hetty Gray loves Jasper/ And longs for him to . . . clasp her.*"

"Never," said Hetty, but the corners of her mouth twitched.

"*Jas-per, were, stir, myrrh, fur, cur—*"

"Stop it." Hetty was laughing now, and Ophelia felt better. "Do you think he's found the prince yet?"

"He'll want to tell you when he has."

Shadow's soft whicker always heralded Ophelia's approach. Alexander looked up from his book. In the hours he spent in the Grays' stable he might have rewritten the laws of Trevigna or proved Fermat's last theorem, if he hadn't spent them thinking of Ophelia and reading the same sentence a few thousand times.

She appeared at the stable door and halted, stiff and distant, her gaze meeting his and sliding away.

He went to her, intending to draw her to the bench, but stopped short of touching her. "Sit."

She obeyed without a word. The care she'd taken to avoid even the most fleeting and impersonal touches had put him on edge.

He busied himself with the horses. Her name had frozen on his tongue, and he feared she would not come back tomorrow, feared this aloof Ophelia.

She was embarrassed, and that was unlike her. He knew instinctively that it was the reason she wouldn't look at him or talk to him. All his imagined conversations, kisses, and touches seemed absurd. With foolish, contrary intentions, he wanted her haughty and he wanted her to kiss him. He finished saddling the horses.

Without a word she came to Shadow's side and stroked the mare's neck gently. They were alone for now, but another groom could walk in at any moment.

He came up behind her. He had to say her name. "Ophelia, look at me."

She shook her head.

He edged around her and rubbed Shadow's nose, more for his comfort than the mare's. "Let me speak, then."

No reply. She leaned her forehead against the smooth leather of the saddle flap.

"If one of us must be embarrassed for our last meeting, let it be me."

She turned her head slightly and checked. He felt his pulse trip in answer to that small concession.

"Ladies who dally in amorous encounters with their servants have the worst of all bad names." Her voice was toneless, as if she were reciting a rule conned by rote.

She was right, of course; it was one of society's most unforgiving rules. Married women were permitted discreet *amores* with men of the same rank, but by society's rules she had sinned on two counts when she had let him kiss her. He'd not thought she could be hurt in this way. She was a rule-breaker, but for some reason she was ashamed of their minor transgression. The game of subverting her authority over him and testing her egalitarian principles had taken an unexpected turn. Because she believed him a groom, she would play by rules of the old world of money and title, not the dream world of the new Trevigna he hoped to build.

But she was wrong to blame herself for what happened. That, he could do something about.

"I started things. You stopped them."

"Not soon enough." Her voice was shaky.

"Painfully soon," he said quietly. She looked over her shoulder at that, the brown eyes, usually so shrewd, now wrenchingly vulnerable. He gripped the strap of Shadow's bridle, tangling his hands in the leather. The steel bit jingled. "Do you think it was your weakness in the garden? It was mine."

She looked skeptical, disbelieving.

"Mine," he insisted. "You don't know what liberties a morning ride allows." He took a deep breath. If he told her his thoughts, she'd never trust him near her, but maybe he could make her laugh. "I can see your elbows always close to the body, your wrists loose and easy. You have perfect hands. And you have a flawless seat. You and Shadow move as one."

"You were moved to kiss me in the Grays' garden because of my superior horsemanship?"

"I suppose other men praise your hair, your eyes, your wit, your grace—"

"My dowry." She said it lightly, keeping her distance with irony. "We must not kiss."

It was nothing less than reason and truth, and he ought to agree and obey and lift her to her horse and ride out into the morning.

"You don't want to kiss me?" he asked. "Or you don't want to admit that you want to?" He waited for her answer, which seemed a long time coming.

"I can't." Her eyes were sad.

His good intentions dissolved. It was not refusal but regret. He had her speaking to him, looking at him, and he wanted more. He edged around Shadow, sliding his hand down the mare's neck, letting Ophelia see that he was going to touch her. At the lip of the saddle he paused, giving her one more chance to back away. When she didn't, he took her gloved hand in his, turning her from the horse, pulling her up against him.

She came like a dreamer, floating, borne along by the current of his will, and their bodies met softly. Then he slid his arm round her waist, clasping her to him, and brought his mouth down on hers. The kiss lasted no more than a few seconds.

Rough voices in the alley made them spring apart. His heart was hammering, but he linked his fingers for her foot and tossed her up on Shadow.

They rode out into the light of mid-morning. The sun had burned away the mist and Ophelia blinked in the brightness. Three men came toward them in the narrow lane, swaggering, joking loudly, filling the space. One moved to allow Ophelia and Alexander an opening, but the fellow in the middle grabbed his arm and stopped him. All three came to a halt, blocking the way.

"Gor, blimey. If it ain't 'er little ladyship." Ophelia's former groom, William, looked from Alexander to her with suspicious eyes. "Still escapin' yer da, ain't ye?"

"Good morning, William. I hope you've found a new post." Ophelia regretted the words at once. The man reeked of sweat and ale, his clothes grimy and streaked with dirt, his collar gray.

"Oooh, it's William, is it?" said the man on his right. They all laughed unpleasantly. Raj's ears went back.

"There's the lady wot got me sacked, boys, fer takin' 'er to 'er friend's 'ouse."

"I'm sorry you were dismissed, William. Someone informed my father."

"Wot good is sorry?" He spat. "A man's situation taken from 'im. It's a crime, ain't it, boys?" The three men laughed again.

"Clagg sacked you, not Miss Brinsby." Alexander spoke in a voice she hadn't heard him use before, quiet and firm. "You've only to lift the bottle in your hand to know the reason why."

William and his companions stopped laughing and studied Alexander. There was an exchange of glances, a subtle shift in their positions, the two men on the sides closing in a bit.

"An 'oo might ye be? Ye talk fancy enough fer a bloke, that's takin' a bit on the side to please 'er ladyship."

"Bet 'e's doing it, too, Bill," said the man on the right.

"This the bottle yer blamin'?" William lifted it to his lips and swallowed. With a glance at his companions, he turned the bottle upside down, shaking out a few last drops, and wiped his mouth along his sleeve. The gesture seemed to signal the men to close in on Ophelia and Alexander.

Alexander nudged Raj between Ophelia and the men. William shouted, smashing his bottle against the ground, raising the jagged end, and lunging forward. Abruptly, Raj rose on his hind legs, advancing, hooves slicing the air, screaming, and the three men fled, flinging bottles and shouting curses and threats.

"Ophelia, are you going to sleep all day?" Jasper's voice at her door woke Ophelia from hot, muddled dreams of Alexander holding her.

She must have managed some answer because Jasper entered and threw himself in an armchair at her bedside. "Did I ruin my chances with Miss Gray forever by being such a dolt at the tailor's shop?"

Ophelia blinked and rubbed her eyes. "What time is it?"

Jasper checked his watch. "Three."

Ophelia fell back against the pillows, her eyelids heavy, her limbs like jelly.

"I suppose she thinks I'm an idiot?"

"Who?"

"Miss Gray." Jasper frowned at her, his handsome brow furrowed.

Ophelia pushed herself up against the headboard. "Not at all."

Jasper snorted. "I run around London searching for a man without knowing what he looks like."

"You did look foolish for a moment, but I'm sure—"

"—Foolish? I looked an ass. A prize ass! So sure of my moment of glory that I brought her along. She saw right through me, I'm sure. She has very . . . intelligent eyes." Jasper slumped, his elbows on his knees, his hands pressed to the side of his head.

Ophelia tipped her head to one side, studying this new self-critical Jasper who recognized the intelligence in her friend's eyes. It was hard to pinpoint what was different about him.

"I know you probably think she's merely quiet. But it's just that she doesn't say everything she's thinking. You can see she takes it all in; she notices."

Ophelia drew her knees up and wrapped her arms around them. "You're right. She *is* observant. It's one of the things I most like about her."

Jasper groaned and jumped up. He circled the room with impatient strides, swearing to himself, and came to a halt beside Ophelia's bed again. "I've got to find Mirandola. Then she'll see I'm not an idiot." He turned away and went to her mantel, looking at himself in the glass.

"Did you find out what he—"

"I'm going to be clever this time." Jasper made an adjustment to his cravat. "I'm going to study up. I've been reading about Italy all morning. Can hardly believe it, of course. Every power in Europe has been trying to get a piece of the place for years. No wonder Mirandola doesn't trust Castlereagh."

"Jasper, that's very sound. If you understand the prince and why he ran away, you're much more likely to persuade him to return to negotiations."

"That's what I thought." He grinned at her in the mirror. "And I won't bother Miss Gray again until I have some definite information to tell her."

"Wise." Ophelia nodded gravely.

"Do you think she likes green?" Jasper turned. "Did you see her last night?"

Ophelia plucked the counterpane, avoiding Jasper's gaze. This new Jasper was more alert than the old one had been. "It was such a squeeze at Marchmont's after the opera." She tried to think of a way to stem his questions about Hetty before he asked about her family. She threw back the covers and reached for her wrapper. "You know, I borrowed a book you probably need. Let me find it."

At her writing table she pushed aside the notes she'd made on Berwick's poem. "Here. Sismond's *History of the Italian Republics*. There's a section on Trevigna."

"Thanks, Sprite." Jasper took the little volume reverently. "This is just the thing." He flipped through the pages and showed her the heading Trevigna. "Well, thanks." He turned and strode for the door.

"Jasper?" she called before he could get away. "Did you find out what Mirandola looks like?"

He looked up from Sismond's book, his hand on the doorknob. "Yes, I saw a miniature that Burke has. Funny, Mirandola doesn't look anything like an Italian prince."

Chapter 11

"**T**o kiss or not to kiss?"

Open and indiscreet, Alexander's question made Ophelia glance round the Grays' stable. They were alone. Alexander, having dismounted, was looking up at her. His perceptive gaze recognized her indecision, while she regarded him from Shadow's back, unwilling to descend and admit she wanted his kiss. To think the word started butterflies of agitation beating their wings in her.

"You mustn't think I come to Hetty's for kisses."

"That's why I come," he said.

Ophelia twisted the reins around her hands.

"We're going to face this dilemma every time you ride, Ophelia. Your groom wants to kiss you."

"How can you admit it so freely?"

"How can I conceal it?"

She thought he could if he could turn the blue of his eyes to something cool and gray. "And if I refuse?"

"You choose," he said with a little bow. "The

lady is sovereign. The man is her servant and must obey her."

"What are you talking about?" she asked.

"The rules of . . . love."

"Love?" She couldn't help looking at him then.

Of course, he'd caught the irony in her tone, and that had started him thinking, wondering. She could see it in his eyes. "What rules?" she asked.

"I read them in a book."

"In your father's library?"

He nodded.

"An amazing library. Your father was a . . . ?"

"Great reader," he said lightly. "You are used to giving me commands. You can command in this, too, if you like. I'll obey."

He led Raj to a stall while she sat, studying her hands. When Shadow moved restlessly under her, impatient now for Ophelia to dismount, Alexander returned and steadied the mare with a touch on her bridle.

It was odd to think of commanding him in this matter. It was nothing to say "Saddle my horse" or "Clean the stalls." Those were not commands of his will, but only of his body. To say "Kiss me" or to withhold permission gave her an odd sense of power. She slanted a glance at him, detecting a finely drawn tension in his mouth. He wanted to kiss her. He had admitted it. Surely that gave her some power over him.

"Very well," she said, freeing her foot from the stirrup. "I agree to your rules."

He put his hands to her waist, catching her as

she slid from Shadow. "You haven't heard them all."

She started to draw back, but the expression in his eyes held her. "If we kiss," she asked, "how do I tell you to stop?"

"Tug on my ear? Step on my foot?"

"I'll tug on your ear," she agreed solemnly.

"Test me."

She nodded, her throat suddenly dry. His hands tightened on her waist, and he lowered his mouth to hers slowly, making a ceremony of her permission. His lips brushed hers lightly at first, then clung, full and open and consuming, different from the hasty kiss they'd shared the day before. This exchange began in acknowledged purpose and led to revelations of longing and need.

She barely remembered their signal, fumbled her hand up from his shoulder to his ear. At her touch he stopped, wrenching his mouth from hers. She could feel his heated breath on her shoulder for a long, pulsing instant. Then he stepped away, turning his back to her.

He reached for Shadow, and under his shaky touch the mare shivered with a jingle of steel. Another groom entered the stable, leading a pair of carriage horses, and Ophelia slipped outside.

Hours later, on their way back to Searle House, she told him, "I'm not fond of rules."

He gave her a wry smile. "These are all to your advantage." They rode side by side in the last stretch of lane before the stables, the horses pulling a little, eager for the comforts of their stalls.

"Tell me the rest, then."

"Love should be kept secret."

"Sensible."

"When made public, love rarely endures."

"That explains the dearth of it in marriage."

"In a crowd, the lover must treat his beloved almost as a stranger."

"Discretion, always wise."

"Meetings of lovers should be difficult to arrange."

She risked a glance at him and then couldn't look away. "How often did you read this book?"

"Once."

"Recently?"

"Years ago."

"And you remembered so much? You've must have been very interested in the subject matter."

"Never as much as now." He flashed her a grin.

"That," she said, trying to ignore a fluttering sensation in her middle, "is mere flattery. What do the rules say about flattery?"

"I forget."

"Liar."

"There is another rule I remember."

"What?"

"Love is suffering."

"That's not a rule."

"It's the one rule every lover obeys." They reached the stableyard gate, and conversation between them came to an end, but she gave her hand to him at the mounting block, and he held it even when her feet were firmly on the ground. Reluctantly, she pulled away.

*   *   *

Ophelia moved lightly among the gossiping groups at the subscription ball. Now that she had added kissing Alexander to her secret offenses against society, she must be very careful to appear as unremarkable as possible. But for once she found it easy to appear shallow and heartless and bored. After all, everyone was doing it.

Fortunately, society had other transgressors to punish, as if who was in or out were a mere children's game of choosing. Lord Byron was out, his sins exposed by his estranged wife. A week before, society had given him the cut direct, ignoring a party in his honor. Brummell was out, forced to flee his creditors. Everyone who remained was full of unspoken self-congratulation at retaining a place among the elite.

Nothing changed among them. They were impervious to ideas, but they danced well, so Ophelia danced, with Dent, who was dull; Ayres, who was proud; and Wyatt, who was merely offensive. He was pursuing a besotted-looking girl in white, but he requested a dance with Ophelia as she stood at her mother's side. She smiled with false sweetness, agreeing to a quadrille, not the waltz he had requested. Jasper found her between sets.

"Have you seen Miss Gray?" he asked.

Ophelia sobered instantly. "She doesn't have vouchers, Jasper."

He was looking about the room, but that brought his gaze back to Ophelia. His brow wrinkled in puzzlement. She could see him thinking, trying to square his high opinion of Hetty with what her inability to get vouchers might mean about her standing in society.

"I suppose this sort of ball is too mercenary for her taste." His disappointment in Hetty's absence was plain. He stopped looking around the room.

Ophelia softened. She could not bring herself to tell him that Hetty would never receive vouchers. "Yes, her family thinks private balls are better for forming attachments," she lied.

Jasper shoved his hands in his pockets. "Well, I just wanted to tell her of our progress in the Mirandola search."

"Jasper, what have you found out?"

"Actually, the Foreign Office received a letter from an Italian named Ferruci. According to his letter, the prince is behind a plan to call a constitutional congress in Trevigna this fall."

"Your prince is oddly democratic, isn't he? What does he mean by this congress?"

"We're not entirely sure, but it puts his disappearance in a new light."

"How so?"

"If he is behind this republican movement in Trevigna, his disappearance at a critical moment in negotiation is a hostile act. A republican government is unlikely to enter into any agreement with England, you see."

"Then what happens to your search?"

"It's more important than ever that I find him."

"What are you going to do?"

"I've set my man to watch the tailor's shop. If there are any suspicious comings and goings, he's to find me straightaway."

"Oh." Ophelia tried to shake off the disappointment she felt at her brother's methods of conducting a search. To think his valet was standing in the dark on a drizzly night while Jasper led debutantes around a ballroom put her out of all patience with her brother. So much for his ambition to rise in the foreign service or even to impress Hetty. It occurred to her that she rather admired Alexander because he didn't have anyone to wait on him. She excused herself when her new partner approached.

Jasper watched his sister join the set, smiling and nodding at her partner as if utterly engrossed by his remarks, which Jasper knew she wasn't. It struck him then that for all his sister's apparent compliance, she actually did pretty much what she wanted to do. She had evaded their parents' efforts to marry her off for nearly two years, and she was being less than forthcoming in the matter of Henrietta Gray.

"Evening, Brinsby," said a voice at his side.

"Wyatt." Jasper acknowledged his companion without turning.

"Is your sister giving you trouble?"

"What?" Jasper looked away from the dancers. Wyatt and his sister had raised expectations briefly in the last season, but nothing had come of them. Now that he thought about it, Jasper found it rather curious that Ophelia never spoke of Wyatt.

"Has she formed an attachment this season?"

"Sprite? Not likely. She hardly pays any attention to her partners."

"She's paying attention to someone, I'll wager."

"What makes you think so?"

"She's got the look of a woman who's been kissed."

Jasper stared at his friend. "Give it up, Wyatt. I ought to call you out."

"Just a friendly warning, Brinsby." He sauntered off, and Jasper was left with a suspicion that his sister was deceiving him. He recalled the night she'd planned to meet him at the Candovers' and hadn't shown. She never answered his questions about Miss Gray. The more he thought about it, the more he felt entitled to some straight answers. If he couldn't get them from his sister, then he would have to ask his mother.

Alexander let himself into the tailor shop by the back door around midnight. He lit a candle in the hall and crept up the stairs to his room. He needed to catch up with his correspondence. There was no telling what Francesca was up to or whether Hume and Tollworthy were doing their part to get the Trevigna Fund going.

At the landing a sleepy Lucca greeted him in a magnificent frogged silk robe and slippers. He wrinkled his handsome nose as Alexander passed. "Majesty, you must stop this peasant work. You are soiling the hands of a king."

"The boots at least." Alexander tossed his gloves on the desk and held up his relatively clean hands. "You aren't offended by honest sweat, are you, Lucca?"

"You joke, but we had visitors. Spies, I'm sure of it."

"Spies?" Lucca was taking the English government entirely too seriously if he thought Castlereagh would trouble to send spies to look for the missing prince of Trevigna. Alexander shed his jacket and cravat.

"A gentleman, *molto signore*, and two ladies. One fair, very pretty; one dark with the eyes of a hawk." Lucca's countenance grew very sad. "The gentleman bought the forest green double-breasted coat."

"The forest green?"

Lucca nodded.

Alexander felt a pang of regret. It was one of his finest coats. The clothes he wore in the stable were showing the effects of daily contact with horses, dust, and mud. He sank onto the bed and tugged at his left boot. "The fellow has good taste, but that doesn't make him a spy."

"The man had the wits of a celery stalk, but the little dark lady, she was like a *lazzarone* with a stiletto, very sharp."

"The government sent a female spy?"

Lucca looked grave. "I think she knows."

"Knows what?"

"That we are selling your coats."

"Even if she knows they're my coats, which I very much doubt, you are selling them, not I. If questioned, you'll say you bought them from a secondhand dealer in Monmouth Street."

Lucca sniffed. "Flies don't enter a closed mouth."

"Don't worry." Alexander set his boots aside and moved to the desk. "You are following all our precautions for sending and receiving letters?"

"Of course."

"Then no one will find us."

Alexander lit the desk lamp. "Are there any letters from Trevigna?"

"From Donna Francesca, they come like cheese on macaroni."

Alexander leafed through the pile. Aunt Francesca was undoubtedly his most reliable correspondent. Where were the others he needed? He settled himself in the chair. "Thanks," he said over his shoulder. He heard the slap of Lucca's slippers retreating down the hall as he opened the first letter.

It was late when he'd sorted out the conflicting demands and suggestions. He had spread five letters in a line across the desk. In the first Aunt Francesca praised Federico Tesio's daughter and explained how well her proxy courtship was proceeding. The girl apparently had the stately dignity of an empress. Her family was aware of the financial uncertainties of the royal house of Mirandola but were prepared to overlook any of Alexander's embarrassments in the service of Trevigna.

Of the other letters, the first was from a nobleman in Aunt Francesca's camp. In his view any effort to develop a republic was misguided and dangerous. He wrote of the uncertainties of the time and of the general opposition in the wake of the fall of France to any republican undertaking. Ferruci was active again, and all of Trevigna wanted a strong government to oppose the bandit. Alexander should not trust anyone who agreed to a constitutional convention. He should take his aunt's very sound advice to marry and get an heir.

Tollworthy's letter was hardly more encouraging. The London Committee for the Restoration of the Italian Republics was divided and floundering. The republican faction in Trevigna, having heard rumors of Alexander's upcoming marriage, was sending a man to London to negotiate independently with the committee. The investors were alarmed. Tollworthy devoted two pages to their fears and questions.

In a shorter missive, Aunt Francesca wrote that she would be arriving in London with Tesio's daughter sometime before the first of May.

Only the last letter was a pledge of support for the constitutional convention Alexander had planned for October. He had fifty letters promising attendance so far. He needed twenty-five more, at least. He would have to send another round of pleas.

"Majesty?" It was Lucca with a tray of bread, cheese, and wine. "You should eat."

Alexander cleared a place on the desk for the tray and leaned back in his chair. "I didn't mean to keep you awake," he said, rolling his stiff shoulders.

Lucca set down the tray. "If you can stay up, so can I." He shrugged.

"Go get another glass, then. You can help me sort out this tangle." He waved his hand over the letters.

They made short work of the bread and cheese and sipped the wine in silence for a while.

"Is the news very bad, Majesty?" Lucca asked.

Alexander was tempted to deny it, but he didn't. "Francesca's meddling has turned the republicans against me. They are sending their own man to London. We have less than a fortnight to convince the committee that there will be a constitutional convention in October."

"They doubt you?"

"Tollworthy wants to know when and where the congress will be held, how many representatives there will be, how soon they can expect a constitution to be adopted, and when we will hold the first general elections." He swore a satisfying oath he'd learned from one of his fellow grooms.

"*Madre della Virgine*, where did you get such a phrase?"

"May not a prince swear?"

Lucca smoothed the folds of his silk robe with offended dignity. "You are angry. You work and work and do not hit one nail on the head. I do not understand why you do not give up the stable. Stay here and write your . . . letters."

Alexander regarded his wine. There was one reason he would not leave his job, but he wasn't ready to tell Lucca about kissing Ophelia Brinsby. He drained his glass. "Thank you for the meal, Lucca. I'm going to write a few more letters tonight. Can you take them tomorrow?"

Lucca rose and bowed. "Of course, Majesty."

The unexpected summons to her father's library came as Ophelia was readying to go to the theatre. She knew without asking that she had been found out in some way. There was no chance to send a warning to the stables lest Alexander be questioned and sacked. She followed a sober-faced footman down the hall to whatever doom awaited her, thinking only that she wouldn't know where to find Alexander if her father had already dismissed him.

At the library door, she paused for a deep breath. She would not give anything away. She knocked, and at her father's call, entered.

Her father stood with his back to a lively fire, his hands spreading his coattails. Her mother reclined on a small sofa with Pet's head in her lap, and Jasper stood in the middle of the carpet, looking miserable and apologetic. Pet roused himself so far as to offer her a low growl of greeting.

"Miss," said her father, "you have some explaining to do."

"Yes," said her mother, stroking the dog. "Jasper says he's met you twice in the company of Miss Gray."

She cast her brother a swift glance, wondering which time Jasper had failed to mention. "We met quite by accident, mother. Miss Gray is free to come and go about London as she pleases. I didn't see any harm in exchanging a few words in passing."

"Hardly the story your brother tells us," her father said.

Jasper cleared his throat. "But I assumed they were together. Perhaps you should have questioned Ophelia first."

Her father turned his most serious you've-let-us-down face on Jasper, who subsided at once. "Ophelia, when you were sixteen, we asked you to sever all ties with Miss Gray. Do you remember why?"

Ophelia had sense enough not to answer.

"Not merely because of your ill-judged foray

into publishing, but because we had your interests at heart."

Ophelia clenched her fists. The temptation to tell them they had no notion of her true interests was very great and would be utter folly. She waited for her father to continue.

"In truth, these new meetings with Miss Gray are more injurious to the family than your earlier association with her."

"How can that be?" Ophelia could not resist asking.

"Do you know who Miss Gray's mother is?" her mother asked.

"What can it matter? She's dead."

"She's not dead. She's very much alive and so notorious that Miss Gray cannot be eligible for even the most modest of matches, and for her to aspire to your brother's hand—"

"She doesn't aspire to Jasper's hand. She has no such thought. And if such foolishness entered her head, I would be quick to point out that a snob like Jasper is beneath a woman as fine and sensible as Hetty."

"Silence," roared her father, startling Pet into furious barking, which lasted several minutes while Lady Searle stroked the dog, soothing him with soft murmurings.

When the room was quiet again except for the snapping of the fire in the grate, her father spoke. "Miss Gray's mother is that novelist, Amelia Hart."

"Mrs. Hart is Hetty's mother?" Ophelia was sure Hetty did not know and that Solomon did not want to her to know. And Mrs. Hart was holding that knowledge over her former lover's head, making him look sick and miserable in her company as Ophelia had seen at their evening gathering.

"Her former liaison with Solomon Gray is widely known and must preclude all possibility of a respectable match for Miss Gray, whatever her personal attractions or merit."

Ophelia stared at the floor. Her mother was speaking, but she couldn't listen. Hetty deserved respectability and love, and Solomon had tried to provide both. Ophelia could not stand by and see her friends hurt, but she hardly knew what to do to help them. Except that she must get out of this room and think.

She looked up into her father's frowning face.

"Do you understand, miss?" he said.

"What?" She glanced around. Her mother was kissing Pet. Jasper was straightening his cravat.

"You will not leave this house except in the company of your mother until the ball."

Ophelia lifted her chin. "And Jasper, who polluted himself with Miss Gray's company? Is he also confined to mother's company?"

"Jasper," said her mother, "has done nothing. You misled him about your friend's character."

"Her character? Her character is superior to the collective character of this entire family." Ophelia threw her hands up and spun on her heel, heading for the door.

Pet came off the sofa, barking furiously, snapping, and circling Ophelia, halting her in her tracks.

"Sit," her father commanded the dog. Pet obeyed, plopping his hindquarters to the rug in front of Ophelia, his bark subsiding into a low rumble in his throat.

"Ophelia, do not add impertinence to your other crimes," her father continued. "You will not walk out on your parents." He beckoned to his wife. With stately dignity they swept from the room, the dog waddling at their heels.

A lump of coal collapsed in a soft hiss in the grate. Ophelia did not trust herself to speak.

"Well, that was uncomfortable," said Jasper. "Father makes a fellow feel like he's in short coats again."

Ophelia didn't turn. "Is that what concerns you, Jasper? The discomfort of it all?"

"No, damn it, Sprite. It's the deception. You should have told me the truth about Miss Gray from the start. You could see . . . you could see . . . Well, devil take it, you should have told me."

"Why? So that you could avoid forming an attachment with an unsuitable girl?"

"Yes, damn it. What if I had come to care for her? Then where would I be? What would Mother and Father say to that?"

Ophelia let a harsh laugh escape her. She faced her brother. "Jasper, you're an idle, pretentious snob. I wouldn't let you marry my friend."

Jasper's mouth opened and closed twice. "I'm a snob? Well, you . . . you are a spoiled, deceitful baggage. Where did you go that night you were supposed to come to the Candovers'? And who have you been kissing? Wyatt says you have that look, and I've come to think he's right. You'd better watch yourself, Sprite, or you'll end up married to Dent before a month is out." He looked around for his hat and gloves, found them, snatched them up, and headed for the door. "Excuse me. I have work to do."

"Work? Your valet does your work. No wonder you haven't found Mirandola yet."

Chapter 12

As Jasper leaned against the stable wall, waiting for one of the undergrooms to bring his cattle round, the quiet of the place made him feel some queer, disagreeable emotion he was sure he'd felt before but couldn't quite name. He straightened and brushed a piece of loose straw from his trouser leg. He was in the heart of London, yet he felt removed from society. It must be the pungent odor of the place— dust, leather and sweat, and underneath a hint of horse piss and rotted hay—smells of honest toil.

Your valet does your work. His sister's words had chafed at him for days. If it weren't for Ophelia, he'd be dining at his club or playing cards or flirting happily with the newest incomparable. Instead, he'd dismissed his valet Plumb from duty outside the tailor's shop, and had taken over the dull work himself. It reminded him of long hours on his own at school, and suddenly he knew what it was he felt—loneliness.

He poked his head through the wide doors to see if he could hurry the groom along, and found

Clagg making entries in the stable books.

"Evenin', sir." Clagg looked up from his work. "Waitin' fer yer cattle?"

"Yes."

"I'll give the lads a hint, sir," Clagg offered, pushing up from his chair.

Jasper thanked him, but Clagg didn't move.

"Bye the bye, sir, been meanin' to speak w' ye about that stallion ye bought."

Jasper nerved himself for some quip at his expense. He'd forgotten the embarrassment of the chestnut stallion that had thrown the stables into chaos.

"New man's worked a miracle on 'im. Sound 'orse. Ye should take a look at 'im someday."

"I will." Jasper felt mildly better. Perhaps his judgment was not so very faulty.

But his four-day vigil outside the tailor's had been fruitless so far. He had detected nothing more suspicious than the Italian tailor's apparent attachment to a saucy shopgirl from the perfumer's establishment at the end of the street.

It seemed pointless, all his hanging about, hoping to catch the prince. Who would care? Lord Castlereagh would hardly notice Jasper's contribution while weightier matters of state were pressing. Jasper would not find himself elevated to the inner circle at the Foreign Office or trusted with delicate dealings with foreign governments.

He sauntered back out to the yard. He couldn't remember why he'd been so determined to find the prince just a fortnight ago. But a treacherous little voice inside whispered that he did know, that finding the prince had mattered when he could tell Hetty Gray about it. And now it didn't matter because there was no chance of seeing Miss Gray's eyes light when he related his success.

For the hundredth time he blamed Ophelia for allowing him to think her lovely friend eligible. Ophelia deserved her punishment. Her defiance of society's rules was folly. He hoped they *would* marry her off to Dent. His treacherous little voice spoke again, telling him he wanted Hetty Gray, and he was jealous of his sister's courage in daring to break the rules. He tried to silence the voice by recalling Ophelia's unfeeling frankness.

As he thought of it, he realized that Ophelia wouldn't change. She'd break the rules again, and find a way to meet her friend. He should be watching his sister, not the tailor's shop. And when Ophelia made her escape, he should follow. She would lead him straight to Hetty Gray. Then he would tell Miss Gray directly what he thought of her presumption. Once he told her his feelings, he would be himself again without this unaccountable melancholy, and he would devote himself to the season's pleasures.

The undergroom brought the horses out, while two stablehands rolled the curricle from its house, but the carriage suddenly bored him.

"On second thought," he said to the groom with the horses, "I'll walk." When they all just stared at him, he added, "Sorry to trouble you."

He reached in his pocket for some coins, and tossed one to each man. As the undergroom turned the horses, a new thought struck him. "Do you know Lady Ophelia when you see her?"

The man nodded. Jasper tossed another coin

his way. "If you see her in this stable, saddle my horse and send for me directly."

He left the yard in a few quick strides. Eventually Ophelia would bolt, and he would be ready for her.

And she did . . . sooner than he'd expected. The very night after he'd made arrangements with the undergroom. The man was as good as his word. Jasper found his mount ready and could see the hindquarters of his own chestnut stallion disappearing down the lane as he left the stable.

It took considerable patience to hang back in the evening traffic, but he was rewarded when he saw Ophelia and her companion enter a house on a modest street in Kensington. He found the mews, stabled his horse with a groom, and went looking for the chestnut stallion. A couple of inquires told him he'd come to the right place. Still, he hesitated at the door, preparing himself for disappointment or embarrassment if he was wrong.

"Miss Gray, please," he said to the mobcapped woman who opened the door.

"Who may I say is calling?" the woman asked.

"Jasper Brinsby."

Her eyes widened. "In here, sir," she said, ushering him into a small, dark parlor. She lit a lamp and vanished. The furnishings were surprisingly tasteful, with a fine landscape painting over the mantel. He laid his cloak, hat, and gloves across the rolled arm of a small, elegant sofa. Things he planned to say to Miss Gray tumbled through his mind. He took a deep breath, trying to settle his thoughts. He had only to put her in her place and he could go.

A whisper of light footsteps in the hall sent his heart skipping. The door opened and Hetty Gray entered, so lovely, that he could think of nothing whatever to say.

She looked stricken; her hands were tightly clasped. "You've come for Ophelia, of course. I'll send her to you at once. But I hope you won't tell your parents. She really shouldn't marry Dent," Hetty finished in a rush.

Jasper swallowed. In the lamp's glow the golden curls around her face seemed to have a light of their own. Her dress made him think of pale champagne. "I didn't come for Ophelia."

A puzzled look came into her eyes, but she said nothing.

He took two careful steps toward her, watching her eyes. "I came to see you." That much was true. He became interested in the place at the base of her throat where her pulse beat.

She spun away from him toward the hearth, looking down into the empty grate. "What you must think of me for concealing my origins from you, I can't imagine."

Jasper opened and closed his mouth unsuccessfully twice. "You must despise me for the most shallow sort of snobbery." It was not what he'd planned to say at all.

She shook her head, the little golden curls swinging.

"Miss Gray." He moved to close the gap between them. "Look at me," he urged her, his throat suddenly tight.

Another little shake of her head. Putting his

hands to her shoulders, he turned her gently. "Hetty." His voice cracked. He tilted her face up to his. "Can we start over again?"

A dizzying moment passed.

When she nodded, he stepped back, holding out his hand. "Very well, I'm Jasper Brinsby, prize fool." Slowly she raised her hand to meet his. "And you are the wise, benevolent Miss Gray?"

A little sob escaped her, she denied his compliment with a shake of her head.

"Of course you are," Jasper said firmly. "Glad to make your acquaintance."

"Your family will be angry and embarrassed that you came to see me." Her eyes grew sad again, and she withdrew her hand from his.

He squared his shoulders and struck a martial pose. "My family will throw great obstacles in our path, but we will overcome them with heroic efforts."

She smiled her wise, sad smile. "Do you think we can?"

"Yes."

She seemed unconvinced, but Jasper wanted no doubts now. "Are you going to invite me in?" he asked.

"You want to join our party?"

"It will probably be a great blow to my pretensions, but yes."

"You won't give Ophelia away or embarrass her?" She looked severe, her brows drawn together, and he forgot to answer her as he realized there would be hundreds of looks to get to know, to catalogue.

"I owe Ophelia too great a debt."

She smiled at that. "Come along, then, and meet the Gray circle."

Jasper didn't know what he'd expected, exactly, but it wasn't Solomon Gray and his guests. Ophelia cast him one horrified glance and exchanged a look with Hetty that apparently calmed her fears. Mr. Gray welcomed Jasper civilly, but with reserve. Amelia Hart stunned him. He saw at once where Hetty got her looks, though he was puzzled at the introduction, for there seemed to be no acknowledgment of Mrs. Hart's relation to the Grays. As for the others, their wit was dry and sharp, their clothes fashionable, and their looks sophisticated. Then Jasper forgot them all, for standing at Ophelia's side, looking little older than his portrait, was a man who was unmistakably Prince Alexander di Piovasco Mirandola.

Chapter 13

Ophelia thought for an alarmed instant that Jasper must recognize Alexander as a groom from the Searle House stable. Then the look of recognition in his eyes passed, leaving only an expression of besotted wonder, which he directed at Hetty. Ophelia had to smile. His snobbery seemed to have succumbed to his admiration, altogether an improvement in his character. She could not fault his manners as Hetty introduced him to her guests.

As Hetty led Jasper around, Ophelia seized a chance to speak with Solomon.

"Where have you been, miss?" he asked. The words were playful, but his eyes had lost their customary mirth.

"I've been caught with your daughter again, sir, and been confined to Searle House."

Solomon's gaze followed Jasper and Hetty. "Is that what's brought your brother down on us?"

Ophelia shook her head. "You can see Jasper's besotted. Apparently he lost his snobbery somewhere between home and here."

"He'll find it again soon enough." Solomon's mouth settled in a grim line.

"Because of Mrs. Hart?" Ophelia asked.

A little flash of alarm in those fierce eyes betrayed the truth. "Did your father tell you?"

Ophelia nodded. The novelist, in a burgundy gown that set off her alabaster complexion, sat listening to Berwick with half an ear, her fingers playing on the carved arm of her chair as if she were waiting for something.

Solomon suppressed a groan. "It's a game to her. She can unmask me to my daughter anytime."

"Why?"

"She never wanted a child. She left Hetty entirely to me . . . until this spring. She saw us by chance in the street, and realized who Hetty was."

"She came out of curiosity, then?"

Solomon took a swallow of his wine. "She can ruin Hetty. All the respectability I've tried to give her . . ."

"Hetty is utterly respectable, lovely, and good. Mrs. Hart can't change that. Nothing can change what Hetty is."

"Miss Brinsby," called Mrs. Fenton. "You must join us, dear. We're speaking of novels." She saw Solomon's face and immediately offered an apology.

Solomon smiled, feigning his usual good humor. "Take her away, Mrs. Fenton." To Ophelia, he added, "Your review of Berwick's poem has come out. It's being quoted here tonight. Berwick takes exception to your characterizing his style as 'diffuse.' "

A few minutes passed before she could really attend to Mrs. Fenton's ideas about the lonely, superior heroine of Samuel Richardson's *Clarissa*. Alexander sent her a veiled, questioning glance, and she gathered her wits, joining the conversation. The Grays' drawing room, Ophelia realized, doubled the narrow realm in which she and Alexander could express their friendship. It was curious that she thought of him as a friend. True, he kissed her. But he had put her in command, and she knew her limits, knew just when the dangerous weakness began—and *that* she would not allow. She had two friends now.

Ophelia smiled at him until Mrs. Hart's gaze reminded her that even here there was a need for caution. No one except Hetty knew that Alexander was her groom, but Mrs. Hart appeared capable of discovering the secret. Jasper, too, could ask embarrassing questions, for which Ophelia would have to prepare herself. For the moment, however, Jasper had forgotten Ophelia. He and Hetty had settled on a couch near the door in a private conversation.

Mrs. Fenton was still defending *Clarissa*. Then Mrs. Hart came to attention, leaning forward, her snowy bosom attracting the gentlemen's notice. "Must the heroine's story always end in marriage?" she asked, directing her gaze at Alexander.

At any other time the question would have fascinated Ophelia, but she saw what it was. Ideas didn't interest Mrs. Hart; she wanted to see character exposed. She was like Wyatt, collecting secrets, making others vulnerable.

Berwick sent Alexander one fierce look, as if

they were rivals, and pounced on the question. "Marriage *is* the heroine's story," he insisted. "She keeps herself pure and unspoiled until the man of merit secures her by valiant deeds. Penelope, Cinderella, the Sleeping Beauty . . . marriage is the end for all of them." He gave a careless wave that summed up the possibilities for women.

Mr. Archer brought his wineglass down with a clunk. "Not Penelope. I'll not allow you to lump her with those witless paragons waiting to be plucked. Her resistance is magnificent."

Others sang the praises of Penelope until Mrs. Hart brought them back to the topic again.

"Berwick's wrong, of course," she said with her charming smile. "The girl in a fairy tale is static, unchanging, a prize. The story has nothing to do with marriage." She cast Alexander another interested glance. "The conflict is always between an old crone and a maiden. The fairy tale is simply the story of a young woman displacing an older woman as a sex object."

Archer choked on a sip of wine. Solomon pounded him on the back while the others protested Mrs. Hart's view with impotent politeness.

She merely smiled and scanned their faces, pausing at Solomon's, daring him to check her, her sly cat glance passing on to Alexander. "Your turn."

Alexander set aside his wine. "I haven't been married," he said lightly. "But I'll venture an opinion. The heroine's story ends in marriage because the heroine's proper opponent is a man, her equal." He watched Ophelia, letting her know the words were for her. Her pulse quickened in reply. "They must tame one another to live in society."

Mrs. Fenton and Mrs. Gardiner applauded, but Mrs. Hart stiffened. "How conventional." She sipped her wine and turned to Ophelia. "Now you, Miss Brinsby, a woman of marriageable age—you must have a reply to Mr. Alexander."

All eyes shifted to Ophelia. Under their scrutiny, she felt Mrs. Hart plucking at the invisible threads of consciousness that bound Ophelia to Alexander. A glance showed her that Jasper's place beside Hetty was empty.

She raised her teacup and took a delaying sip. Mrs. Hart had roused everyone's suspicions of them by her pointed questions. "The heroine's story should end with her choice, whether to marry or not. Marriage, as it is, has too much to do with property and rank. A woman must be able to refuse marriage if there's no love in it."

"Love or nothing? Miss Brinsby is a romantic." Mrs. Hart leaned back in her chair, letting her amused glance wander to Alexander. "Back to you."

Berwick broke in at once. "Ridiculous for a woman to think of refusal. Marriage is the imperative for women—biological, social, economic. What else are they to do?"

"Write?" Mrs. Hart asked, her thin brows arching upward.

Berwick sputtered incoherently, and laughter drowned his defense. When the laughter died, Mrs. Hart turned to Hetty. "Miss Gray agrees with me, I think?"

Hetty smiled softly. "About writing, yes; but about marriage, no." Hetty had that serene in-

ward look that came over her when she was
thinking about a poem. The room went quiet and
some of the tension left it. "I imagine marriage
is one of those deep, simple necessities in which
life renews itself."

"Come now, Miss Gray." Mrs. Hart's mouth
became a thin, contemptuous line. "Marriage is
absolutely mired in formality and legality."

Hetty shook her head. "We build elaborate
churches, but prayer remains a simple cry of the
heart. We give marriage forms and ceremonies,
but that doesn't change what it is."

Ophelia held her breath. In some way her
friend had broken Mrs. Hart's indefinable control
of the room. There would be no unmasking tonight. Mrs. Pendares sailed in so promptly with
the tea tray that Ophelia suspected her of having
listened at the door. Everyone moved to the refreshments, and Ophelia realized that Jasper had
slipped away. When she looked for Alexander,
he beckoned her to the door.

In the garden they paused to adjust to the freedom and consciousness of being alone together.
Ophelia recognized now how awareness of him
wakened her senses to the immediate, to damp
stones under her slippers, the scent of sweet violets and hyacinth, the cool air against her
cheeks, the sharp divisions of shadow and moonlight in the garden. His gloved hand found hers,
and thus linked, they started down the path.

His hand was a firm, warm clasp around hers,
solid, real, an extension of the man himself, his
frankness and generosity, his habit of offering
comfort and strength. This joining of hands dif-

fered from all the times when he'd offered his
hand as she'd mounted or dismounted Shadow.
This was a meeting of equals, another gift of the
Grays' drawing room. Their unhurried footsteps
on the path had a companionable sound.

"Does Miss Gray know that Mrs. Hart is her
mother?" he asked.

Ophelia turned quickly. "How did you
guess?"

"Little things. Their looks. Mrs. Hart's hold
over Solomon Gray. I suspect she could hurt him
only through his daughter, and you've been worried about the Grays all evening." He gave her
hand a squeeze.

"Apparently Mrs. Hart is threatening to reveal
her secret."

"Do you think she will?"

"I think Solomon should tell Hetty himself and
free them from Mrs. Hart."

"He must fear to lose her if he tells."

"It will be worse if he doesn't."

Alexander didn't answer, but Ophelia liked
sharing this other secret with him. It seemed to
fit the new experience of joining hands.

At the gate he reached for the latch.

"You're not going to kiss me?" she asked, half
teasing, half in earnest.

"You didn't command it," he said in a low
voice, his hand on the latch.

"I do now."

He let the latch fall with a click, and turning,
leaned against the gate, drawing her into his
arms, cradling her with his body.

She closed her eyes, burying her face in the
folds of his cravat, breathing the scent of him,

but pressing her forearms against his chest, keeping a little distance. She would not spoil the closeness by letting him discover the betraying peaks of her breasts.

He put his lips to her hair, his hands to her waist. "I lied about why I kissed you that first time."

Ophelia started to pull back, but his hands trapped her.

"It wasn't solely your riding ability. It was this," he said, kissing her hair. "And this." He spread his fingers, framing her waist firmly, settling her hips against his.

She stiffened. Pressed against each other, she would know if his body changed.

"Am I too bold?" he asked, his lips at her ear. "I have no experience at kissing ladies."

Ophelia lifted her head. "You can't tell me that you've never kissed before."

He laughed. "Do you want me to confess my amorous adventures to you?"

She supposed it was an odd thing to want to know, but she knew he would tell her if she asked. "May I command it?"

"Yes." His voice was a hoarse whisper.

"Then I do."

His chest rose and fell under her as a he took a deep breath.

"Alexander's experience of love. A very short narrative. An innkeeper's daughter taught me boldness, and a courtesan taught me a few refinements."

She wanted him to say more. Sometime she would ask him about that interesting, wicked-sounding word *refinements*. He plainly knew more than she did about sexual congress, but he seemed to think what he knew did not apply to ladies.

"Are you going to confess your experience?" he asked.

She gasped. "No."

"At least tell me what you like, so I don't offend you. It's one of the rules. A lover should never give offense."

"I like kisses," she said.

"Nothing more?" She could hear the dismay in the question.

"Just kisses."

"Because I, your humble groom, am so far beneath you?"

"You are a most unhumble groom."

"Still, I am your servant in love. I do what you bid me." His fingers found her chin and tilted her face up to his. Then he paused, holding her mouth inches from his, as if to test himself and let the longing build.

It was a sweet relief when his lips met hers in a long, slow kiss. One kiss led to another. He didn't force or press, but drew back each time until their mouths seemed to meet again by mutual accord. Ophelia could stop at any time. It was like turning the pages in a fascinating book, the story unfolding so that one could not find a pause, longing written on every page. Just one more, her mind whispered.

His hands kneaded her waist, bunching her gown, the silk sliding over her fiery skin. She felt the hungry press of his body against her belly and a terrible impatience to move. She could not hold still another minute. She squirmed, wanting to release her arms.

The voice spoke in her head. *You're one of the hot ones, Ophelia.* She hated the smug voice, but she couldn't stop the words. She twisted in Alexander's hold. His hands slid urgently up her ribs, and she tugged desperately at his ear. He broke their kiss with a groan, holding her in an impassioned clasp, as she stood shaking and shamed.

Above them a bird ruffled its feathers.

"You're cold," he said. "Let me take you back to Searle House." Abruptly he opened the gate, grabbing her hand and pulling her into the lane.

They moved through the dreamy, unreal landscape, where they were free to join hands, toward the plain square of light cast by the stable lamp, where they must return to the differences that separated them. Ophelia regretted that she'd stopped him so soon. Maybe it would not have been so very foolish to linger a few minutes more in the garden.

Maybe there was some way that Alexander could become her equal. There were men lower in rank than Alexander who mixed freely with their betters, men like the champions of track and ring valued for their narrow, limited excellence. Alexander's excellence was general, his speech and ideas those of a gentleman. It was insulting to him to compare him to race touts, riders, boxers. Perhaps if he owned horses or bred them, he could move in society. She could buy him a horse. He should possess Raj, he already did in a way.

She was thinking of it when a rush of footsteps

broke the silence. Alexander spun, freeing her hand. Two black shapes hurtled toward them.

"Run, Ophelia—"

The clash of bodies cut off his command. One black, burly figure shoved Ophelia hard and she went reeling. Her shoulder slammed into stone. She rolled groggily back against the wall, getting her breath, trying to clear her head.

From the writhing shadows in the lane came grunts and curses. The two shapes were wrestling Alexander up against the opposite wall. She heard a thud.

"Got 'im, Bill. Cut 'im! Cut 'im," shouted a high, thin voice.

A third black shape emerged from a deeper shadow under an opposite eave, moving slowly toward the pants and grunts.

Ophelia glanced toward the stable. The little square of light seemed impossibly distant, but she began to edge toward it, hugging the wall, staying in the shadow. Damp weeds caught at her feet, and her ankle came up against the sharp edge of something. *Please, let it be a stick.*

"Come on, Bill," said the thin voice. "Can't 'old 'im a bleedin' week."

The slow moving figure closed in on the others. "Where's yer fine 'orse, boyo? Not so 'igh now, are ye?" There was a sickening thud, followed by a tight rasp of breath. "Take my place. Use a 'orse against me."

"Cut 'im and ha' done w' it," said a third voice, flat and calm.

Ophelia slid down the wall, keeping her eyes on the dark mass opposite, groping with her fingers for the thing in the grass. She found the flat edge of a stick, maybe an old barrel stave, as wide across as her palm. She tugged it free of the weeds and straightened.

She could see the black shape that was Bill stretch out an arm. At the end of it, a flash of metal gleamed in the moonlight. She braced herself, raising the stick, then made a swift dash from the concealing shadows. With a savage cry she brought her stick crashing down on the offending arm. Her stick landed with a crack, the force of the blow reverberating through her body. Bill shrieked and whirled, his arm flying, knocking her to the ground with a jarring impact.

She scooted back across the dirt, tangled as she was in her cloak, until she could get her feet under her and scramble into the shadows.

From across the lane came a hail of blows and a sickening thud. Then a sudden snarl and a keen whistle of breath. Ophelia pressed her fist to her mouth to stifle a cry.

One of the black shapes staggered to the center of the lane, doubled over, wheezing. "Damn ye, Bill." It was the flat voice. "It's *me* ye've stuck."

The three shapes came together and passed down the lane, only the low rumble of their voices coming back.

Ophelia could hear Alexander's short, fast breaths.

"Alexander?" She crossed through the moonlight to the opposite shadows and reached for him against the wall. He grabbed her hand and pulled her tight against him.

"Are you all right?"

She bobbed her head against his chest, feeling

the pounding of his heart and his labored breathing. She could smell his blood, hot and coppery.

"Come into the light," she urged, lifting her head from his chest.

They stumbled into the stable, and she pushed him down on the bench. She could see at once that a cut above his eye had bled freely and his lower lip had been split. She pulled off her gloves.

"I'll get Raj," she told him.

The stallion's eyes were rimmed with white, his nostrils flaring. He tossed his head, making her struggle to get a bridle on him.

"The smell of blood makes him nervous." Alexander's voice came from directly behind her.

She looked over her shoulder and let go of the bridle. Her stomach plunged wildly. He'd stripped off his gloves and removed his upper garments and was wrapping his cravat around a long gash on his arm. Ophelia looked away from the fair smoothness of his shoulders and the dark golden "V" of hair on his chest.

He came up beside her, calming the horse with his voice and hands until Raj accepted the saddle.

"Let's get you to Searle House," he told Ophelia.

She watched helplessly while he slipped into his coat, easing the sleeve over his makeshift bandage. He was showing calm sense and judgment. But to part now with the sickening thuds of the attack still in her ears, her own throat raw from the cry she had uttered, his wounds un-

tended, seemed to give the victory to their attackers.

"Not there, somewhere else," she pleaded.

His eyes burned, making her think the impossible—that there could be hot blue seas.

"I have a room above a shop, where I go sometimes to . . . think."

"Take me there."

Chapter 14

~~~⌒⌒~~~

Ophelia didn't recognize the streets or the turnings. The moonlight made an unreal city where black shadows wavered as if they might break loose at any moment and rush forward to attack. At a rickety gate off an alley, Alexander swung down and led Raj into a small enclosure.

When he had taken care of the horse, he led Ophelia through a back entrance into a plain brick building. She waited impatiently in the dark, deprived of the peculiar pleasures of his nearness, the scent of his skin, the rhythms of his pulse and breathing. He returned with a candle and a decanter of spirits.

"Who lives here?" she whispered.

"Just a shopkeeper."

The candle lit their way up two narrow flights of stairs to a small, neat room with moonlight spilling through an uncurtained casement window over a desk and a bed.

His room. His things. Ophelia stopped in the doorway, aware that he was offering her a glimpse of his secrets. His circumstances were not as hopeless as she'd thought. She could see the dull gleam of metal on the dresser, the faint pink of the moonlight-blanched counterpane on the bed, and stacks of books on the desk, their titles hidden in the shadows. The quiet, bookish room suited him, revealed the simplicity and dignity of his taste. Like her, he had found an escape in the midst of London. Here there was no one to order him about. Even her pretense of commanding him would be a mockery. She kept her gaze on the books and crossed to the desk, a safe object of scrutiny.

"Your father's library?"

"A bit of it," he said.

The door clicked shut behind her, and a current of anticipation passed through her. The privacy of the place and the late hour conferred new freedoms. There would be more than kisses. William's attack had pushed them past the careful boundaries she had drawn around all their previous encounters.

He came to her side and set the candle and the decanter on the edge of the desk. Gold lettering gleamed on the spines of the books. She lifted her gaze to his. The first freedom of the room was this—to look openly at each other.

Under his regard she felt herself transformed. How odd to feel lovely in ruined slippers and a muddied cloak, with soiled gloves, her curls wild! A quivering started deep inside her, and she clenched her fists to keep the trembling concealed.

His fingers tugged the strings at her throat, and the silken cloak slid down her back with the lightest whisper of sound.

"I like you in evening wear," he said in an altered voice.

Ophelia stared helplessly at his absorbed face. Even with a cut on his brow, a split lip, and a fierce red welt on his cheek, his face had a rare sort of perfection, an elegant sensuality that was not jaded, like the faces of other men she knew. Her awareness narrowed to the expression of unmistakable longing in his blue eyes, dreamer's eyes, with golden lashes, like bars of sunlight. In this room he dared to dream things she could only guess at, while she schemed merely to break society's rules. She felt petty and imperfect and retreated into talk.

"This is a snug room," she whispered, her throat dry.

He smiled. "It must seem small and plain to you."

"Not at all. You have your desk, your books . . . it's like a safe hiding place." She ran her hand along the edge of the desk, observing the fine wood. "Does one of these books contain the rules of love?"

"I remember all the rules we need."

"Do we need rules?"

"We do," he said firmly. "Because you're afraid of the bed in the corner."

Her gaze flew up. "You have some conceit to think your bed interests me."

"I am a conceited fellow where you're concerned. There's a permanent print of your cheek right here." He tapped his chest. Candlelight burnished the golden brown hair where his torn shirt gaped open.

"That's because you crushed my ribs as we rode."

He smiled, a slow curve of his mouth, warm and amused. "Even if you admit you like me, Ophelia, you don't have to fear the bed. We haven't reached that stage."

"You make it sound as if we're lumbering along like an antique post chaise." She drew a circle on the polished surface of the desk. "What stage have we not reached?"

"The fourth stage of a lady's love. First, there's giving hope, then granting a kiss." He swallowed. "Then allowing the enjoyment of an embrace . . ."

Ophelia's throat was dry. "That's three."

"I'll tell you about four when you're willing to consider three."

She lifted her chin and tried for a light tone. "Why should I?"

The answer flickered in his blue gaze.

He took the stopper from the decanter of spirits, releasing the fiery scent of brandy in the air, and poured a measure of the amber liquid in a glass, offering it to Ophelia.

"To dispel the shock."

"Oh, I'm quite over it, I assure you."

"Really?" He caught her unresisting left hand and folded her fingers round the glass. Then he took her right hand, turned it over in his, and brushed his fingers across the dirt-streaked palm of her glove. She gasped as a thread of sensation uncurled up her arm even to her breast. He seemed not to hear her as he popped the tiny wrist button free of its loop and peeled the glove down her arm. He freed her hand and lifted her scraped palm to his mouth.

"Drink your brandy."

She raised the glass, and he broke away and stepped into the shadows of the corner. There was a splash of water and a clink of porcelain. Then she heard the rustle of his jacket as he shed it. She turned to offer her help, felt a peculiar weakening of her limbs, and told herself it was the brandy.

Moonlight melted on the smooth curve of his shoulder. Shadows defined the long hollow of his back and the ridges of his ribs. She was used to the padded elegance of fashionable men, the layers of wool and silk and cambric, the frills on cuffs and shirts. Here was elegance of line.

"Let me see to your injuries," she said, tugging at her remaining glove. He glanced at her over his shoulder and went still. The heavy rhythmic beating of her heart marked off the pause before he moved, bringing a basin and towel to the desk.

"We'll need more light." She laid her gloves on the desk.

"This is good," he said. He pulled out the desk chair and waited for her to sit. Then he sat, angling his knees opposite hers and offering his arm. Permission to touch.

Ophelia's stomach did a queer flip at the thought of touching him freely, because she wanted to, with no disguise of accident or purpose to hide behind. In Searle House, maids and valets helped mistresses and masters with hair and clothes, a mockery of intimacy, a professional touch, like bakers frosting cakes. Only

Lady Searle touched anyone with affection, and then only the dog.

She began unwrapping the makeshift bandage. A single long gash, sticky with blood, marred the curve of muscle that tapered to his strong wrist. The swift, ugly violence of their attackers came back to her.

"You need a surgeon," she said with certainty.

"Just you," he said calmly.

She took his wrist in her shaking fingers. "My vast nursing experience consists of putting a poultice on Shadow's hock."

He laughed. "Shadow survived, and so will I."

Fresh blood welled up, and she pulled the stopper from the decanter and poured spirits on a clean corner of the towel she held. A little spasm shook his arm as the alcohol made contact with the wound.

"You like this, don't you?" he asked through his teeth.

"I like you humble and obedient." She gave him a wry smile. "For a change."

"When have I ever been otherwise?"

"Only when you've been cheeky, proud, arrogant, utterly assured." She reached for a piece of linen and began wrapping his arm, binding the edges of the wound together. He was watching her closely, a new tension in him.

"The day we met, from your manner with the horses, I thought you owned Raj. The first time we went to Hetty's you explained Prinny's failings as if you were above everyone in the room."

He lowered his gaze. "I've always obeyed your commands."

"Some more willingly than others." It was a

provocative thing to say, and she took refuge in tying the ends of the new bandage and rinsing out the soiled cloth, wringing it dry, the dripping of the water the only sound between them. "Let me see your hand."

She spread his fingers, washing away the blood, and discovered the scraped knuckles. She wanted to kiss them, an impulse so compelling she froze, his fingertips resting lightly against her palm. He sucked in a breath and his fingers curled, stroking her palm. When she looked up, his eyes blazed into hers and he withdrew his hand.

"It's a mistake for you to be here," he said tightly. "I'll take you home."

"Let me finish," she said briskly, holding up her rag. "Your face."

As she pressed the damp cloth to the cut on his brow, her fingers brushed against his hair. His eyes closed, and a barely perceptible tremor shook his limbs, passing to her hands so that she dropped her rag. It was silly to think she could continue any useful tending of his wounds. "Kiss me."

The whispered plea hit Alexander like a breath of air coming up from the coast on a summer's day, scattering the winnower's chaff. Just so, a dozen reasons he should not kiss her were blown out of his mind.

He'd meant no more when they'd set out than to spend another evening pushing her acceptance of him as friend a little further. He had not come to any conclusions about when to stop his deception. It had been instinctive to go on spinning out their time, a fragile, glittering web of moments. Never mind that it could be dashed apart in an instant. A few more days of her company, a few more kisses, had not seemed so wrong until this night.

In the garden she had censured Solomon Gray for keeping a secret from his daughter, and Alexander had meant to take her home after that. Then she'd commanded that he kiss her. She was impossible to refuse, and obeying her command stirred him more than he'd expected. Still he was resolved to take her home until they'd been attacked. For a few minutes he'd been overpowered by the thugs, pinned to the wall, half mad with helplessness and fear for her. When she'd flung herself into his arms afterward, he had been unable to let her go, as he was unable to let her go now.

With slow, deliberate motions, he rose and pinched the candle out. Moonlight took over the room, seeping into the corners, transforming Ophelia's pale gown into something glowing. Winking gleams of brightness sparkled from the threads, the jewels at her throat, her eyes. She was as delicate and elusive as a night fairy.

He pulled her up into his arms and brushed his lips over hers. Then he moved his head, dragging his mouth across hers, feeling a pull like a tide, drawing him deep as dreams, his caution slipping away. A few more minutes were all he asked. He let his hands skim up and down her back, feeling her shudder beneath his fingertips. Her elbows, pressed against his chest, kept him from her breasts, a deliberate shyness.

He liked that. She didn't know how to calculate the effect of a look or a touch. She guessed some, for her wit was sharp, but there were things he could teach her.

He drew back, taking her hands and flattening them against his chest, letting her feel the heat of his skin, the tautness of his nipples, and the beating of his heart. Hesitantly she moved her hands, her palms arching in slow circles across his chest, her expression soft as it had been when she'd gazed at his battered knuckles.

A low, inarticulate sound came from his throat. He had to touch her in return. His conscience made extravagant promises of self-denial if he could have just one taste of her sweetness.

He pulled her hands from his chest and led her to the bed. She sank down on the edge of the mattress, looking up at him uncertain, defiant, and caught as he was by longing. In a flash that showed the full extent of his desire for her, he saw himself pressing her down into the mattress, covering her as he had in the grass of the park, free to kiss and touch and join his body to hers.

To block the image, he dropped to his knees, encircling her waist with his arms, laying his head in her lap. After a minute she moved, skimming her hands across his shoulders and threading her fingers through his hair.

"I want to touch you," he confessed.

Ophelia paused, on the edge between restraint and abandon. Her body felt strangely divided, weak and powerful at once. The slightest friction of the silk bodice against her breasts sent hot spikes of sensation through her. If he touched her, he would know. He would feel the tiny peaks with their stiff readiness.

But he was her friend, his head in her lap, his

bandaged arm about her, smelling of blood and brandy. They had shared each other's escapes. Now he confessed a weakness to equal hers, and she could not turn away.

He lifted his head, giving her a look of hot reverence.

"Touch me," she whispered.

Moonlight made him a glowing figure. His hands closed around her back, releasing tiny buttons. He rubbed his cheek against hers, his lips tasting her ear, making her shiver. Then he drew back, absorbed in his task. His fingers worked the tiny puffed sleeves of her dress down her shoulders, pinning her arms to her sides. He kissed the places he'd exposed, transformed by moonlight and by him. The tiny bodice flattened and freed her breasts above the stiff support of her stays.

His breath caught, and on the exhalation he murmured, "So pretty."

He cupped her breasts and drew his thumbs over the peaks. The touch like a single concentrated drop of scent seemed to flood her senses. She filled her lungs, arching to meet his hands, and he clasped her to him, breast to breast, with a shaky laugh, breathing her name before his mouth found hers for an ardent joining.

From somewhere came a voice and steps and a light knock. It was like waking from a dream. Ophelia tried to hear above their ragged breathing and the pulse pounding in her veins.

"Majesty?" the voice inquired.

Alexander broke away and the bed sprang up. He strode to the door, his finger on his lips. Ophelia stared after him.

"Majesty," the voice came, more insistent now. "There's blood on the floor."

Alexander cracked the door, and a beam of light fell on silver and brass on the dresser. Ophelia saw herself revealed again in all her abandon, her breasts brazenly bared, her skirts arranged primly over her knees, her hands clenched in her lap.

"*Madre della Virgine!* What happened to you?"

Ophelia went cold, icy where a moment before she had been burning. She knew that voice. Instinct made her pull up her sleeves. She tried to restore her bodice to order, but the cold made her clumsy. She clamped her teeth shut to keep them from chattering and stood on shaking legs.

"It's nothing. Footpads. I'm fine," said Alexander.

"You must let Lucca tend you," said the voice.

Ophelia pressed her fist to her mouth. Images fluttered and beat in her brain, leaving her dizzy. Alexander holding the horses, speaking at the Grays, telling her the rules of love, dropping a book in his pocket. She'd been blind for weeks. Now she saw clearly—the way he spoke, his bearing, his confidence. The quiet room was now transformed by brass and silver, gold and crystal, and the rich fabric of counterpane under her fingers to a prince's quarters.

He'd deceived her. Her friend. All along, the game he'd been playing had been for his amusement.

She couldn't believe it was happening to her again. Worse that she had exposed not only the desires of her wanton, treacherous body, but those of her heart.

"I'm not alone," Alexander said.

Ophelia stooped to gather her cloak and gloves, trying to don them with furious haste, her clumsy fingers knotting the strings at her throat.

The door clicked shut. "Don't go just now." His voice sounded raw.

She looked away, pulling on her gloves. "I think I must." She curtsied, a brief dip of her unsteady knees. "Your Majesty."

He froze while she stood fumbling with the gloves. "You have it wrong, Ophelia. You are sovereign here."

She shook her head. Her throat and chest ached. "I've been here before, you know. I came with my brother, looking for you." She thrust her chin up. "Alexander di Piovasco Mirandola. What a good joke to hide under my brother's nose in his own stable, tending his horse."

"I never met your brother before tonight. Why is he looking for me?"

Ophelia choked on a bitter laugh. "He's with the Foreign Office, Your Majesty, assigned to find one missing prince." She walked toward him as she spoke. It was necessary to leave or she would break down in front of him and complete her humiliation. "A vain, ornamental fellow, fond of his coats."

His hand on the doorknob blocked her way. "I had good reason to hide."

"Did you have a good reason to mock me?"

"To tease you, to make you laugh. You were so haughty, but you claimed to believe in equality. I tested that, and you proved your principles tonight, by coming here. You kissed me as if you meant it."

Alexander watched her retreat into someplace where he couldn't reach her. Their time was up. He couldn't keep her any longer.

"I'll take you back," he said wearily.

She shook her head. "Get me a hackney."

He stiffened. "You'll come with me on Raj, and we'll get you back into Searle House without notice."

There was no opposing the authority in the voice. "Very well, Your Majesty."

The moon was down, and they parted in the deep shadows of the stableyard.

"Ophelia, say you'll ride in the morning." Alexander whispered in the hush. She listened only because he caught her hand and held it.

"You deceived me."

"About my circumstances. Not about . . . my feelings."

"Good-bye, Your Majesty."

He released her hand, and she slipped away in the darkness, an ending so abrupt and bitter that he could never have foreseen it when the evening began. He had always known their friendship would end, and he'd meant to put his mind to the problem of parting when the time was right. He had imagined that there would be a way to send her back to her world happy, glad for having known him. He had thought of the days between their first acquaintance and their separation as infinitely expandable. He had drawn them out in fantasies of a thousand encounters.

He had not felt himself poor in the hills, or the tailor's shop, or even in Lord Brinsby's stable, but he would be the poorer for this night. The great riches the earth afforded the common man—the moon, the stars, the deep blue of the sea—would be for him reminders of Ophelia. Enchanted objects his night fairy had touched sunk to ordinariness again without her.

He led Raj toward the stall, moving like a sleepwalker.

"Your Majesty," said a voice in the shadows.

Alexander froze.

"Alexander di Piovasco Mirandola?" the voice asked.

"Who wants to know?"

"Jasper Brinsby." A flint was struck and light flared in a lamp. Brinsby strode forward. "I can help you, Your Majesty."

Chapter 15

～⌒♡⌒～

In a flowing dressing gown and tasselled cap, Lucca offered their guest brandy with hostile punctiliousness, every gesture an attempt to remind Jasper Brinsby that he was in the company of a prince. Brinsby, edgy and impatient, accepted the drink, watching Lucca with a slightly puzzled frown.

In Italian, Lucca inquired whether Alexander had lost his senses, bringing Brinsby to the tailor shop.

"What a country for insults!" he complained. "More insults than the church has saints. A royal prince living in a shop, attacked by footpads, pursued by fools."

Lucca lingered, stabbing the logs in the grate, and Brinsby cast a questioning glance at Alexander.

"He stays," said Alexander. "Lucca, sit, or leave us."

Lucca gave a contemptuous sniff, set aside the poker, wrapped his silk dressing gown about him, and settled in a chair by the door with a bit of mumbling.

247

Alexander turned to Brinsby. "You offered to help. What did you have in mind?"

"I could arrange rooms for you at the Pulteney Hotel, courtesy of His Majesty's government, would you accept them?"

Lucca nodded. Alexander shook his head.

Brinsby frowned. "We should at least offer you protection."

"Thank you, protection isn't necessary. I have Lucca."

"Where was he tonight? When I saw you at the Grays' party you didn't have these wounds."

"Footpads. I'm not likely to meet them again." Alexander met Brinsby's gaze. The man was taking his measure. "Was your offer of a place to stay your idea of helping me?"

"No." Brinsby leaned forward, his elbows on his knees, his eyes snapping. "Why did you disappear, Your Majesty?"

Alexander permitted himself a short, mirthless laugh. Did Brinsby know anything about his employer's tactics? "What do you want for your country, Brinsby?"

Brinsby straightened, looking as if the question made no sense. He spread his upturned hands in a helpless gesture. "What do you mean?"

"If you were . . . buying a birthday gift for your country, what would it be?"

"A birthday gift for England? I suppose it would be . . . peace, prosperity . . . that sort of thing."

"Anything else?"

"Respect, power . . ."

Alexander looked his guest directly in the eye. "What about freedom? Justice?"

"Of course."

"I want no less for my country." Alexander waited. "Can you help me get those things for Trevigna?"

"Now, look here, Your Majesty. Are you suggesting that England doesn't respect Trevigna's sovereignty?" Brinsby's voice was cold, his posture stiff.

Lucca snorted, and Alexander shot him a quelling glance.

"England wants access to the port of Laruggia and a stable situation in Trevigna." Alexander couldn't keep the contempt out of his voice. "England appears to be indifferent to what Trevigna wants."

Brinsby opened his mouth and closed it. "You must agree, Your Majesty, that after invasions by the French and Austrians, a stable situation would be good for Trevigna."

Alexander leaned back in his chair. Brinsby knew more than he thought. "A stable situation would be death to Trevigna."

"With all due respect, Your Majesty, I don't understand you."

"Your foreign secretary would make us a nation of children, not of free men, with a vassal king constrained to obey England."

"Your Majesty, we are trying to develop an alliance and negotiate a safe harbor for the English navy in a dangerous part of the world. You make us sound like feudal overlords imposing a tribute."

Alexander raised his glass. "Just so." Brinsby sputtered and fell silent.

The fire in the grate crackled. Alexander could

see Brinsby rearranging cherished opinions. He waited until his guest looked up from the flames.

"I want a dynamic situation in Trevigna, a nation where free people choose their rulers and govern themselves."

"Don't you want your throne back?"

"Not if I must be a puppet king whose power depends on England. A king's power should derive from those he serves, not from foreign masters."

"But without England's support, Trevigna could be taken over by Austria or France within a year."

Alexander took a swallow of brandy. "I know. As you said, I need help."

"What exactly do you want?"

"I want a constitutional convention in October."

"You want a republic?"

"Yes."

"I beg your pardon, Your Majesty, but what role does a prince play in a republic?"

"Citizen."

"*Madre della Virgine!* Your father spins in his grave, Majesty."

Brinsby glanced at Lucca. "Even your servant questions that notion, Your Majesty. Castlereagh's never going to go for a republic of Trevigna."

"The excesses of France have given republics a bad name, but believe me, Brinsby, the idea of free men governing themselves won't go away."

"Free men govern themselves in England with a prince on the throne."

Alexander had no reply. It was true.

Brinsby seized the opportunity of Alexander's hesitation. "What about your nobles, Your Majesty? Don't they have some say in this?"

Lucca straightened, and Alexander sensed his interest in Brinsby's view.

"More than other men? Where's the democracy in that?"

Brinsby didn't answer at once, but swirled the brandy in his glass. "Trevigna has centuries of tradition. Perhaps you need some blend of the old with the new."

Alexander had considered it. A constitutional monarchy—with an upper and lower house, like England's—might be the best compromise between the traditions of the past and the demands of the new century. But he had to be certain that the people wanted it.

"Without a convention, there'll be no participation by the people, no way to guarantee that the government derives its power from them."

"Then talk to Castlereagh; make him understand your concerns."

"I talked to him for months. He didn't seem to hear me. I'd rather deal with the Committee for the Restoration of the Italian Republics. They're prepared to offer financial support for a constitutional convention."

"I suppose you mean Hume and Tollworthy. Do you trust them?"

Again Brinsby proved more knowledgeable than Alexander expected. "They are predictable. They'll pursue a profit."

Brinsby leaned forward. "What you need is an unofficial meeting, to reestablish communication.

If I could get Castlereagh to listen, would you agree to talk with him?"

"How do you propose to get an unofficial meeting?"

"My mother's giving a prenuptial ball for Princess Charlotte and Saxe-Coburg. Castlereagh will be there, and all the foreign ambassadors. You could come, a sign of your goodwill toward England. It would do much to smooth things over if you appeared on your own initiative."

Alexander didn't answer. The thought that came to mind with stunning clarity had nothing to do with the future of Trevigna. Instead, he saw himself dancing with Ophelia in a grand ballroom.

"And I'll arrange to get you some time with Castlereagh."

Alexander jerked his mind back to reality. Ophelia would not dance with him. He had asked her to trust him with her person, and his betrayal of that trust might never be forgiven. Nothing would be easier in a crowded ballroom than for her to ignore a foreign dignitary. He made himself consider Brinsby's proposition. It was clever. The committee's banquet was set for early May, just after the royal wedding. This ball might be Alexander's one chance to meet with Castlereagh in time to come to an agreement. "It might work," Alexander conceded.

Brinsby's expression was open, eager. "We can make it work. If you're willing to trust me."

Alexander winced at the idea. He had asked for Ophelia's trust and broken it. It seemed fair that he should have to trust her brother. What choice did he have? He could trust Brinsby or flee farther into London's hidden places and rely on the profit-seeking investors of the committee.

They sat locked in silent appraisal of each other while the fire snapped in the grate.

"You've been riding my horse for a month," Brinsby said.

"You've been wearing my best coat."

Lucca mumbled in Italian.

Alexander finished his brandy. "Whose side are you on, Brinsby?"

"Are there sides between allies? We'll make this thing work."

"I'll trust you."

Brinsby grinned. "Now, you've got to tell me what you want. What the non-negotiable points are, where we start from."

There was gray light at the shop window and Lucca was snoring, a loud rumble, when Jasper Brinsby finally stretched and put down his pen. They had a working document, a list of points Brinsby was willing to push for. Alexander was stunned by it. After months of addressing Castlereagh with all the effect of speaking to a brick wall, he was amazed to have someone listen to him.

He watched Brinsby gather his notes together. "Thank you."

Brinsby looked embarrassed. "Don't thank me yet. I'm only trying to be less of an idiot than I was a few weeks ago when I started looking for you."

"You're succeeding, then. No one else in the Foreign Office has troubled to learn so much about Trevigna."

Brinsby shrugged. "I wouldn't have, either, if

I hadn't made such a cake of myself in front of Miss Gray."

Alexander rose and stood in front of the dying fire. The mention of Miss Gray brought Ophelia to mind with a powerful wave of regret. In one night his hopes as a private man had plunged, while his hopes as a monarch had soared. He felt strangely divided, as if he had split into two selves.

"Your Majesty, if I may be so bold, there's a question I must ask you."

Alexander turned.

Brinsby studied his papers. "A rumor reached the foreign office this week that you've contracted a marriage with the daughter of a nobleman."

"Miss Tesio arrives in London any day now."

"That complicates our negotiations somewhat, as we don't want to offend the royalist faction in your country."

"I know."

"It also forces me to ask what your intentions are toward my sister."

Alexander flushed. "What can they be? I have no money. Unless I persuade Castlereagh to my way of thinking, no kingdom. And if I do succeed, a most uncertain future, nothing to offer a woman of rank and wealth."

"Do you have a heart?"

Alexander felt that organ lodged somewhere in the pained region of his chest. "It belongs to Trevigna."

Brinsby looked as if he were weighing his diplomatic coup with his sister's honor. "And my sister's heart," he persisted. "Have you left it whole?"

"She's under no illusions about me."

"Sprite knows who you are?"

"Sprite?" The name caused a stab of pain.

"My pet name for her. She was always so little and lively, and the name Ophelia seemed so grand and tragic."

"Sprite suits her." He liked it. It summed up the quickness and caprice of her nature, his sense that she was full of tricks.

"When did she learn your identity?"

"Tonight."

"Well, it's probably best that she knows. I'm sure we can count on her discretion. She wanted to help me find you, and of course, in a way, she has." Brinsby gathered up his coat, hat, and gloves. He seemed full of energy in spite of the long evening they'd spent hammering out the details of their scheme.

"Your Majesty, I take my leave. I think you can rest assured that your dealings with the British government will be very satisfactory from now on."

Alexander bowed. He wished he could share Brinsby's optimism.

Jasper waited impatiently in the Grays' little sitting room. Not that there wasn't pleasure in being there, seeing Hetty's things, recognizing her spirit in the arrangement of flowers on a table or a group of watercolors on the wall. It was just that he had such news to tell her, he thought he would burst with it. He checked his pocket for the stiff white card of invitation to his mother's ball. When he heard the light footfall approaching, he spun toward the door.

She entered smiling, and he was lost for a moment just looking at her, wondering how soon he could reasonably ask her to marry him. He managed a bow and a greeting and found himself seated opposite his love on a Chippendale armchair.

"I came to tell you about my search for Prince Mirandola."

"Did you find him?"

"Yes. Yes, I did. Thanks to you."

"To me? How did I help?"

"Well, you see . . ." Jasper was determined to give credit where credit was due. "I would not have thought to ask about his appearance without your suggesting it."

"It was very forward of me. I knew nothing of your search or your methods."

"It was very intelligent of you," said Jasper. "Your good sense made me ask the right questions. And it turns out that the prince's friend Burke actually has a miniature of the prince, done when they were at Oxford. So I was able to recognize him when I saw him."

"You saw him?"

"And for that I have to thank you, too." Jasper knew he was grinning idiotically, but he couldn't help it. She was so pretty and she looked so admiring. He felt his heart swelling with joy. "Mirandola was here last night."

"Here?" Her eyes clouded with a momentary doubt, as if he'd taken leave of his senses.

"Mirandola is, was, Ophelia's groom. What did he call himself? Alexander?"

Hetty pressed her hands to her mouth and stood abruptly. She circled the room, moving in quick agitated steps. "Does Ophelia know?"

"Yes. Apparently he told her himself, sometime last night."

Hetty came to a halt, her eyes still troubled. "Well, it's probably all right, then." She took her seat again, smoothing her skirts. "It would not be good, you see, if he lied to her, because she trusted him."

Jasper hardly understood what she was saying, something about his sister, to which he should be paying attention, but it was hard to think about Ophelia while Miss Gray's lovely face was troubled. He reached in his pocket and drew out his mother's card of invitation. He'd been very clever, he thought, to manage the extra invitations under Graves's nose.

"What will happen now that you've found the prince?" she asked.

"That I'd like you to see for yourself, Miss Gray. The prince will be attending my mother's ball for the royal wedding, and I'd like you to be there, too." He handed her the white card.

"Me?" She frowned at the card, turning it over in her hands. "Thank you," she said, "but you know I must decline your invitation."

Jasper pulled his chair closer. "Don't." He reached out and stilled her hands on the card. "This is a great chance for us. I know my parents have foolish notions of rank, but they don't know you. They will see you at this ball in all your loveliness, and they won't be able to—"

"You didn't tell them I would be coming." She sounded faint.

"No. I know better than that. I can't win them over by argument, only by showing them that you are every inch a gentlewoman. They can't miss that once they see you."

"But they won't see me. They'll see a tradesman's daughter. They'll condemn me for my presumption. You would, too."

"No, I wouldn't. I've changed, and so will they."

Hetty smiled sadly at him. "I don't think so."

Jasper wanted to deny it, but he had to admit his parents were unlikely to change. There was no point in a dream picture of the duke and duchess being gracious to Hetty Gray and her father. He had to build his new life on reality. His parents were snobs and likely to remain so, and they might take nasty financial measures against him if he chose to disoblige them in the matter of marriage. He took a deep breath. So be it.

"All right. They won't change. My mother may create a scene. Will you brave it? Will you enter the lion's den?"

Hetty studied him.

"I have another reason for wanting you to come. Prince Mirandola will be there. I've arranged a meeting for him with Castlereagh. He'll need a friend in that crowd. And I can arrange to get you into the ball undetected by my parents."

"Unfair tactics," said Hetty.

"I want to dance with you in the ballroom of Searle House at least once. Say you'll come."

"I'll come."

Chapter 16

O phelia watched a footman on a ladder, directing him in the placement of one of the fragrant green swags festooning the Searle House ballroom. Lady Searle had decided appropriately on a May Day theme for her ball. Every servant who could be spared from his or her duties had some occupation in the ballroom. Two men placed chairs, music stands, and candle braces on the dais under the direction of the orchestra leader, while the gardener arranged a bank of violets and lilies of the field below. Three girls pushed wide dustmops across the polished floor, while grooms wrestled potted fruit trees into position beside the tall terrace doors. Others bustled to and from Lady Searle with an alacrity a general could admire.

Ophelia stood in the middle of the room with an armful of lists, trying to keep her mind on the details of preparation and not on one treacherous prince. She hadn't decided yet what she should say to Jasper about him. Anger was better than wretchedness, and she struggled to keep it burning in her breast. She could not believe she'd been so blind to his obvious rank. From the first he had held the horses like a man accustomed to possession. His groom's accent had been accurate enough, but his courtesies, his lack of submission, had been the qualities of a man of power in the world. Then the books, the education. True, a poor vicar's son might have such an education, but when he'd spoken at Hetty's, quoting Machiavelli, no less, she should have seen him for a prince.

And she, was she such a snob that she deserved to be tricked, mocked? She certainly hadn't taken advantage of her position as mistress, at least, not after the first day. Days. Once they had begun to go to Hetty's, they had been on an equal footing, or at least, as equal a footing as circumstances allowed. But he had deliberately let her believe he was leagues below her in rank and fortune. He had made a game of all their kisses.

And then, most unforgivable, he had coaxed her to yield to him, had made it seem as if giving him this bit of herself was a great gift, was water to a man in the desert, when all the while he was lying, amusing himself, knowing he was above her. Her thoughts had followed this same track for three days, always coming back to the black moment when she'd heard the voice in the hall and realized Alexander had taken her for a fool.

The footman attached the swag and waited for her approval. She nodded and checked her list again. Sharp footsteps made her glance up. Jasper came striding across the ballroom.

"Sprite," he called. "Glad I found you." He

grabbed her about the waist and whirled her in an impromptu waltz.

"Jasper, stop." The footmen had turned to watch them, and she pulled back from her brother's arms. "I'm busy."

"So I see. Looks like you're turning the place into a greenhouse."

"May Day, in case you've never seen it," Ophelia said. She gestured to the footman to move his ladder more to the right.

Jasper took her arm. "Can we talk?"

Ophelia frowned at him. "Go ahead, talk."

He shoved his hands in his pockets. "You're in a surly mood."

"I'm sorry," she said. "Mother's making everyone edgy with her lists." She held up her loose sheets of paper.

"Well, it's the party I want to tell you about," Jasper whispered. "Thanks to you, Sprite, the party is my big chance."

"Big chance for what?"

"To prove myself to Castlereagh." Jasper glanced around the ballroom, but there was no one near them. "I found Mirandola, you know. Or rather, you did. Right under our noses. Ironic, isn't it?"

"Very." Ophelia hugged the lists to her chest and concentrated on the footman's placement of the next swag. One dilemma solved. Jasper knew about him.

"He's remarkable, really. What he wants. How he's held out for months. Castlereagh and the others had him all wrong, thinking he was just some idle fop who could be satisfied with a decorative role. You know, he's written an entire framework for a constitutional convention."

Ophelia stared at her brother. "You've certainly changed your mind about him."

"Well, we talked most of the night, night before last. After you left the stable."

"Oh." Ophelia stared at the floor. Why did it hurt so much to think that Alexander had spent hours chatting with her brother while she had been fighting tears of humiliation and wretchedness? She swallowed the ache of unshed tears in her throat. "Did you take him to Castlereagh?"

Again Jasper glanced around. He leaned toward her. "No one knows I've found him yet. I have a plan."

"Are you sure you know what you're doing? Won't Mirandola just disappear again?"

Jasper shook his head. "He won't."

Ophelia could hear the new certainty in his voice, a confidence that wasn't merely show.

Jasper put an arm around her shoulders and squeezed lightly. "I owe this to you, Sprite, and Miss Gray. You made me wonder why he was hiding, made me curious enough to read about Trevigna. It all made sense to me as I listened to him. I think I understand him—more than the others, at least."

"Really?" She couldn't help the sarcasm in her tone. Alexander wasn't worthy of her brother's faith or sympathy. Alexander was false and self-serving, and his idealism a sham. "Then what is your plan?" she asked.

"He's coming here."

Ophelia gasped.

"To the ball. I've arranged an informal meeting with Castlereagh. It's perfect." Jasper went on explaining the beauties of the plan while Ophelia tried to gather her wits. She saw so clearly an image of herself dancing with Alexander, whirling about the floor in a dizzying waltz. She fought the image. Prince Mirandola would be in some antechamber, negotiating his country's future, while she was dancing with Dent toward some future of her own, quite separate from his.

"And that's not all, Sprite. Hetty—that is, Miss Gray—is coming."

Ophelia spun toward her brother. "What? Jasper, mother and father will never admit Hetty here, especially not to a royal ball."

Jasper straightened. "She's coming. I've arranged it. Whatever they do or say, I will dance with her here." He glanced around the ballroom.

"That's a lovely dream, Jasper, but are you thinking of Hetty? Of what people may say, or how they may snub her? You don't know how cruel our classmates were in school."

"You are her friend. Can't you see to it that she's welcomed?"

"Oh, Jasper, don't you think I want Hetty here? But she doesn't know about Mrs. Hart's being her mother. And that's the first thing our mother will say to her. If Hetty gets through the receiving line!"

"I've arranged that. She'll be like Cinderella, arriving and departing mysteriously, with no one the wiser."

"Has Solomon agreed to this folly? He's sick with worry that Mrs. Hart will reveal herself to Hetty."

Jasper looked away. "Solomon's not to know."

"Jasper, I think you're being selfish. You want to show her off, but you're likely to cause her embarrassment and pain."

"I thought you'd be on my side in this, Ophelia."

"I am, but—"

"Then say nothing, and be a friend to Hetty—"

"Miss, miss!" Ophelia turned as a footman with his wig askew slid to a stop on the polished floor, breathless and flushed.

"What is it, James?" she asked.

"Beg pardon, miss. Cook says t' find 'er Grace."

Ophelia glanced around. "Lady Searle's here somewhere. What's wrong?"

"It's the dog, miss—'e's gone stark mad in the kitchen, 'e 'as, jumping on tables, barking at everyone. Cook and the others are 'iding in the larder."

"Oh dear. Thank you, James. Jasper, excuse me. I've got to find Mother." She started toward the far end of the ballroom.

"Ophelia, you owe me a silence," Jasper called after her.

"Very well," she called back over her shoulder.

Alexander could just see his aunt reflected in the cheval glass over his left shoulder. She was enthroned, the only word for it, in one of the Pulteney Hotel's best chairs, and had been complaining steadily about her quarters, the wine, his outfit for the evening. He refused to wear the splendid princely uniform and dress sword she'd brought from Trevigna, but he agreed to a sunburst pin that had been his father's, which Lucca was trying to fix to the right breast of his black evening coat.

Alexander felt like two people. His formal public self stared back at him from the glass. Even without the uniform that made him look like a toy soldier, he could not reconcile the image of the monarch in the mirror with the man he felt himself to be inside, a man he'd known only a short while, whose hopes for the evening had less to do with the fate of a nation than with the smiles of a capricious, spirited girl and his plan to steal a few minutes of time alone with her at a ball.

When he turned from the mirror, Francesca's brows were pinched above her thin nose and her eyes were a glacial blue. Her face was set in elegant, haughty lines that proclaimed her dissatisfaction with him.

Lucca, in Trevigna's blue and gold livery, adjusted the fall of Alexander's cravat and the placement of a sapphire stud.

"Stop fussing over the boy, Gavinana," Francesca said. "If he's not going to dress like a prince, what does it matter how many folds he has in his neckcloth?"

Lucca finished with the pin and straightened. But he could not resist tugging Alexander's shoulder seams to make sure the coat lay flat.

"The boy looks prettier than his betrothed."

Alexander nodded to Lucca, who rolled his eyes discreetly and retreated.

"Aunt, you're not too fatigued to attend this ball?"

"I'm never fatigued. We must have your betrothal to Tesio's daughter known . . . the sooner, the better."

It was the answer he expected. Aunt Francesca's arrival had been as inconvenient as possible. Even one day later and he'd have been able to put her off, but as it stood, he was going to have to escort her to the ball at Searle House, and once there, Francesca was going to do her best to spread the news of his betrothal.

"I'd rather wait to announce any betrothal, Aunt," he said quietly.

Her blue eyes became piercing. "You've waited long enough. What have you accomplished in England? People wonder if you've forgotten how to be Italian." Her sharp glance swept his black evening clothes.

"Appearances are deceiving, Aunt. I have been most productive in England."

A careful look came into Francesca's eyes. "Good terms from Castlereagh, I hope."

"I'm meeting him tonight."

"Ah." Francesca's eyes snapped back and forth. "At this ball?" Alexander nodded. "Ah. Is he going to support the house of Mirandola?"

Alexander strolled to the hearth and picked up the poker. "He'd be happy to—in exchange for the port."

"Well, it can't hurt to have the British navy anchored at Laruggia. It will keep the damned Austrians out."

"I agree." Alexander stirred the fire to life.

Francesca sighed deeply. "But you didn't ask for that, did you?"

"How is Miss Tesio?" He watched the flicker on the edge of the coals.

Francesca allowed him to switch the subject, but her gaze told him she would not forget his evasion. "Your betrothed is not romantic, but quite regal. She should suit you, and you will behave toward the girl. She speaks no English."

"Aunt, I cannot dance attendance on her this evening. Most of my time at the ball will be devoted to ... Lord Castlereagh."

"Of course. It will be my duty to let your intentions toward the girl be known."

Alexander stiffened. "I must ask you not to say word about a marriage."

"I've brought a priest with me, Alexander. Father Leonardo is prepared to marry you this evening, if you like. We've arranged a license. We can have the rite here, if the hotel staff is up to it." She looked around the rather spacious room. "We'll have all the pomp and display in Trevigna when you return."

"Aunt, I won't marry the girl before the fund banquet."

"Well, you could at least bed her, start her breeding."

Alexander laughed. "Poor Miss Tesio. Does she know how you see her?"

"She's a dutiful girl."

"Aunt, I've not met her. We don't know that we'll suit."

"Suit? What does that matter? What matters is that if you'd not delayed, she could be months along by now and everyone's confidence in the House of Mirandola restored."

Alexander grasped the mantel. "Is she clever? Witty? Sweet?"

"You're not balking now over mere feminine charms. You've always done your duty. What you need is a girl who'll do hers. Someone compliant, dignified, and fertile. Miss Tesio's two married sisters have produced six healthy babes between them."

Alexander turned to his aunt. "Francesca, even kings can make disastrous marriages. Tell your priest to plan nothing before the banquet."

Francesca adjusted her shawl, avoiding his gaze. He realized she was concealing something. Miss Tesio was probably an extraordinary beauty, and it was Francesca's way to tease him into thinking otherwise and then surprise him with the reality. She opened the strings of her beaded bag and withdrew a letter.

"Here. Read this."

Alexander took the letter. It was from Baron di Rondo, an old friend of his father's. The man was ill and not expecting to see the harvest of almonds blossoming outside his window. He was sick at heart over the state of Trevigna. He described the bickering of the nobles, the disorder of the republican faction, and finally, the outrages of Ferruci and his bandits. This mild, gentle old man, a scholar, could make no sense of the chaos and suffering the new century seemed to bring.

Alexander folded the letter. Trust his aunt to twist the knife in his heart.

Lucca knocked at the door. "The carriages await, Majesty."

Alexander returned the letter to Francesca. He helped his aunt to her feet. "Let's go meet this paragon of Italian virtues," he suggested. "But understand me, Francesca, no marriage before the banquet."

The sidewalks around Grosvenor Square were crowded with royalty watchers, awaiting the passage of their royal highnesses the Prince Regent, his daughter, Princess Charlotte, and her betrothed, Prince Leopold of Saxe-Coburg. One Italian prince and his entourage in their hired carriages could slip past without too much notice.

Cords kept the onlookers back from the entrance to Searle House, but once Lucca emerged to lower the steps in his magnificent livery, the crowd turned their way. Miss Tesio drew gasps and applause when she alighted. As Alexander had suspected, the girl was a beauty Botticelli would have been happy to paint, tall and stately, with a perfect oval face, golden skin, wide, lashless amber eyes, thin brows, and honey-colored hair. Her serenity was so complete that Alexander doubted she had ever experienced anything so troubling as a thought. She moved with languid grace, and waiting for her to make her regal and somewhat glacial descent from the hired carriage, Alexander tried not to think of the quick flash of movement and wit that was Ophelia. *Sprite*, her brother had called her.

She was third in the receiving line, between her brothers and her parents, in a gown of celestial blue with silver brocade and virtually no bodice. Instantly Alexander was back in his bedroom in the moonlight, baring to his gaze and his touch what wasn't his and never could be. The moment he had the thought, she looked his way, in her eyes a flash of pain. Then she dropped into a deep curtsy before the guest she was greeting, showing Alexander only the top of her head. But he knew the feel of that delicate head in his hands, the texture of those unruly curls.

Sin was punished. If he'd ever doubted it, he knew it now. He shepherded his aunt and Miss Tesio forward to meet their hosts. Jasper clasped his hand and leaned close to tell him to watch for a signal as soon as the Regent arrived. To his right above the babble of greetings he heard his aunt presenting Miss Tesio as his betrothed.

In the next minute he was holding Ophelia's gloved hand while she turned to someone in line behind him. She wore a welcoming smile, but he could see the shadows under her eyes, the pinched look to her cheeks he'd detected on their morning rides. She was like one of those delicate pink flowers in the rock pools along the shore that closed at a touch. His touch had made her retreat.

Chapter 17

❝It's May Day," said Hetty, entering the Searle House ballroom on Jasper's arm. "How clever of your mother."

He expected the crowd in the ballroom to fall silent at her entrance, but he couldn't look away from her delighted eyes to note anyone's reaction. "Marry me," he whispered in her ear.

She sobered at the words, instantly self-conscious, looking at the hundreds of guests, her steps faltering. Jasper had a sudden doubt about the glories of his world. It seemed not glittering and brilliant, but garish and overscented.

"Oh my, that's the Regent."

"Are you shocked?" Jasper thought she might be by the Regent's exaggerated girth, displayed in scarlet regimentals and white breeches, a parody of a soldier, the Prince of Whales.

Hetty shook her head, setting her golden curls bouncing. "He looks like a proud papa."

"Do you wish to be presented to him?"

Her gaze searched those around the Regent. "He's speaking with Prince Mirandola, isn't he? That means your plan is working."

Jasper grinned. Speech was beyond him. This lovely wise girl saw his triumph. They stood indiscreetly in the middle of the ballroom where his mother might see them, and the devil with it. When he considered everything that could have gone wrong, the delicate nature of the personalities involved, the careful timing required, the unpredictability of their royal guests, he wanted to shout.

"I owe this success to you," he said.

"Is Lord Castlereagh here?" she asked.

Jasper pointed out a sober-suited gentleman to the Regent's right.

"You must start your meeting soon," she said.

"As soon as you dance with me."

A set was forming to honor their royal guests. Saxe-Coburg was leading Princess Charlotte and Mirandola, his Italian beauty. Jasper manuevered Hetty into the line before she could protest standing up with royalty. He watched her concentrate on her steps until the pattern of the quadrille brought him near enough to speak for her ears only. "Marry me," he repeated.

"Your parents will never permit it."

"It's your father who might object. I haven't much of an income if my parents cut me off." The dance parted them, but Jasper could see the furrow in her brow. To defend her father, she would have to side with Jasper.

"Money will never weigh with my father." They joined hands again and passed into a square with the princess and her betrothed. Hetty fell silent.

When the dance shifted them to less exalted

companions, she asked, "Shouldn't you be thinking about the meeting?"

"Agree to marry me first."

"Impossible."

"Then tell me why you reject me."

"You know why." They came together, parted,
and came together again.

"I don't. Is it because I'm not literary?"

"No, of course not."

"Perhaps I should present you to the Regent
to further your literary career." He watched her
color instantly at the suggestion, a lovely pink
above her pale gown, like a blossom.

"You wouldn't."

"Then marry me."

"It will hurt your career to marry beneath your
station."

"It will help my career to marry an excellent
hostess, a woman of wit and sensibility and
beauty."

"Do you truly believe that?"

Jasper managed a nod. "It will help my career
to be happy and to have a woman of sense ask
me clever questions when I'm off making an idiot of myself."

They moved into the last figure of the dance.

"You can't deny that you've helped my career
already."

"Jasper, you'd best go to your meeting."

"Say yes and I will."

She dipped into the final curtsy of the dance
and came up, saying "Yes."

The dance dissolved around them as he took
it in, elation swelling in him. But as he moved
toward her, uncertainty dawned in her eyes. He

was an idiot to ask her here, where everyone watched them and he could not seal their pledge with a kiss. Later, he would draw her out on the terrace, hold her, make her feel his confidence.

"You won't be sorry," he promised.

"Go to your meeting."

"Find Ophelia. She'll look out for you until I come back."

Jasper's plan to turn their mother's ball into a diplomatic mission guaranteed Ophelia misery. It was more painful than she'd imagined to watch Alexander open the ball with the Italian girl. The implications of her presence and the aunt's hovering attentions were not lost on Ophelia. It was only then, as she saw him there in black pumps and pantaloons, snowy waistcoat and careless cravat, with a black coat and a single starburst pin, that she realized the self he'd shown her was false in every way. His imperious aunt, the aloof beauty, and his magnificent liveried servant claimed him as theirs, the Prince of Trevigna, with a destiny far from her own.

She did her best to smile when Dent claimed her for the set. There was nothing to do but to get through this ball and the next one and the one after that. Sally Candover interrupted these gloomy reflections by asking who Jasper's mystery partner was.

"Everyone's dying to know," Sally said, as they crossed to opposite partners. "Such pointed attention to the girl."

Ophelia looked up the row of dancers and saw what Sally meant. Jasper leaned intimately toward Hetty, saying something in her ear that made her blush and protest.

"Miss Gray is an old friend of the family," she said, hoping the casual answer would turn aside curiosity. It wouldn't save Hetty from their mother's wrath, however. Lady Searle must already be aware of Jasper's indiscretion, and Ophelia would have to get Hetty aside as soon as the set ended.

As she extricated herself from Dent's cloying politeness, Sebastian took her arm. She found him wearing gold-rimmed eyeglasses that gave him an astonishingly intelligent air.

"Sebastian, you look much . . . happier in spectacles."

"Yes, well, one must see." He turned her away from Hetty toward the little grouping of seats, hastily arranged for the Italian girl and the aunt, an imitation of the grander arrangements made for the British royals.

"As host I should ask Miss Tesio to dance, don't you think, Ophelia?"

"She's most likely intended for Prince Mirandola, Sebastian. I don't imagine she cares to dance with anyone else."

Sebastian frowned, but his gaze remained fixed on the tall beauty as Alexander sent his servant on some errand, no doubt for the lady's comfort. "Actually, I don't think she cares for the prince."

"What?" Ophelia quelled a silly spurt of hope.

"She doesn't look at him." Sebastian sounded defensive. "She seems to be in a world of her own." He pushed his new glasses up the bridge of his nose.

"She doesn't speak any English. She probably feels utterly alone surrounded by strangers."

"Exactly," said Sebastian. He cleared his throat. "One would expect her to turn to her countryman and engage him in conversation. But she doesn't. And she's not smiling."

"Sebastian, you're making something of nothing. She doesn't look like the smiling sort of girl."

Sebastian drew himself up. "As host I think it my duty to make her smile." He straightened his waistcoat and cravat. "I speak Italian, you know."

Without another word he started across the ballroom, bearing down on Alexander and his partner. Ophelia froze. Her snobbish brother was bent on exposing himself to a set down. He would be rebuffed, embarrassed. The prince's party saw him coming. Sebastian bowed to the girl, said something, and then to Ophelia's astonishment Alexander offered the girl's hand to Sebastian. The instant Sebastian clasped the girl's hand, Alexander's gaze found Ophelia's. *I'm coming for you*, his eyes said.

Her heart hammered in her breast. Her shameless body grew warm. She slipped into a knot of guests, threading her way through the crowd toward the tall terrace doors, and found Wyatt.

"Sprite, all grown up, in feathers no less." He caught her wrists. "Has Dent already driven you to distraction? I can help."

"Excuse me, Wyatt." She looked pointedly at his hands. "I have guests to attend to."

He glanced over his shoulder at the open expanse of the terrace. "On the terrace?"

Ophelia smiled. "I'm to see that all the torches are lit. My mother's orders."

Wyatt laughed. "You don't lie very well, Sprite." He leaned forward. "Who's waiting for you? Ayres? Haddington?"

"No one." She pulled free of him, but he caught her chin with one gloved hand.

"You've been kissing someone, Sprite. It's a thing I'm never wrong about, and I can find out who."

"Wyatt, you may be the only man who makes me wish I could change my sex." She smiled. "So I could plant you the facer you deserve."

"Brave words, Sprite, but a rumor about you could be ugly."

Without a further word she strode past him out onto the terrace, where all the torches burned bright.

She walked the length of house, returning to the ballroom by another door. Blocking her way was Alexander's man Lucca, magnificent in blue and gold satin, with a tray of glasses aloft in one hand. He bowed slightly.

"It is the lady who makes His Majesty so much misery and confusion. Here." Lucca pressed one gloved hand to his heart.

"I beg your pardon." Ophelia shifted course.

Lucca pursued. "Will you talk with him?"

"He made a game of me."

Lucca shook his head slowly. "His Majesty never makes games."

Ophelia, still retreating, bumped into a young gentleman from Miss Mercer-Elphinstone's set and accepted his arm, allowing herself to be pulled into their gossip and jests. When she was

sure Lucca had gone, she returned to her search
for Hetty. Jasper, Alexander, and Lord Castlereagh had disappeared, so Jasper's meeting must
be in progress. Sebastian was dancing with Miss
Tesio, and the girl was actually smiling. But
Hetty was nowhere in sight.

By midnight Ophelia was ready to conclude
that Hetty had left, but in the middle of the last
waltz before supper, as the tide of guests flowed
toward the refreshment room, a subtle movement among those who remained made Ophelia
glance toward the dais. In the far corner she saw
the plumes of her mother's headress bob vigor-
ously. A cluster of ladies broke up, and Ophelia
saw that her mother had cornered Hetty. Then
Dent whirled Ophelia down the ballroom.

Alexander emerged from the quiet tension of
the library, where care governed every word, expression, and gesture, into the bright ballroom
and the mad whirl of a waltz. The ball had
reached that stage where even the dullest sallies
drew peals of laughter from those who heard
them. The strange feeling of having two selves
left him. Castlereagh had listened. He wanted to
see Alexander crowned, but he did not object in
principle to a constitutional convention or to the
development of a parliament. He wanted to
know only how Alexander meant to fund such a
venture. They agreed to meet again. He had done
all he could for Trevigna this night.

It took but a minute to find the particular celestial shade that meant Ophelia. It was the deep
blue of the sky at dusk, glimmering with winking lights like the first stars. His night fairy. She
whirled in the arms of a vapid-looking blond

gentleman, her face wearing its pinched, unhappy expression.

He studied the terrain. Between him and the girl were his fellow sovereigns, his aunt and her candidate for his hand, and even a few of his school friends. One of his aunt's favorite phrases came to mind. *Andare in brocca!* Aim straight for the mark.

While Ophelia spun down the far side of the ballroom, Alexander paid his respects to the Regent and his glowing daughter. The Regent's pleasure in his daughter's coming marriage made him expansive, but Alexander kept the conversation to a few brief civilities. As Ophelia and the blond gentleman turned up the near side of the ballroom, he slipped past his aunt with a smile and a nod. As Ophelia's partner bowed over her hand, Alexander promised the last of his school friends he'd meet him for dinner soon. Ophelia was unaware of his approach. She would not elude him. He started across the ballroom when she turned and with quick steps headed for the far corner of the dais. Unnoticed, he came up behind her as she addressed Lady Searle.

"Mother, what are you doing?"

"I've asked Miss Gray to leave. For her own comfort, of course."

Ophelia linked her arm through Hetty's. "I'm sure she's perfectly comfortable here."

It was a patent untruth. Hetty Gray's pretty face was pale, and she clung tightly to Ophelia's arm.

Lady Searle's diamond choker sparkled. "This is your design, Ophelia, bringing Miss Gray here to embarrass us. She's conspicuous in this company where the distinction of rank is so apparent."

"The only distinction here is in the material advantage of your guests. You've surrounded yourself with people who proclaim their consequence with rock collections and the plumage of dead fowls. There's no real merit or talent in any of them. Hetty is inferior to none."

Alexander could not help smiling. Passionate conviction made Ophelia shine.

Lady Searle batted her fan. "Ophelia, we have resolved this issue. Return to your guests. I have summoned Miss Gray's carriage. Her connections are so decidedly beneath—"

"Mother, it's beneath you to behave with such incivility to a guest."

"Miss Gray is not a guest, but an interloper who procured a card of invitation by some devious means and entered the ball surreptitiously."

"I believe Miss Gray is with Jasper."

Lady Searle's cold gaze swung to Hetty. "Miss Gray, I warn you, your parentage makes any connection between you and my son unthinkable."

"That is for your son to decide," said Hetty, clinging to Ophelia. "My father is a gentleman in manner and mind, if not by birth or profession."

"It is not your father that sinks you, Miss Gray. It's your mother. The woman's a trollop and a scribbler. Byron is possibly the only fellow who's not been her lover."

"Mother!" Ophelia stepped forward as if to ward off a blow. "Come, Hetty," she said. But

Hetty didn't budge, her gaze fixed on Lady Searle.

"Whatever do you mean, Your Grace? My mother's dead."

A cunning look came into Lady Searle's eyes. "You are sadly mistaken, Miss Gray."

"Mother!" Ophelia warned sharply.

"Ophelia, return to your guests."

Ophelia gave Hetty's arm an urgent tug, trying to draw her away.

With ashen cheeks, Hetty froze in her tracks. "What do you mean, Lady Searle, that my mother is alive?"

Ophelia groaned.

Lady Searle drew herself up, a fierce gladness in her eye. "Amelia Hart is very much alive and living in Bloomsbury with her latest paramour."

Alexander stepped forward. "Your Grace, Miss Gray, Lady Ophelia." He bowed. The three women dipped into a curtsy. "I beg your pardon, ladies, but Miss Gray is a particular friend of mine and promised to go in to supper with me. Will you excuse us?"

His eyes met Ophelia's and in hers he saw gratitude. He wanted to prolong the silent exchange with her, the moment of shared feeling for a friend in distress, but he had to act.

The duchess glanced from Hetty to Alexander, obviously doubting the possibility of a connection between the prince and the untitled girl. Alexander concentrated on the tense, shaken figure of Hetty Gray, willing her to accept the fiction he'd created. He offered his arm, and Ophelia helped her friend to take it. He glanced at Ophelia, hoping for another moment of understanding between them, but she didn't look up.

Gently he turned Hetty toward the doors at the far end of the ballroom. Her arm trembled on his as she looked the length of the room.

"Miss Gray, keep your eyes on me." When she obeyed, he put his hand over hers.

"Your Majesty, you're very kind. I cannot go to supper here. Truly I cannot."

"No matter. We're going to walk the length of this room, chatting with apparent amiability and composure. No one is to see your distress." Her expression told him that she'd prefer crossing a bed of hot coals. "Ready?"

She took a deep breath and they began their stroll.

"I must go home at once," she said, when they were less than halfway down the room.

Alexander glanced round for Jasper, but he was probably still conferring with Castlereagh. "Your carriage will be ready."

"Thank you."

In the marble foyer her knees gave way, and Alexander led her to a small bench. He sent one servant for her cloak, and another to find Jasper. The girl huddled where she sat, withdrawn into herself, apparently unaware of the flurry of activity around her. Alexander stood at her side, shielding her from the stares of servants.

Abruptly she stood. "Does Jasper know who my mother is?"

Alexander didn't know.

She started for the door, and Alexander caught her hand. "Oh, do let me go, Prince Alexander. I must get away before . . ."

"Your Majesty," said a footman, "the lady's

coach is here." Alexander released her, and
Hetty dashed through the door, down the steps,
and into the waiting carriage.

"Left her cloak, she did." A footman handed
Alexander the abandoned garment as Jasper
came striding into the hall.

"Where is she?" he asked.

"Fled. Lady Searle told her Amelia Hart was
her mother. She's in shock. She didn't know."

"My God! I've got to go to her."

The Regent and his entourage were preparing
to leave. Footmen passed through the crowd
with trays of champagne glasses for the final
toast to the young royal couple. Royal attendants
cleared a path for the Regent and his party. Lord
and Lady Searle and their sons gathered round
their royal guests, preparing for the last formality. The orchestra played a brief fanfare.

If Alexander could get five minutes with
Ophelia now, he could explain. The situation
wasn't hopeless. Her glance over Hetty Gray's
head showed some fragment of their friendship
remained intact, an ember in the ashes. He
would blow on that small coal until it burned
brightly again. Alexander paused, searching for
Ophelia in the crowd, as the resplendent monarch lifted his hand to wave to his subjects.

Ophelia sank into a curtsy with the assembled
lords and ladies in the suddenly hushed ballroom. Once the royals were on their way, she
could find Jasper and send him after Hetty. Her
father lifted his glass. Everyone followed. Charlotte and Saxe-Coburg were enormously popular.

Her father started speaking in his heavy mournful rumble. "It is an honor, a deep honor, for Searle House to mark in this humble way this occasion of great felicity, great felicity, for all Englishmen and -women."

Shrieks of laughter coming from the supper room abruptly pierced the solemnity. Lord Searle frowned and continued speaking, but Ophelia could no longer hear him as the shrieks came closer. The Regent jerked toward the sound, the bowed heads came up, a footman dashed out.

A lady screamed at the doorway. The crowd parted with ungainly shuffling, leaving an open stretch of parquet straight to the Regent's party. There was a moment of baffled expectation. Then Pet erupted into the open space, covered with streaks of icing and blobs of cream and flower petals. Before the stunned faces of the guests, the creature skidded on the polished floor, plopped his hindquarters down, and went into a long, gliding spin, smearing a purple streak of icing like a snail's track in his wake. Nimble lords and ladies leaped aside to protect skirts and spotless pantaloons. Champagne sloshed from fluted glasses.

The long slide slowed. Pet scrambled to his feet, and with a series of short, happy barks, launched himself into the silken skirts of the Duchess of Searle.

Silence, awkward and amazed. Then a lady tittered, a gentleman choked on a laugh, and the sound spread and grew until the ballroom erupted in hilarity.

That instant a strong hand closed on Ophelia's wrist.

"Come with me." Alexander dragged her through the laughing crowd, ignoring her protests.

At one of the tall doors he stopped and said in her ear, "Five minutes. Where can we go?"

She refused to answer, and he flung the door open. They were under the stairs at the back of the entry hall. He swore. She expected him to release her then, but as he looked at two opposite doors, clearly trying to decide which to take a chance on, Lucca appeared.

"This way, Majesty."

Alexander strode after him, his grip firm on Ophelia's arm as he guided her past the servants crowding the ballroom entry to catch a glimpse of the duchess's humiliation, through the door, down the steps, and into a waiting carriage.

"We will talk," he said.

Chapter 18

"**W**hat can you hope to accomplish by abducting me?" Ophelia pressed herself into the corner of the coach as far from him as she could get. She crossed her arms, trying to cage a treacherous longing to let him hold her.

On the opposite seat Alexander twisted, shedding his evening coat. "I want to explain why I concealed my circumstances from you as long as I did."

"Your servant revealed your circumstances inadvertently. You never intended to tell me the truth. Did you plan to walk away from the stables saying nothing?"

"I couldn't walk away, though I should have after I took you to Miss Gray's that first time."

"Well, now that I know who you are, there's really nothing to explain. Take me home."

"There's a great deal to explain." He offered her his coat.

Her chin went up. "Write me a letter. I promise to read it."

"I have a better idea. I'd like to tell you a story."

She stared out the window. "I won't listen."

"You read Berwick's poem," he reminded her. "You were moved by the adventures of Prince Azim. Won't you listen to a true story?"

She turned on him then. "Truth from you? Unlikely."

With a sudden lunge he crossed to her seat and pinned her against the squabs with his coat. She twisted and squirmed, knocking her feathered headdress askew, but his body trapped hers. She fixed her gaze on the flicker of lights beyond the coach window, trying to block him from her mind. But his breath ruffled the curls at her cheek, a faint disturbance that threatened to crumble her defenses.

"I'll make my story as plain and honest as I can. You be the judge, Ophelia." His voice cracked a little.

She pressed her lips together, but her glance strayed to his.

"I won't try to deceive you about the least detail. I'll answer any question you ask." He waited, unmoving. He knew stories were her weakness. Words on the page, books, drew her.

She nodded solemnly.

"Take my coat." As abruptly as he had joined her, he pushed away, returning to the other seat. The coach wheels made a low rumble beneath them.

He led her from the carriage to his room, and seeing it again, she felt a bewildering mixture of hope and humiliation. He had shown himself to her that night, as she would have realized had she not been so besotted. Tonight he lit a plain lamp. There was no moonlight to turn the scene to one of enchantment. She removed her slipping headdress and set it on his desk. She would be hardheaded and would judge his story on its merits as fairly as she had judged Berwick's poem. The storyteller's handsome face would not turn her brains to butter.

He was handsome with the lamplight gilding his hair and lashes and slanting across the lines of his face. They took two seats, like a student with his tutor. He leaned forward in his chair while she pressed back in hers, keeping her gaze on his clasped hands hanging down between his knees.

"Once upon a time," he began, "in the faraway land of Trevigna, a prince was born. His mother the queen died the same night, and the king, grieving for her, vowed that her monument would not be some marble tomb, but the care of their son."

He told the story as if it were a familiar tale from childhood, the words conned from repeated hearing.

"Trevigna was troubled by enemies on all sides. When the prince was still a boy, two armies invaded the land, so the king sent the prince and his servant to England, where the prince could grow to manhood in safety. Every week the king wrote his son letters, teaching the boy how to be both a king and a man. And one by one the king sent the books he considered important to a ruler's education."

Ophelia risked at glance at him. When he spoke of his father, there was a slight but noticeable alteration in his voice. Her gaze passed to the old volumes on his desk with their gold lettering.

"The prince loved England. He might have been lonely, except that on his first day there, the carriage passed endless green fields full of horses. If the prince had a weakness, it was horses. And he liked the school, his first, and wanted to do well so that he'd be ready to go home. Some of the masters reminded him of his father, men of learning who exercised an amiable, effortless control."

"Surely it was not easy for you to begin school here. Did you speak English at all?"

"Some." His mouth turned up for an instant. "It was harder for Lucca. For the first month, everyone thought he was the prince. He tried to correct their mistake with his fists."

Ophelia straightened her skirts, avoiding his gaze. She would not smile. She'd made a mistake taking the coat. It was as if she'd wrapped herself in his arms. She thought she could shut him out, but somehow he got inside her and understood as if by magic what she was feeling. "How were you discovered to be the true prince?"

"Francesca came and straightened everything out."

There was more to that episode than he was telling. She could see the autocratic Donna Francesca taking on the masters of Winchester.

"While the prince studied in England, the French and the Austrians divided Trevigna between them. The king, in hiding in the mountains, wrote more letters, encouraging the prince to continue his education. Then, in the summer of 1808, the old king, fleeing from Austrian troops, was captured by the bandit Ferruci, sold to the French, and executed as an enemy to France. A gentleman—"

"Stop." Ophelia's eyes stung and her throat ached. His tone betrayed nothing. He'd used the plainest words, and yet she felt the thing that haunted him—the lonely indignity of a father's death.

She swallowed hard. "Why didn't the French allow your father to be ransomed?"

It was a moment before he answered in the same toneless voice. "They believed he was a symbol around which resistance forces would rally."

Ophelia took a deep breath and turned away. After a pause he went on.

"A gentleman from the Foreign Office brought . . . me the news at Oxford and advised me that I could expect the protection of the British Crown. I declined, and rather against the wishes of the Foreign Office, returned to Trevigna to join the rebel forces in the mountains. I had to learn to know my country again, and I had to study the ideas that divided Trevigna into republican and royalist factions."

"How old were you then?" She tried not to look at him, but her gaze was drawn against her will.

"Two and twenty. With the defeat of France in 1814, I saw the first hope of reclaiming Trevigna. I sent friends of my father's as ambassadors to the Congress of Vienna and returned to England to raise money."

"What happened when Napoleon's escape broke up the Congress?"

"The one piece of good fortune for Trevigna in twenty years. She was overlooked. The boundaries of France and Austria were redrawn without her. She was free, but her coffers were empty, her people divided. No council, no parliament, no court had operated for over fifteen years. No village schools, no newspapers."

Ophelia toyed with the buttons of his coat. He was coming to the part of the story that involved her.

"In England I tried to keep Trevigna's plight before Lord Castlereagh. But until last fall, no one in the Foreign Office was particularly interested in meeting with me. I ran out of money. I sold my house and my horses. Then a Turkish gunboat fired on an English frigate. England's control of the seas was threatened, and the foreign secretary summoned me to a meeting the next day."

Ophelia did not have to look at him to know the ironic twist his mouth would have.

He stood and moved to the hearth, picked up the poker, and idly stirred the dead coals.

"And the rest?" Ophelia managed to ask.

"Castlereagh wanted to restore me to the throne immediately, by force, if necessary, in return for the port and whatever funds I needed to maintain a government. I stalled as long as I could. Then a group of London investors approached me. If their bond scheme worked, Trevigna could be independent of England. I needed to avoid Castlereagh until the bonds sold, so I disappeared."

He turned and Ophelia found herself looking

straight into his hot blue gaze. "Why a tailor's shop?"

He laughed. "The tailor was bankrupt, and all I had left were my coats, dozens of them, and a servant who's clever at alterations."

"What did you think to gain by hiding?"

"Time and money and support at home for a new government."

It made so much sense. Ophelia's spirits sank. She could not fault him for his actions in the service of his country. They were honorable. So why had his treatment of her been so dishonorable? She did not want to follow that thought.

"How did you end up working in my father's stable?"

He moved to the desk chair, resting his hand on it's curved back. "I missed horses. I just wanted to be around them. When I came upon Raj, he was blindfolded and four of your father's grooms were trying to hold him on long leads. I thought, *I know just how you feel.*" He shrugged.

"Clagg offered you a job."

He nodded. "You were not in town. He'd sacked William that morning."

She knew it was more than that. Clagg had seen the obvious empathy between the man and the horse. It happened sometimes that a horse and a rider understood each other so completely, that like strings of a perfectly tuned instrument, they vibrated in harmony with one another.

Alexander was looking at her intently now, and her fingers stilled. He had explained it all, except the parts that had to do with her.

"Thank you," she said. "You've been candid and plain, and your explanation makes good sense." She sat up straight in her chair and reached for her headdress. It was time to end their visit and take her leave. She had done her part in listening to him, really, far beyond the five minutes he had asked of her. A quick glance at his face showed her he had other plans.

"There's more, Ophelia," he said.

"Don't." He shouldn't say her name like that. It was unfair.

"Ophelia," he repeated, his voice treacherously full of longing.

She took a deep breath and gripped the edge of the chair. "Go on, then."

"When Clagg described the girl I was to accompany to the park each morning, I pictured a twelve-year hoyden."

She flashed him a sharp glance.

He smiled. "When you appeared, I thought you'd see through me. You spotted the clothes, the accent. I thought I'd have to quit and desert Raj."

"But I wasn't so clever, was I? Even then you had me fooled."

"Not fooled. I just realized that for all the details you spotted about me, you couldn't know how to add them up. You had to take me for a groom." He came around his chair and stood directly over her.

"So you decided to amuse yourself at my expense." It was painful to say, but she wanted it clear. She wanted him to acknowledge the thing he'd done. She wanted to put all the times he'd called her by name or touched her or kissed her into a sealed box, like one of the red Foreign Office dispatch boxes. Then she could put the box away in some deep closet of memory unopened.

"No." He sounded surprised, and she looked up. "I want you to marry me."

His expression was earnest, his eyes that beguiling blue. For a stunned moment, Ophelia's spirits soared, a swift uprush of joy. Then the humiliation and hurt returned. He could ask her to marry him here, where he'd betrayed her not three days earlier? She jumped up, clutching her absurd headdress.

"Marry you?" In spite of her effort at control, her voice trembled. "I cannot marry you. You were my friend and you betrayed me."

"I never meant to deceive you. I couldn't tell you the truth at first, and then . . ." He reached for her, but she jerked away, knocking her chair back with a scrape. He caught her shoulders in an unforgiving grip, and his mouth descended on hers in a scorching kiss that made a mockery of resistance. Ophelia felt hers melt like frost in sunlight.

"You are not indifferent to me, Ophelia."

He made her weak and witless, and she struck back with the first weapon she could grasp. "Have you forgotten Miss Tesio?"

"My aunt's candidate for my hand. There is no attachment there."

That was probably the truth, but it didn't alter necessity. "Prince Mirandola must marry for political reasons." Ophelia set her mouth in a firm line.

"Prince Mirandola is as penniless as a groom. If the fund fails, he'll be a puppet in an uneasy kingdom. If it succeeds, he'll have work to last a lifetime trying to restore his impoverished nation. There'll be no palaces or pomp for him." His blue eyes took on their heated aspect. "But there could be love."

Ophelia's mind stopped working sensibly. Anger, hot and furious, took over. "Is that what you're going to say now—that you love me?"

He released her shoulders. "It is a customary part of a marriage proposal."

"Well, I don't believe you. You shouldn't marry me, anyway. You need someone regal like Miss Tesio, not someone . . . like me."

"I want you."

Ophelia shook her head and turned her back. After a brief silence she heard him cross to the door and unlock it.

"Lucca will make things as comfortable for you as he can."

"What? You're keeping me here?"

"Until you think seriously about my proposal."

"I don't need to think about it."

"But you might, if you had time." His mouth quirked up in a brief smile.

"You can't keep me here."

"Yes, I can."

Ophelia saw that she had something to learn about crossing a royal will. "Jasper will come for me. He'll figure out where I am."

Jasper admired the way sunrise brought a pinkish cast to the upper windows opposite Hetty's door. He liked her street. The cobbles were bright, the facades regular and elegant. There was a kind of meter in the way the arched doorways broke the line of shiny black iron railings, a rhythm that seemed fitting for a poet's dwelling.

When he'd been refused admittance to the Gray house at one, he had quite stubbornly sworn he wasn't leaving the front steps until he could speak with Miss Gray. A rash utterance, but he was glad he'd made it and stuck to it. The cool night air had soon cleared the fumes of success from his brain and allowed him to think.

His mind had been idle for so long after he'd left school that when Lord Castlereagh had given him the assignment to find Mirandola, he'd been paralyzed. Underlying his inactivity and wasted motion had been the fear that he really was the frivolous imbecile that his colleagues in the Foreign Office took him for. Then he'd met Miss Gray, and the encounter had completely addled what was left of his brain.

The accident of finding Mirandola under his nose and the success of the planned meeting between the prince and the foreign secretary had made him giddier than he'd ever been as an adolescent with a bottle of claret. Just before Hetty'd arrived at the ball, Castlereagh had rested a hand on Jasper's shoulder and given him one of his lordship's rare smiles.

Jasper had felt invincible. He could do anything, have anything, and there was Hetty Gray, and he'd proposed, rashly, bluntly, with no thought for the obstacles to their union. He'd forgotten the inflexible opinions of his parents and his class. His own snobbery hadn't evaporated in the warmth of love. He would still hear a humble accent with a superior ear and note blunders of taste with a superior eye. He would no doubt embarrass his love in such moments.

And he hadn't thought to ask her father's permission to pay his addresses. He had swept away her origins and treated her as if she'd sprung from his own fancy. He would do better this morning. The clear, cool night had given him time to know himself and to devise a strategy.

He stood and stretched his limbs, shaking off the stiffness of his long vigil and straightening his coat and cravat. He rubbed his jaw, feeling the stubble, and ran his fingers through his hair. Flawed and humble, he would offer for her again.

The housekeeper opened the door to his knock. "Miss Gray is not at home," she said, her sweet face flushing with evident discomfort at the common social evasion.

"I'd like to see Mr. Gray, if I may." Jasper saw at once that he'd caught her unprepared for such a strategy. She backed up, opening the door, and he seized that moment of polite behavior to step inside.

"Wait here, sir," she told him, gesturing to the little room where he'd spoken with Hetty twice before. He smiled as he crossed the threshold. Unless Solomon Gray had a pistol and the will to use it, Jasper wasn't leaving until he saw his love. He took a stand with his back to the hearth and waited.

Solomon Gray appeared promptly. Facing the older man's intense gaze and grim countenance, Jasper squared his shoulders, regretting his unshaven chin.

Solomon spoke without preamble. "What do

you mean, spending the night on my doorstep, sir?"

"I beg your pardon, Mr. Gray, I owe you an apology or two."

"Go on." Solomon's glare was unencouraging.

"Last night I offered for your daughter without first applying to you for permission to pay my addresses. I beg your pardon."

"If my daughter's refused you, what's the purpose of an apology now?"

Jasper thought he'd rather face a pistol than that level gaze, after all. "Actually, sir, Miss Gray accepted my proposal last night."

The fierce expression left Solomon's eyes. "My daughter had a painful shock last night, apparently at Searle House."

Jasper took a deep breath. "I am entirely to blame for that, sir. I invited her to my mother's ball, exposing her to the snobbery and bad manners of my family. I deeply regret having caused her pain."

Solomon Gray was now looking at the floor. He moved one booted toe slightly. "Actually," he said, "I am more to blame than you are, for concealing from her so long the truth about her mother." He sank onto the sofa, his features slack and drained of forcefulness, and gestured for Jasper to take the chair opposite. "The problem remains, however, that Hetty is distressed."

Jasper leaned forward. "Sir, with your permission, I would like to assure her that her mother's character and reputation cannot alter my feelings or my determination to make her my wife."

"With my permission? I fear I've lost the power to influence my daughter in any way."

Jasper took another deep breath. "I don't believe that, sir. You may be the only parent to approve a marriage between us, and I want to assure you that should Lord and Lady Searle dislike my marriage and cut me off, I will still be able to support a wife."

"It seems you've thought of everything."

"It was a long night."

A wan smile transformed Solomon Gray's face. "For what it's worth, you have my permission to address my daughter." He stood, offering his hand.

Jasper rose and clasped the offered hand. "Thank you, sir."

"I'll send her to you." Solomon's face became serious again. "But be advised, she will not recover easily from the blow of this discovery."

Half an hour later Jasper decided she wasn't coming. He stood at the window, watching the street fill up with vendors and carriages, trying to think of the next phase of his strategy.

A click of the door latch made him turn. She was utterly pale, her eyes and even the tip of her nose reddened, the hollows in her cheeks exaggerated, her hair pulled back in a simple clasp at her nape.

He forgot all the careful things he meant to say, crossed the room in two strides, and took her in his arms, pressing her head against his chest.

"When you left last night, I lost my head. Nothing mattered. Not Mirandola, or Castlereagh, or my career."

She gave him an embrace so brief he might

have missed it, and the tightness around his chest eased a fraction.

Words tumbled out of him about need and hope and the hollowness of his life before he met her. "I was wrong, careless, to expose you to my mother's cruelty. I hope you will forgive me in time."

"Jasper," she said, addressing his right arm, "did you know who my mother was when you . . . when you asked me to marry you?"

He swallowed. "My mother told us when she forbade Ophelia to come here. I thought you knew."

He pulled her closer and steeled himself to confess a further selfishness. "The day of the ball, Ophelia warned me that you didn't know about your mother, but I wanted you there, even as I anticipated the danger to you."

She let out a short breath. "Neither you nor Ophelia is to blame for keeping the truth concealed from me. My parents did that."

Jasper heard the pain and knew he had no remedy for it except his love. He was willing to stand and hold her for as long as her heart ached. Gently she pulled away from him.

"I've no more tears for now, I think," she said. "You must realize that my . . . origins make it impossible—"

Jasper reached out and stopped her words with the press of his fingertips against her lips. He shook his head. "Don't say that today." He released her lips. "All your life you have been Amelia Hart's daughter. It has never made you less lovely or less good or less worthy to be my wife."

She lifted her stricken face to his. "But now I know who I am."

Looking into those despairing blue eyes, Jasper felt in his bones the cold of those long hours in the night air. "I want to marry you, Hetty. Don't say no to me until you've lived with this truth awhile."

She clasped her hands and lowered her gaze. Jasper stepped forward and took her shoulders. He kissed the top of her head. "I'll come back soon."

Chapter 19

Ophelia woke, stiff and chilled, to the smell of coffee. She lifted her head from her arms, pushing back from Alexander's desk, where she'd fallen asleep over his writing sometime before dawn. A thin curl of steam rose from the spout of a silver pot on the table beside the hearth.

She groaned. By falling asleep, she'd obviously missed a chance for escape. Mirandola or his servant must have opened the door within the last few minutes.

She eased to her feet, shivering in the prince's coat and her crumpled silk dress, and moved quietly to the door. The lock was the sort that could be worked by a key from either side of the door. She rattled the knob to see whether the key was in place. It was.

Disappointment made her stand stupidly for several minutes before she could bring herself to examine the contents of the tray. When she had put herself to rights as much as her situation allowed, she curled her cold toes under her in the arm chair and wrapped her hands around a cup of coffee, feeling its welcome heat through the delicate porcelain.

He had asked her to marry him, and the idea of it would not leave her mind. For nearly two years, she had been avoiding marriage and all it would entail—hearing the banns read, balls, parties, wedding clothes, standing up in St. George's, Hanover Square. But none of those things came to mind with Alexander's proposal. Wicked images had come to mind, and she had avoided the wicked visions through the long night, by walking, by thinking of Hetty's shock and distress, of her mother's embarrassment, of the dog, and finally, by reading his papers—his "Declaration of the Democratic Principles of Government by the People." He was a careful writer, crossing out words, recasting phrases, working toward a taut elegance.

She absolutely refused to consider his proposal. The cynical voices she had heard all her life reminded her that he had not asked her to marry him intentionally. Her anger had prompted his offer. And he had asked her only after he'd seen her family's connection with the Regent, after her brother had helped him rescue his country.

It was plain that he would do anything for Trevigna: sell his horses, his house, his coats. Marry—Miss Tesio, his beautiful, wealthy countrywoman—or Ophelia, with her dowry and connections. Then she remembered her dream.

She had dreamed of sea-bathing in one of the machines at a resort. She trembled on the bench in the damp wooden hut, her heavy bathing costume clinging to her limbs. The slits in the plank walls admitted narrow, piercing bands of sunlight. The attendant lashed his horse, and the cart lurched forward down the shingle until gentle swells lapped against the sides. The dipper, a portly woman, knocked on the door, calling to her in a coarse voice. Timidly she emerged, but instead of her expected assistant there was Alexander, and then she was in the sea, her pale limbs naked and free, the water a caress against her skin.

She shook off the lingering effects of the dream. She felt suspended in time, taken out of her usual pattern, almost like the sleeping princess in the fairy tale, for whom even the flies on the walls stopped their buzzing. Judging by the sunlight streaming through the window, it was nine or ten. Everyone in her family would sleep late, especially after the debacle of Pet's eruption into her mother's party. She could probably return to Searle House unnoticed except by the servants as late as midday. It was Jasper she was counting on. How soon would he miss her, and would he look for her here?

As the coffee warmed her, she tried to feel confident. Her situation was ridiculous but certainly not hopeless. The prince would have to release her. He could not carry on delicate negotiations with the British government while keeping a subject of the Crown hostage in his rooms. Whatever madness had seized him the night before, daylight was likely to bring a return to rationality. Her gaze drifted to the stack of papers on the desk. As for herself, she understood perfectly now why they could not marry. She had seen him for what he truly was—no fairy tale figure with a dress sword like Prince Azim's, but that rare leader, a practical man of dreams, with a destiny far from hers.

The lock rattled. She swung her feet to the floor, banged down her cup, and lunged for freedom, coming up short under Alexander's nose. He caught her by the waist and pushed the door shut behind him. As she looked up into his eyes, the fixed certainty of her refusal crumbled. The ringing "no" she meant to deliver faded like the peal of a distant church bell. She wrenched herself out of his hold and stalked to his desk.

"You can't keep me here."

"Did you sleep?"

She glanced over her shoulder. She saw the weariness in his face and his unshaven chin. That roughness tempted her hand. "Did you?"

"Not much. I was thinking of ways to court you."

"A fruitless exercise." She picked up the loose papers on the desk. "I used my time more wisely. I read your writings."

He looked away. "If you marry me, you can attend the constitutional convention."

Ophelia turned to face him, holding the papers against her chest. "I can't marry you. We wouldn't suit."

His expression gave away nothing. "Dukes' daughters do marry princes."

"True." She looked at the floor. "In the eyes of world it would be an acceptable match. You are pledged to Miss Tesio, however."

"My aunt's idea. Why do you think we're unsuited?"

Ophelia's throat tightened. She looked at the papers she was holding. "A Declaration of the Democratic Principles of Government by the People." She paused so as not to betray herself by the least quaver of her voice. "You have these grand dreams for the nineteenth century, Your Majesty. You would bring down all the old regimes not by war but by reason. You would plant democracy in Trevigna and spread the seeds of it to the most feudal corners of Europe."

"You don't like that dream?" He stood still as stone.

"It's a beautiful dream." His words had made her weep for the vision of men free, equal, and at peace with each other and with nature. "It is too grand a dream for me. I've never been more than a . . . schemer." She put aside the papers. "I don't dream. I plot. I break a few rules for my own independence."

He smiled. "I like that in you." He advanced, closing the distance between them, his gaze unwavering. "I like your shrewdness and your tricks, and your refusal to be bound by mindless conventions."

There was nowhere to go, just as he intended. Ophelia pressed back against the edge of the desk. "You can't want me."

"I can. I do."

The blue gaze was melting her will. Ophelia wrapped her arms across her chest. At the gesture, he checked, a sudden alertness coming into his eyes. She tried to undo the motion, straightening her arms at her sides, but she hadn't fooled him.

"It's something else, isn't it?" His voice was

taut, his eyes penetrating. "You've been hiding, too."

"I've nothing to hide."

"You were hiding a secret life at Miss Gray's."

"I just wanted more freedom than young ladies are customarily allowed."

"No, that's not it." He was reading her, gathering certainty from each detail. "You wanted a place where you were most yourself, where you could be as bookish and quick-witted as you liked."

"Don't." She flattened her hand to his chest, holding him back, a mistake. Beneath her palm she could feel the swift beating of his heart and the tight stillness of his body in response to her touch. "You'll be feeling sorry for me, and you shouldn't. I've always found ways get around the rules."

"I'm trying to tell you I admire you, but you're holding back. That's why you shrink from my lovemaking."

"Maybe you overrate your lovemaking."

He smiled wryly. "You like my kisses, but when I want to touch, it's always the same—you close like one of those pink underwater flowers. It makes me wonder. Did something happen to you?"

"You imagine things. You don't know me at all. A few weeks of flirtation. What do your rules say? A lady may withdraw without blame up to the third stage. Well, I'm withdrawing. Surely, it is the man's part to accept my decision."

He took her hand from his chest, holding it in both of his, rubbing a thumb over her knuckles. "But I don't accept it, Ophelia."

"You won't get me to marry you by compromising me." Her voice was thin. "I have the right of refusal."

He released her hand and turned away, and perversely, her hand felt abandoned. From the door he looked back. "I've already compromised you, as Jasper knows."

"What?" She couldn't keep the surprise from her voice. "Then why keep me here?"

"Because I'm going to find you out as you found me. I'm going to unmask you."

When Jasper did not appear by late afternoon and a wary Lucca had come and gone with a lunch tray, Ophelia decided she had to escape. Alexander would have to go out, had perhaps already gone. His concern for Trevigna demanded that he now court London society.

She set her mind to thinking about the problem, which meant thinking about the locked door and Lucca. She must lull him, then surprise him, taking advantage of his weaknesses. She paced the narrow room, picturing the man in her mind, the haughty countenance, the instant obedience to Alexander, the magnificent livery he had worn to the ball and still wore.

When he brought a tea tray around four, she was ready. She lifted a tear-streaked countenance as the door opened and pretended to search madly for a handkerchief.

"Miss," he exclaimed, hastily depositing the tray and offering her his own immaculate linen. Under her lashes Ophelia saw the door swing almost closed, the little key on the edge of the tray.

"Forgive me," she said, taking his handkerchief and giving him her tremulous smile. "I didn't mean to become a watering pot. It's just that it's been a long day."

Lucca frowned. "His Majesty regrets leaving you alone."

Ophelia shook her head. "I'm sure he forgets me entirely."

"Never. He has the memory of an elephant. Come, you must have your tea." He bowed, and she rose from the desk chair. It was almost too easy to cover the little key with the handkerchief and lift it from the tray.

She turned back to Lucca. "Will you join me?"

As he drew himself up for a stiff refusal, she picked up one of the delicate cups with the blue coat of arms. "The royal plate of Trevigna?" she asked.

"His Majesty's mother's set."

"He was very close to her?" Ophelia feigned ignorance, turning the cup in her hands.

Lucca gave a tragic sigh. "She died when he was born, but always he keeps her china and her paintings." He pointed to a watercolor over the mantel. Ophelia felt a pang. His mother's things, his father's books—little enough to hold onto when his parents were lost to him.

Ophelia raised her gaze to Lucca. "This must have been a difficult time for you."

A suspicious gleam came into his eyes, but Ophelia persisted. "Living here, above this shop. Bringing the royal plate into such low surroundings. The hiding, knowing your prince was doing common labor in a stable."

Lucca shuddered. "Miss, please, the tea will grow cold."

"If I take my tea, will you stay?"

"Yes, miss." He was looking at the tray as if he found something odd there.

"But you must not hover over me. I could not bear that."

Lucca brought the desk chair over to the little table while Ophelia poured her tea, watching as her reluctant companion adjusted the fall of lace over his wrists. She kept her head lowered, gazing into her teacup. Her plan was working.

"You must be pleased, now that Prince Mirandola will return to his throne."

Lucca's eyes took on their tragic aspect again. "His Majesty does not want to be king. He wants a republic." Lucca spoke the word as if it were particularly disagreeable. "He wants to be a citizen."

"I know. I read his framework. But that's not what you want?"

Lucca leaned forward conspiratorially. "His Majesty should be a king. A monarch should not be this fat prince of yours or that old fellow of France. He should be a leader, a man of courage and honor, a man who is generous, not like these Bourbons who devour their people."

Ophelia forgot her plan for the moment in Lucca's unexpected vehemence. "Is Prince Mirandola a soldier?"

"The best. In the mountains he led many raids against the French, the Austrians. Always successful. When the French stole from our farms and the people were starving, His Majesty went and stole all the cows back, even the chickens, the ones that were left."

Ophelia felt her heart contract. He was more gallant than the fictional Azim. His were not fairy tale adventures, but true hardships. He had endured cold and hunger, faced death, even, for his people. What had he been thinking that night at Hetty's when she had defended the Regent as a man of taste?

"If Lord Castlereagh has his way, His Majesty will be crowned this summer."

Lucca looked away. Something disturbed him about the idea. "I know."

"You will not be sad to leave London, will you?" Ophelia asked.

"No." Lucca's voice was firm, and he squared his shoulders dutifully, but Ophelia still detected some reluctance in the expressive eyes.

She refilled her cup, letting the silence go on. Lucca sighed.

"Yes?" She hoped she sounded suitably sympathetic.

"There is one thing I would ask you, Miss Brinsby."

"Of course."

"Would an Englishwoman ever leave England?"

Ophelia gave him a sideways glance. He didn't mean her. She smiled into her teacup. There was a woman in Lucca's life.

"It's doubtful," she said. "Would you consider staying in London to make your fortune on Bond Street? You have a talent that has made others rich."

Once again Lucca straightened, but his expression remained bleak. "It is my fate to serve the Mirandola."

Ophelia leaned forward. She had got him thinking a bit with her suggestion about Bond Street, and she judged it almost time for the last phase of her plan.

"Even if he refuses to be king?"

Lucca's misery was so genuine that Ophelia's resolve nearly cracked, but the door was just beyond him, and if Prince Mirandola couldn't have her, perhaps he would wed Miss Tesio and live happily ever after on the throne of Trevigna. With a carefully choreographed move, she jiggled the cup in her hand, splashing tea over Lucca's white satin breeches. He jumped back and she dashed for the door. In the hall she shoved the key in the lock and turned it. Almost at once she heard the rattle of Lucca's attempt to open the door. She leaned panting against the wall, grateful that she understood nothing in Italian.

By mid-afternoon, when Alexander paid his call, an impressive display of cards of invitation lined the mantel of Francesca's sitting room at the Pulteney Hotel. His aunt and Miss Tesio had been busy making calls and receiving visitors. Returning to London society would be less difficult than Alexander imagined.

"*Andare in brocca!*" Francesca advised.

Alexander studied the cards one by one, looking for names he'd heard in the stables when Lady Searle had called for her carriage. Eventually he chose a familiar-sounding name and agreed to accompany his aunt and Miss Tesio to an evening entertainment at Lady Marchmont's. There would be gossip about Lady Searle's ball, and Alexander meant to hear it.

For the rest of his visit Alexander worked at engaging Miss Tesio in conversation, failing miserably. Her needlework clearly excited her interest more than he did, and her composure slipped only once when he mentioned the approaching dinner to initiate the fund. She made her disdain for the republican faction in Trevigna evident, but even then he had the impression that his effect on her was something like the disturbance a leaf made on a still pool, a momentary ruffle in the calm.

At six he left the ladies to their preparations for the evening ahead and walked up Piccadilly from the hotel, considering how he might bring Ophelia around to the idea of marrying him. Miss Tesio's heart, if she had such an organ, would not be broken by his refusal to wed her. The embarrassment to her family he would overcome somehow.

He met two school friends, passing the other way, and agreed to join them for dinner at their club. Burke was a round, rosy-cheeked man of thirty with a sweet tenor voice and a fine mind concealed by unfailing amiability. His passion for horses nearly equaled Alexander's. Rowley appeared so languid that a lifted brow was for him a major exertion, though Alexander knew he was one of the finest amateur boxers in England.

"Glad you can come, Prince," said Burke. "It's a regular thing this dinner. Good company and an excellent meal. It will set you up for the evening ahead."

"You can't escape," said Rowley. "Burke will plague you to death, if you try."

Alexander found he enjoyed both the dinner and the company of old friends. But after the covers were removed, he thought he would return to Ophelia before escorting his aunt and Miss Tesio to their engagements. He was about to make his excuses when he caught the gleam of rivalry in the gaze of a dark-haired gentleman down the table, a man who had danced with Ophelia Brinsby.

Alexander leaned forward across a semi-recumbent Rowley to refill his friend's glass. "Rowley," he asked. "Who's the dark-haired fellow at the other end of the table?"

Rowley didn't move, but his glance flicked down the opposite faces and back. "George Wyatt." After a moment he added, "Keep him away from your sister, if you have one."

Alexander was about to press Rowley for an explanation when a round of toasts began. Burke was thoroughly ribbed for his new title and good fortune. Then he suggested they had to toast Alexander, too.

"Getting married, aren't you?" Burke asked.

Alexander tensed. His aunt's tactics were working. People already thought of Miss Tesio as his betrothed, though nothing had been announced.

"Is that cause for a toast, Burke?" someone called. "Or a dirge?"

Burke rose shakily to his feet, holding his glass aloft, looking down the table at Alexander. "I suppose you've got to do it for your country.

Same thing happened to Prinny, you know."
Burke stared at his glass. "Sad."

"Burke, you're drunk," said another voice.

"I know it." Burke laughed. "Marriage is the
end of conviviality."

"Who's the lady?" asked another man. Alexander thought it was the fellow named Haddington. "The stunning Italian?"

They were all looking at Alexander, and he
knew wagers would be placed on Miss Tesio's
chances of wearing a crown.

"Beauty isn't everything," said Burke, with a
claret-induced air of gravity.

"Burke wouldn't know," said Wyatt. "He likes
them soft, round, and ample."

"We won't discuss your tastes, Wyatt," said
Rowley.

"No," Haddington added bitterly. "Wyatt
doesn't care what a woman tastes like, as long
as he gets the first taste."

Wyatt's glance met Alexander's, and Alexander felt himself go cold, then hot.

"To each his own, Haddington. Apparently
you don't mind coming after me." Wyatt rose
lazily, as if the conversation no longer interested
him.

"Here, here," said Burke, still standing with
his wine glass. "We were going to toast the
prince."

There was a scraping of chairs as the party
rose to its feet. "To the prince."

After Alexander had been given his due, gentlemen began to drift toward the cardroom or the
exits. Alexander settled back down next to Row-

ley. Through the doorway he could see Haddington and Wyatt having words.

"Want to tell me what that's about?" he asked Rowley.

Rowley didn't bother to look. "Some heiress Haddington wants. Last year Wyatt subjected her to his interest. Haddington thinks Wyatt trifled with the girl."

Alexander schooled himself to patience with his laconic friend. "Just what does Wyatt do?"

Rowley actually lifted his glass and sipped the wine. "I've seen him work a room. He picks one girl, the newer to society the better, singles her out, stands close, but doesn't touch, at first. His eyes linger. He finds out her interests. He flatters her. He repeats the treatment soon and often."

"And what happens?"

"Wyatt won't say." Rowley turned his head, looking straight at Alexander. "If he has taken advantage, what lady can expose him without harming herself more?"

"No one's called him out?"

Rowley watched him closely, no sleepiness in the eyes. "Dueling is illegal, Prince. And with the war there was no place to flee. The Continent is just now open again. But if you've no evidence to go on, what can you do?"

Alexander stood. "Who was this heiress last year?"

"Don't even think it, Mirandola." Rowley pushed to an upright position in the chair.

"I'm not thinking of a duel," Alexander said quietly. "Who was the girl?"

"Lady Ophelia Brinsby."

Alexander let the hot flash of rage pass

through him. He thought of her as she must have been in her first season, entering the ballrooms of London with her too-clever mind and her warm heart. There she had become Wyatt's quarry—hunted, inevitably caught, and apparently humiliated. Alexander guessed that Wyatt had taught her kisses and caresses before she'd discovered his game. With her quickness she'd have seen through him sooner than other girls, but for all the sharpness of her mind, she was vulnerable. What had she said to Alexander? That he'd been amusing himself at her expense.

Alexander came back to the present. Rowley appeared as indolent as ever, but he was watching the two men in the other room.

"Rowley, have you drawn anyone's cork lately?"

Rowley came to his feet with a slow unfolding motion. "No, I haven't, Prince, but now that you mention it, I think I need a good bout. If I can arrange one, would you like to be there?"

"Thanks, Rowley. I would like that."

"I'll see what I can do."

From the club Alexander returned to the Pulteney. He escorted his aunt and the dutiful Miss Tesio to a series of evening entertainments. At Lady Marchmont's he danced and chatted and fetched wine for Miss Tesio with apparent delight, secure in the knowledge that Ophelia was waiting for him. At Lord Twillen's he laughed at no fewer than six variations of the tale of the dog and the duchess and answered dozens of ignorant questions about Trevigna.

At three he returned to the tailor's shop, and before he reached the top of the darkened stairs, he knew that Ophelia had escaped.

Chapter 20

At his bedroom door Alexander found the key in the lock. He released Lucca, who began to complain at once of Ophelia's perfidy.

"Duped. Sold holland for cambric. Taken in by a hollowed cheese." Lucca went on muttering as he treated the satin knee breeches to a careful process of stain removal.

Alexander spotted her feathered headdress and gloves on his desk. Just the sort of fragments a night fairy would leave behind—a puff of blue gauze and drooping plumes, limp gloves. He took up her abandoned gloves and pulled the soft kid across his palm. In his mind he followed her fleeing form, deciding that she would not go to Searle House but to Miss Gray, her friend.

That's where he had failed her most, as a friend. He had seen from the beginning the lengths she would go to for friendship's sake. He had wanted such a friend himself. He had taken her hand in the Grays' garden, letting her believe that she could share her secrets with him. But he had kept their friendship in a separate compartment of his life, as if it were a chapter in a novel, whole and complete in itself. He had known he would leave the stable and go back to being Prince of Trevigna.

Each time he'd left her, he had come to this room to write his letters. He had led a strange double existence, planning for a convention in Trevigna and imagining hours with Ophelia, pretending that he did not have to choose. Then, when he'd least expected it, his deception had been revealed. He had told her his story, hoping she would see how he'd become trapped in his imposture, but he hadn't apologized.

Still, if he had concealed a truth, then so had she. When her secret was told, then they could begin again on an equal footing.

He saw the pattern of all their encounters now. Passion flared between them like dry grass catching fire from a windblown ember, and then she closed up. Whatever Wyatt had done to give Ophelia a disgust of her own passionate nature, Alexander had unwittingly added to it. He had to undo the damage.

Alexander's own sexual initiation had come from a generous if flawed woman. She had taught him to understand his body, given him names for acts and desires that before had been vague whispers in the darkened box of the confessional. She'd convinced him that what he found awkward and embarrassing pleased her. And she'd not taken his pride. He had to show Ophelia that he admired and wanted her passionate nature.

Lucca's voice intruded on his thoughts.

"She is beneath you, Majesty. This girl." He held up the ruined breeches. "She will put more nails in your heart than in the cross."

"I want her."

"Majesty! How will you wear the crown with such a girl beside you?"

"Lucca, do you know where to find Aunt Francesca's priest?"

"Who in Trevigna will obey a king who cannot control a wife no higher than a penny's worth of cheese?"

"Find out where the priest lodges, Lucca."

"*Madre della Virgine!* You have a banquet to attend."

Alexander regarded the plain comforts and good taste of Hetty Gray's parlor as an auspicious sign. It was a room where an ordinary man might propose to his love and be accepted.

"Your Majesty." Hetty dropped into a curtsy.

Alexander lifted her up at once, shaking his head at her.

"I owe you a great debt for the other night," she continued, keeping her gaze lowered.

"One you can easily repay," he said levelly. "I know Ophelia must be here."

Hetty's head came up. She sighed. "Your Majesty, she doesn't want to see you."

"She's made that plain, but I owe her an apology, and she owes me a truth."

"She believes you belong in separate worlds."

"I don't think we can live apart."

Miss Gray smiled wanly. "You want to argue with her, I see."

"I do," Alexander acknowledged. "Tell me, Miss Gray, does the name Wyatt mean anything to you?"

He did not miss the quick intake of breath. "You know?"

"Wyatt made her the object of his attentions last season. He makes a game of pursuing young women. I think Wyatt stands in my way as much as the politics of Trevigna."

Miss Gray shook her head. "I . . . I can't speak for Ophelia."

"Will you persuade her to speak with me?"

Miss Gray studied him, measuring his intentions with her serious gaze. "I will do my best, Your Majesty."

He knew a flash of triumph. "I'm prepared to wait."

Two lifetimes later the door opened and closed behind Alexander as he stood at the window looking down into the street. He turned and stared. He'd never seen Ophelia in a day dress before, an ordinary dress, soft and yielding, with just a hint of pink in it from some pattern of the cloth. It must be a borrowed gown, he realized, but the pink did extraordinary things to her skin, warming it, hinting at the sweetness of her person. A wisp of a creamy shawl hung over her arms, and the dark curls about her face looked tousled. Everything about her was sweet and fresh, except for the tight fists at her side and the vexed look in her eyes.

She gave him a nod, but stayed at the door. "Your Majesty, how good of you to call. As you can see, I suffered no harm from my brief captivity in your lodgings."

"You must have known I would come after you."

"I can't think why. We've settled every question between us and may now meet as common and indifferent acquaintances."

Alexander moved toward her slowly, without apparent intention. She glanced at the sofa as if she contemplated stepping behind it and pressed back against the door, one hand closing about the knob.

"I doubt it," he said. "When we meet, you'll make me forget everyone else but you."

She laughed, an artificial sound unlike her usual laugh. "Well, we're unlikely to meet after all. You'll be society's darling now. My brother has seen to that. Even Castlereagh will find it hard to deny you anything you want for Trevigna. You certainly don't need me. Your plans and dreams are far from here."

It was a carefully composed farewell speech. He let her finish, even as he came closer. "Give me your hands, then, for farewell."

She looked confused at his apparent acceptance of her dismissal, but she obeyed.

He took her small hands in his, rubbing his thumbs across the knuckles, holding them until he felt a tremor of response. "Such strong hands." He interlaced her fingers with his. "It's entirely noble and self-sacrificing of you to release me from our friendship, now that my title seems above yours."

"I'm not the least bit generous or self-sacrificing." Her chin went up. "I don't like you." She inched backward, pressing against the door.

He studied their laced hands. "I don't believe

you," he whispered, lifting her hands to his mouth.

"Don't."

But the protest came too late. He kissed her knuckles. "You are behaving like Aunt Francesca, trying to tell me whom to love." He tightened his grasp, slowly spreading his arms, pulling their locked hands out to the side, forcing Ophelia nearer.

The slow stretch of his arms brought them within inches of touching. Her cheeks glowed pink with that quality of her skin that made it seem as if the light came from within her.

"I want you." Alexander forgot about apologies, arguments, explanations. "I want the girl who escaped the vanity and idleness of her class. The girl who tricked me and ordered me about. The girl who accepted me as her friend when I had neither rank nor wealth."

He held her there, looking his fill, letting his eyes linger on her dark hair, her glowing cheeks, her trembling mouth. His gaze dropped lower to the curve of her throat, the "V" of her bodice, the little gathers against which her breasts strained.

"Let me tell you what I see."

She twisted her shoulders, fighting desire and him.

He took a careful breath, slowing the fires inside. They were equals in this, he wanted to say. "I can't touch you, Ophelia. My hands are bound as yours are."

She looked at him with sharp alertness then, as if she understood.

He pushed his hands farther out and her body

came up against his, just meeting, muslin to wool, a surface friction that sent sparks of sharp feeling crackling through him. Her shawl slipped away. He bent his head to kiss the side of her neck, just under the jaw, where the heat of her skin freed her scent and he could breathe her like an incense.

He allowed himself just that, the press of his lips to the sweet place behind her ear. Then he moved, tracing her collar bone with brief kisses, dipping down to the hollow where the light dress covered her breasts.

Her breathing quickened, and she quivered from the strain of their spread arms.

"I can't marry you, you know," she said, her ragged breathing at odds with the calm words.

He laughed, dragging his mouth across her collarbone.

"Truly." Her body arched upward. "I've got into the habit of ordering you about. I would dislike all that kneeling and bowing in your royal presence."

"You have it wrong, Ophelia. When you marry me, you get both a servant and a lord."

He brought his mouth to hers to show her how it would be, how there was no mastery for either. Her lips opened under his, and he had to taste her.

Ophelia was swimming, as she had been in her dream, her skin tinglingly alive, touched everywhere at once, her limbs fluid, boneless, melting. She felt borne along, lifted and pulled, tumbled and righted by swells that roared in her ears.

He broke their kiss and dipped his head, pressing his lips to the swell of her breast.

Through the muslin she felt his touch, drawing her nipple into a tight bud of exquisite sensation. She rubbed her chin over his hair, the tiniest response. He murmured something inarticulate in his throat.

"You are unmasked, Ophelia," he whispered. "You love me."

Too late Ophelia twisted her head, fighting him. He made a rack of his stretched arms, holding her, taking light kisses from her mouth, making it harder and harder to struggle. He pressed her against the door and bent his knees, brushing her thighs with his.

When her knees gave in shameful weakness, he pushed one thigh between her legs, bearing her up, rubbing the hard muscle against her woman's place, making her body throb with longing. Against her hip she felt the unmistakable ridge of his arousal. An aching warmth spread through her, and she moaned. His mouth came down on hers in a searing kiss.

The doorbell rang.

Alexander froze and lifted his mouth from hers. She wrenched herself from his arms. He backed a few feet away, breathing hard. Her shawl had slipped to the floor, she snatched it up and gathered it around her, trying to control her own ragged breaths.

Mrs. Pendares's footsteps passed in the hall. She exchanged commonplaces with the postman while the strange, heated blue of Alexander's eyes held Ophelia motionless. She recognized it now, the fire of the dreams in him. He was a living ideal, a prince who could lead Europe away from blood and injustice to liberty and equality.

Then her gaze dipped and she saw the ridge of his man's part straining against his breeches. Unmoving, he let her look. Her eyes flew up to his.

He swallowed. "No masks. No prince, just a man who wants you."

The front door closed and Mrs. Pendares passed the little parlor again. Ophelia had her hand to the knob.

"Marry me, Ophelia." His voice was a hoarse whisper.

"Never."

He seemed to take the word like blow, but after a moment he spoke again. "Tonight the Committee for the Restoration of the Italian Republics holds its banquet. I have a speech to write. Will you come to hear it?"

Ophelia shook her head. "When your plans succeed, you will be glad I refused, glad you have Miss Tesio at your side."

"Never."

Three silent people sipped coffee in the Grays' morning room. There was no more sound than the occasional clink of a spoon against a cup or the rustle of a page of the paper being turned, and outside the rattle of a passing carriage. After a few minutes, Solomon Gray sighed heavily, made his excuses, and left.

Mrs. Pendares came in to remove Solomon's dishes, stacking china with slow, spiritless motions. There was a silent reproach in her manner. The Grays were hurting each other, and Ophelia could not sit idle and let it happen. When the door closed, she turned to Hetty.

"We have to talk about your mother."

Hetty put down her cup. "Only," she said resolutely, "if you agree to talk about the prince."

"We need more coffee, then." Ophelia poured two fresh cups. After Alexander's call the day before, she had gone out into the garden, speaking to no one. She had been at her weakest in the little sitting room when he had stretched out their joined hands. In those moments she had been so tempted to believe that he loved her, that she was the woman he wanted. She must not weaken. Perhaps if she explained it all to Hetty, she could win Hetty's support.

"Where shall we start?"

Hetty straightened with a deep breath and folded her hands in her lap. "With my mother, I suppose."

"Have you seen her?" Ophelia asked.

Hetty nodded. "She called here the day after the ball. She didn't know, of course, that I'd heard the truth. I told her straightaway." Hetty paused. "She was very gay. Sorry if the truth had hurt me. She'd had her reasons, and that was all she meant to say about the matter. After all, my knowing the truth didn't really change anything, did it?" Hetty's eyes were dry, but the expression in them was bleak. "I tried to explain that I wasn't hurt by the truth or ashamed of her, whatever others might think, but I was hurt by the concealment. I don't think she cared at all."

Sunlight whitened the table linen, a brightness that made Ophelia's eyes water. She reached out and took her friend's hand in hers.

"Before we knew her connection to you, we both admired your mother," she said. "We admired her independence, her daring, her wit, her work. The way she didn't let herself be bound by the rules."

"But how can I respect her now, esteem her? Her dishonesty has been such. She concealed who she was to avoid responsibility, to make father vulnerable."

"She left you, deserted you, and lied about your connection, but she's the one to be pitied."

"You think so?" Hetty gave Ophelia a doubting glance.

"I do. She chose independence over love, and does not even know what she's sacrificed, though I think she must have guessed when she saw you with Solomon. I think she must have been jealous."

Hetty shook her head in firm denial and took a slow, meditative sip of coffee. "I think I can forgive her more easily than him. She made no pretense of affection or respectability."

Ophelia smiled. "Hetty, you will forgive your father sooner or later. I'm afraid it's inevitable. It is your nature to forgive, and if he's erred, it is only through wanting what is good for you."

Hetty said nothing. Ophelia gave her hands a squeeze and released them. "I suppose your father, having once concealed the truth, found it difficult to know when to tell you. How does one judge another person's readiness for such startling news?"

Hetty laughed. "Ophelia, it's very wrong of you to be so knowing of my character."

"Then I fear I'm going to offend you further.

I think you should accept my brother."

"No. Your parents will be so very much against us. And I have not even the faintest claim to respectability now."

"You do. You are as respectable as you've ever been. And you certainly should not consult my parents as models of happiness, to be guided by them in this matter would be the height of folly."

Hetty looked unconvinced.

"Oh Hetty, if you had seen my mother's face when Pet threw himself into her skirts in front of the most elevated members of society."

"What's become of Pet, do you think?" Hetty asked.

"He's probably been locked in the dungeons of Searle House."

"The poor dog."

"Hetty, if you can pity that beast, you'd better be prepared to be kind to my brother when he next offers for you."

A sly look came into Hetty's eyes. "Prince Mirandola has offered for you, hasn't he, Ophelia?"

Ophelia looked away. "Yes, he has."

"And you've refused him because . . . ?"

Because he makes me weak and sick with longing. Because he's everything shining, glittering, and good, and I've been a selfish creature all my life. "We would not suit," she said woodenly.

"Ophelia, you put me out of all patience. I don't think you've meant a word of what you've said to me this morning."

"How can you say that? I . . ."

"What have you been saying about my mother? She's to be pitied for her inability to love, right?"

"Yes."

"Then don't be like her."

"I'm not. I do love him." Ophelia felt her face burn at the admission.

Hetty grinned. "Good. The next time he calls, I hope you'll accept his offer."

Hetty rose, and with a rustle of skirts, headed for the door, but as she reached for the knob, the door flew open.

Jasper strode in without ceremony, threw down two copies of the *Morning Chronicle*, and after a brief bow to Hetty, flung himself into a chair.

Ophelia reacted first, reaching for one of the papers.

"The banquet?" Hetty asked.

"A disaster," Jasper said. He propped his elbows on the table and buried his head in his hands.

Ophelia, scanning the news columns, found the story. "Miss Tesio denounced him?"

Jasper's head came up. "Stood up before the lot of them. Called him a traitor to his country. Refuses to marry him. Wants to sue him for breach of promise."

"I thought she spoke only Italian," said Hetty.

Jasper's face turned furious. "She does, but our own dear brother, Sebastian, translated the whole of her outburst. The fund will never fly, and the prince will be lucky to get his throne. He'll be Castlereagh's puppet."

"Here's his speech," said Hetty, looking over Ophelia's shoulder.

Ophelia read, her throat tightening around the words. "It is the participation of citizens in government, and not the name of republic, that constitutes liberty. It is above all the reign of laws, the public administration of justice, equality, and the removal of all shackles on religion, education, and thought."

Ophelia sat numbly. She never dreamed he could fail. He couldn't fail. She thought of how his eyes must look without the dream in them. He would not go to Trevigna to be a crowned puppet. He would run away again.

"Where is the prince?" she asked Jasper.

"At the tailor's shop, I suppose."

Ophelia stood up. "Jasper, find him. Bring him here, now."

Jasper rose, moved by her urgency, but looking confused. "Ophelia, what are you thinking?"

"We have to do something. We have to make the fund work."

"It's a bit late for that now."

"It can't be."

"What can we do?"

"Write," said Hetty.

Ophelia spun to her friend. "Yes! Tell his story in every afternoon paper. In broadsheets."

"It might work," said Jasper doubtfully.

Both women turned to him. "Get the prince."

Chapter 21

～❦～

"He's not at the tailor's." Jasper spoke quietly. Ophelia looked up from the writing desk where she worked in the Grays' morning room. Her sleeves were pushed up, and ink marked her fingers. Her eyes had a softness he'd never noted before. He made up his mind not to tell her about the message he'd received from the prince, a brief scrawl that had said merely, "Rowley requires my presence in Staines." The note baffled Jasper; he could see no reason for the prince to leave town with a school friend, but he wanted to believe some explanation would come to light.

Ophelia put down her pen. "The shop was closed? Did you knock? Did you talk to the neighbors?"

"I did."

She straightened the pages on the desk. "What about his aunt and Miss Tesio? Did you call on them at the Pulteney?"

Jasper avoided Ophelia's gaze. "They haven't seen him. They have removed to Searle House."

"Really?" Ophelia stared.

"Sebastian insisted." That drew a faint smile. "There will be an announcement in the papers soon. Mother will have a grand wedding to plan."

"There's no sign of the prince, then?"

"None." Jasper regarded his sister closely. He had never seen her in such low spirits, so quiet, so without motion. "Most likely the prince is occupied with Hume and Tollworthy in some effort to save the fund. Do you have any articles ready for me to take to the printers?"

"Just give me a few more minutes."

He nodded, and when she didn't respond, he let himself out.

Ophelia stared at the lines she'd written. She thought it odd to find clarity in a moment when action seemed fruitless. What she had once feared, that he would make her weak and even wanton, seemed unimportant. More important was the fear that he would disappear into London's vastness, into some other life, without her knowing where he'd gone, with no bell to ring, no way to send an imperious note that would make him stay to do her bidding.

The comfortable illusion that he was her servant had vanished in his true identity. But perhaps one last time her words would reach him and call him back. She bent to her task.

In the days that followed, the task of writing to save the fund filled her mornings. According to Jasper, all of London had read "An Argument for an English Alliance with the Ancient State of Trevigna," which appeared in the *Times*, written by D.D., the reviewer of "The Prince of Balat." The argument emphasized the role of Prince Mirandola in the future of his nation and implied that with such traditions, such allies, and such a leader, Trevigna could only prosper. Readers with other tastes would find an ode by one H. L. Gray dedicated to Prince Alexander di Piovasco Mirandola. In it the poet followed the arc of a thrush into the free air and imagined the arch of the wide sky from England to Trevigna, the same sky for everyone who desired freedom.

New places to send her writing, and new people to appeal to as potential investors occurred to Ophelia almost every hour. In the afternoons there were calls to pay on Hetty's friends, who had met Alexander and discerned his unusual qualities, and who now wanted to hear the story of how he had come to be Hetty's guest and what he hoped to accomplish in Trevigna.

Then there were details to resolve about Ophelia's having removed herself from Searle House. She consulted with Solomon Gray's solicitor and wrote her father of her intentions. With help from Jasper and her former maid, she managed to collect some of her clothes. She worried about Shadow.

Ophelia and Hetty even visited Mrs. Hart in Bloomsbury, questioned her closely about how she had managed her finances, and met her lover, a coffee merchant, who watched them through lazy-lidded eyes as he told shocking tales of the Amazon.

Jasper came in the evenings to play backgammon with Solomon and stare at Hetty until she blushed and he remembered to look away. He had not renewed his addresses to her, but Ophelia was confident he would.

By Saturday morning Ophelia had but a few inquiries left to write. She sat in the morning room with her pens and paper, pretending. There was no point in trying the papers, for they were given over to pages of details of Princess Charlotte's evening wedding to Leopold of Saxe-Coburg.

The *Times* explained how the crimson drawing room of Carlton House, the Regent's residence, had been fitted with an altar, where the Archbishops of Canterbury and York would preside. Other details of the grand event included descriptions of the route Prince Leopold would take from Clarence House to the wedding in his plain green carriage and of the princess's elaborate silver dress. The fifty select guests would join the aging queen and her children, the royal dukes and the Princesses Augusta, Elizabeth, Mary, and Sophia. Castlereagh would be there with the rest of the cabinet, but Ophelia knew that her parents would not. Her mother's disastrous encounter with Pet had made the duchess a figure of fun in the print shops.

The wedding had caught hold of London's fancy. Portraits of the enormously popular young royals adorned teacups, boxes, and cards in dozens of shops. There was even a "Coburg hat" offered for sale as a fashion tribute to Leopold.

As the morning wore on, Ophelia felt her spirits sink even lower. It was excessively silly, and she was vexed with herself. Had she accepted one of the offers made her in her first season or encouraged Dent, she could read in the papers a description of her dress, her plans for a wedding breakfast, her guests, her proposed wedding journey.

Marriage was the end of every story she had envisioned for herself, and yet she had spent two seasons avoiding it. Reading about Princess Charlotte, Ophelia knew why. Charlotte's marriage was different from any that Ophelia had been offered. The plump princess, with her doughy arms and loud manner that Miss Mercer-Elphinstone mocked, had found love. All London rejoiced in her happiness. Wyatt and Mrs. Hart were wrong when they laughed at love. It was real, and one needed only the courage to trust in it. Of course, that was precisely what Ophelia had lacked when Alexander had asked her to marry him.

She was reflecting on this dismal truth when Mrs. Pendares knocked on the morning room door to tell her she had a caller.

George Wyatt stood with his back to the parlor door, his face to the window. Bright sunshine streamed into the room around him, but he seemed indifferent to it, leaning his hands on the ledge, his head down.

Ophelia tried to master her surprise. She could not be glad to see him, but she was curious to know how he'd found her and what he wanted. "Good morning, Wyatt."

He didn't turn. "You must wonder at my coming here."

"Won't you sit down?"

He shook his head. "My visit will be brief."

Ophelia took a seat herself, deciding to ignore Wyatt's apparent rudeness. "May I ask why you've come?"

He gave a bitter laugh and turned toward her silhouetted by the brightness of the window behind him with his face in shadow. "To beg your pardon, Ophelia."

Looking into the light, Ophelia wanted to lift her hand to shade her eyes and see his face, but she wouldn't give him the satisfaction. "An apology? Why now?"

With a slow, arrogant stroll he came toward her, stepping out of the stream of sunlight. Ophelia gasped. Circles of brownish purple and livid yellow ringed his eyes, one no more than a slit in puffy folds of bruised flesh. A piece of sticking plaster made a bar across his nose. His upper lip looked lopsided.

"Who did this?" she couldn't help asking.

His brows rose in a grotesque parody of gentlemanly wit. "You can't guess?"

"I cannot."

He looked surprised, or she thought he did. It was hard to read the expression in his slitted eyes.

"No matter," he said. "It's my one opportunity for redemption."

She studied his ruined face, trying to look past the bruises to gauge his sincerity. "Very well. Apologize. I'll listen." She folded her hands in her lap.

Wyatt took a deep breath and plunged his hands into his pockets. The cynical lines of his face showed through the swollen, discolored flesh. "In society one can be a scoundrel or a fool, and I chose to be a scoundrel. Women of our class want to bind a man in marriage. A woman sets a trap for him, and once he's won, she goes her own way, draws on his bank account, takes her lovers, and lets his friends snicker behind his back. That was not for me."

Ophelia thought it odd how much he sounded like Mrs. Hart.

"I set out to play a different game, to make my own harem, if you will, to teach pleasure to girls who would be my lovers when they married." His good eye closed briefly and opened again. "You have no idea how many brides have turned to me, dissatisfied with the marriage bed."

Chilled, Ophelia pulled her shawl about her. This had been Wyatt's plan for her, that she would marry someone like Dent and become Wyatt's lover.

"But you were different, Ophelia."

"Please, don't flatter me," she said, unable to control a flash of temper.

"It's not flattery. I was affected by you, Ophelia, and I pushed you too far, too soon. I wanted you to respond with the . . . same passion I felt. Instead, you stopped me cold."

"This is your apology?" she asked.

"I thought you'd appreciate the piquancy of it, the biter bit, the vile seducer hoisted on his own petard." His mouth twisted in a wry smile.

Ophelia stood. "I suppose I must thank you for your apology and tell you I forgive you, but your chief regret seems not to be any injury you've done me, but your own loss of yet another lover. Good day, Wyatt."

She turned on her heel and crossed to the door.

"Wait, Ophelia. I want to offer amends."

Reluctantly she faced him again.

"The gentlemanly thing to do, and in my case,

the selfish thing as well, is to offer for you."

"What?" She stared in disbelief.

"You could marry me, Ophelia. You don't need your prince."

"He's not my prince," she said carefully, wondering how Wyatt knew about Alexander.

"The devil he's not, Ophelia. I didn't end up with my face rearranged for nothing."

"Alexander did this? Alexander sent you?"

Wyatt's mouth closed in a sullen line.

Ophelia's heart lurched crazily. He wasn't gone. He had been somewhere, thinking of her, acting on her behalf. Though how he knew about Wyatt she couldn't guess, he had certainly known where to find her. The sunbeams from the window seemed to dance. In her heart she felt answering twinkles of happiness that threatened to escape in skips and leaps and unrestrained smiles.

With an effort she kept a sober face and fixed her thoughts on Wyatt. Whatever compulsion he was under to apologize, she doubted Alexander had encouraged Wyatt to make her an offer of marriage.

"Thank you, Wyatt. There was a time when your offer would have been most welcome to me. Even now I am sensible of the honor you do me, though I must refuse."

"He's poor, Ophelia." Wyatt gave her what she supposed was a measuring look, though it was hard to tell from his ruined face.

"He offers me what I require."

Wyatt removed his hands from his pockets. "There's no point in my staying any longer, then.

Thank you for hearing me out, Ophelia. I wish you every happiness." He gave a curt bow and strode toward the door.

Ophelia made no move. The door opened behind her, and he spoke again. "Tell him I called."

"Good-bye, Wyatt," she said. "I wish you happiness, too."

The door closed with a quiet click.

Ophelia was still watching the merry sunbeams when Hetty knocked and entered. "Mrs. Pendares says George Wyatt called for you."

"It was the strangest thing," Ophelia said. "He came to beg my pardon."

Hetty sat down opposite Ophelia, her brows drawn together in a frown. "Wyatt apologize? You never expected that."

"No. Neither did he. From something he said, I think Alexander put him up to it."

"Oh," said Hetty, with a quick flush.

"What do you know that you've not told me, Hetty?" Ophelia could see that Hetty was considering whether her scruples permitted her to reveal this particular information.

"When the prince came and spoke with me, he knew Wyatt made a habit of misleading girls and that Wyatt had paid attention to you last season. He must have talked Wyatt into speaking."

Ophelia was silent. So Alexander had known about Wyatt that day that he had spread their hands and held her captive to his lovemaking. He had been showing her how equally powerless they were in love. Wyatt and Mrs. Hart insisted on power and mastery when what was needed was this mutual yielding.

"Ophelia? Are you well?" Hetty asked.

Ophelia brought her gaze back to Hetty's. "Yes. Perfectly." Or she would be if Alexander returned.

Chapter 22

Jasper found Hetty in her garden late in the afternoon on the day of Princess Charlotte's wedding. He had good news to report. He'd just met Mirandola on the Grays' doorstep and seen Mrs. Pendares direct the prince to the morning room. Altogether it was one of the most hopeful moments of his life.

The daily revelations of this other life had given Jasper a strange confidence. His life need not be confined to Mayfair. If he looked up at the stars from a narrower street, the sky was still as wide. At breakfast he had informed his father of his intention to marry Hetty.

The duke had begun his favorite lecture on the tide of presumption sweeping the town and then broke off abruptly, staring at Jasper as if really seeing him. His valet, Plumb, had given notice on the spot. His mother had listened to him in cold silence from her bed and informed him that she could do nothing whatever in the way of a betrothal party or wedding breakfast if he chose to make such a mésalliance. In that moment Jasper had had a sudden sense of Ophelia's spirit

345

and had recommended that Lady Searle make the most of Sebastian's wedding.

The look on his mother's face had given him such satisfaction that he had gone directly to Rundell and Bridge for a ring. The little velvet box was tucked in his coat pocket.

Hetty sat on a bench, a pencil and notebook in hand, a flat, wide-brimmed straw bonnet shading her face from the afternoon sun. At the sound of his footsteps on the gravel path, she looked up, no alarm, no hesitation in her gaze. Jasper felt his heart expand slightly. He stopped just in front of her, enjoying the way she tilted her face up to his, leaving the curve of her throat exposed. The heat of the day had dampened the curls at her temple and brought a lovely flush to her skin. Her hand pressed to the crown of the floppy hat gave him a view of the creamy underside of her arm, and the cloth of her bodice, stretched across her right breast, defined the sweet swell of that utterly feminine shape. A heat he had not yet allowed himself to feel in her company, unfurled lazily in his loins.

"May I join you?" he asked.

"Please." She made way on the bench, pulling her skirts close and sliding to one side.

He dropped down beside her and indulged himself in looking at her until she laughed.

"What?"

"Jasper, you'll make me vain if you stare so."

"You've progressed to my name," he said.

She played with the pencil between her fingers. "I confess I've been rather free with it from our first meeting. In my mind."

Jasper gripped the back of the bench, steadying himself. He had a vision of snatching her arm and pulling her onto his lap. "Then you're willing to accept my suit."

Her glance came up, met his, and descended again. "Yes."

A little gust tossed the branches over their heads, and a startled bird flitted away. Jasper waited 'til he had a reasonable measure of self-restraint, then reached for her hand. "You do me a great—"

She put her fingers to his lips, shaking her head. "We honor each other."

He lifted her hand from his mouth and slowly drew her toward him, making no disguise of his intentions. "Close your eyes," he whispered. He worked the ribbons of her hat and set it aside.

The tip of her nose was pink from the sun. He kissed that spot first. Then he slid one hand up her back and with the other pulled at her waist, drawing her closer, taking her lips in a long, slow kiss.

Her body arched to meet his naturally, inevitably, the way a flower turned to the sun. They drew apart and immediately came together again with more hunger and impatience. Lips brushed and clung and parted, and Jasper drew back, surprised to find himself trembling. He pressed her head to his chest and rested his chin against her bright hair. He had never dreamed he would find himself so aroused by kissing a fully clothed virgin on a garden bench.

She pressed closer, her arms circling his back. "I had no idea that kissing would be so . . . stirring. I suppose you have a vast deal of experience with this sort of thing."

"Not with this sort of thing," he said, allowing his hand to drift up and down her back. Her scent enveloped him now, clouding his brain. "Not with love."

"It's odd," she said. "I suppose we could not be closer, and yet . . ." A little sigh escaped her, and Jasper wanted to catch that puff of breath. "I want to be closer. I want . . ."

Jasper tightened his arms around her in a fierce embrace. "Hetty, stop." His innocent love had no idea of the effect of her words. "We can be closer. I promise we will be when we are wed."

He told her his parents' position on their marriage and begged her not to be saddened by it. "Their opposition means we can please ourselves with a long engagement or a brief one."

"Definitely a brief one," she said, lifting her head and smiling at him.

"We can have the banns read for the first time this Sunday, if you like."

"I would like that."

The little furrow between her brows appeared, tempting Jasper to smooth it with a touch of his finger. "Do you think Prince Alexander will see our writings?"

"He's here, with Ophelia."

A bright smile lighted her eyes, taking Jasper's breath away.

"How lovely. But Jasper, there is one creature I'm worried about."

"Creature?"

"Your mother's dog."

"Pet?"

Hetty nodded. "I wonder—if he's in terrible

disgrace, perhaps your mother would part with him."

Alexander entered the Grays' morning room soundlessly. The steady, urgent scratching of Ophelia's pen filled the air. He took a moment to look over her shoulder as she wrote. Apparently not satisfied with arguing his case in the papers, as Jasper explained she had, she now addressed the editor of the *Quarterly*, inquiring whether that august journal would be interested in a piece on Prince Mirandola's vision of a new Europe.

He put his hands on her shoulders. "Ophelia."

She stopped writing instantly and a choked sob escaped her.

"I thought you'd gone," she said.

He kneaded her shoulders, feeling the knots of tension in the muscles. "I had to leave town for a while."

"But now you're back."

"I've come from Hume and Tollworthy. They will give the fund a few more days before they withdraw the offer. There is a chance."

She turned to him then, a little light of gladness in her eyes, and he kissed her swiftly once because he could get away with it.

She made a flustered rearrangement of her pens.

"Thank you for writing on my behalf," he said.

"You don't know whether I've done your cause any good."

"You've given me hope. If your writing campaign works, dozens of investors may purchase shares of the fund. Trevigna will not perish as an independent nation."

"When that happens, I'll expect an official thank-you, Your Majesty." She made a light thing of it. "When you are crowned, will you knight me or honor me with Trevigna's Order of the ... Olive?" He watched the interesting way she faltered under his regard.

"Trevigna has no honors for me to award, though I could invent an 'Order of the Pen' for you and Miss Gray." His attention seemed to settle on her mouth. "I would rather thank you personally, Ophelia."

"Unnecessary, really. Hetty and I were glad to write." Ophelia turned away, retreating to the window, looking down on the pavement as if the regular pattern of the stones fascinated her, her heart beating uncommonly fast. "If you succeed, will you have your constitutional convention?"

"It seems likely. Even Castlereagh agrees that it will be in England's best interest to have Trevigna as an ally whether she is a monarchy or a republic."

"Your tactics worked. With cunning and patience you've brought England to her knees."

He came over to the window and leaned his right shoulder against the wall, facing her. "What I remember, Ophelia, is kneeling to you."

She looked down, pinching little pleats of her skirt between her fingers. "That was a strange evening. The attack in the alley, the moonlight ... you could not be sure of your feelings in such circumstances."

He crossed one foot in front of the other, his hands in his pockets. "You would be right, I think, if I had not loved you for so long before that night."

Her head came up.

"I think I must have started loving you the very first day."

"You couldn't have. You hardly thought well of me at all, abusing my groom as I did."

"I liked you for it, for making things go your way, for your impertinence and determination and disdain for the rules. I had been overly cautious for months, and you freed me from that."

"I never thought of you in what I did. I'm too selfish."

"I've always seen you generous with Hetty and with me."

She turned her back on him and pressed her face to the wall. "Are you going to ask me to marry you again?"

He laughed. "Are you going to refuse me again?"

"I don't know." Her fingers closed and unclosed on the window frame. "I should."

"Why? Because I deceived you, betrayed our friendship? I'm prepared to apologize, to beg . . ."

"No." She drew a deep, ragged breath. "You had sound reasons for your imposture. I see that now. And once you'd begun, I suppose you were trapped, like Solomon with the secret of Hetty's birth."

"Then why?"

She turned to him then, her eyes bright with unshed tears. Her chin went up.

"You said yourself that you liked me because I abused you and ordered you about, but if we marry, if I wed a prince and then see you in all your splendor and you kiss me and hold me, you will make me like Pet." She turned away, pacing the length of the room with rapid strides, flinging her hands up in a wild gesture. "I will be good for nothing except to lie pressed to your side on a silken cushion, letting you stroke"—her hands flew up again—"my belly." She came to a halt, her back turned to him, her arms crossed, her shoulders shaking a little.

Alexander shoved away from the wall, strode across the room, and seized her shoulders, spinning her into his arms. "You do not know what a tempting image that is." He tilted her face up to his and kissed her until her lips parted for his entry and her arms came around him.

"You will never be Pet though I hope you will let me stroke your belly," he said, resting his chin on the top of her head. He felt her surprise in a quick breath that pressed her breasts against him.

"You are my night fairy, my Sprite. If I can catch you and keep you, I'm lucky. Even then I know you will bedevil me the rest of my life. And if you think I make you weak, what did you do to me to keep me laboring like Hercules at the Augean stables just for a glimpse of you?"

"Do you love me?"

"I do."

"Lucca!" The shop bell tinkled.

"Majesty?" Lucca appeared, elegantly dressed and holding a single red rose. He glanced from Alexander to Ophelia, comprehension dawning in his eyes.

"You're going out?" Alexander asked.

Lucca acknowledged it, lifting the rose in a brief salute.

"Bring Father Leonardo back with you."

"Majesty! What will Donna Francesca say?"

"Nothing that will change my mind. Miss Tesio is marrying Sebastian Brinsby. I'm free."

Still Lucca stood, unmoving. "But if you do not have the nobles on your side, or the republicans, what will . . ."

Alexander half led, half pulled Ophelia through the velvet curtain toward the stairs. "Lucca," he said over his shoulder, "the priest."

"Yes, Majesty!"

The familiar room above the shop was deep in shadow, with one bright bar of sunlight across the head of the bed and corner of the wall. Alexander looked once at that temptation and then away, pulling the room's two chairs up to the hearth in a conversational arrangement.

Ophelia took the seat he offered her. "With this marriage you gamble everything."

"No less than you," he said, settling himself in the chair opposite hers. He needed her and wanted her and had nearly lost her. He had waited weeks for their coming together, but he remembered what she'd suffered at Wyatt's hands and would observe the proprieties today.

"Oh, marriage is no risk for me. I've left home. I can always live with Hetty—well, at least until she marries. Then I'm sure I'd be welcome to stay with Solomon."

"And if he marries Mrs. Pendares?"

"Do you think he will?"

"As soon as he can manage after Jasper marries Hetty."

Ophelia laughed. "How can you be so sure? You were not around them very often."

"But I saw enough."

Ophelia straightened her skirts over her knees. "What did you see?"

"I saw a man look at woman the way he does when she's before him every day and he cannot have her."

"Oh." As if of their own accord, Ophelia's hands stopped their smoothing motion, and she pressed them hard into her lap. She could feel her cheeks burning.

Alexander jumped up. "I should have had Lucca make us some tea. I can go down and get some."

"No. I'm sure he won't be gone long, will he?"

Alexander shook his head. "Father Leonardo is lodged not far from here."

"Maybe we could pass the time in reading. You and I are both fond of books."

Alexander pivoted and went right to the desk. "A good thought."

Ophelia watched him studying the titles. The shaft of sunlight from the casement window passed just across the top of his head, lighting the gold strands in the brown. He reminded her of little brown butterflies in a summer garden, looking humble and common until the light caught their wings.

He came back to his chair with two volumes and handed one to her.

"*The Republic?* What have you got?"

"*The Rights of Man.*"

Ophelia straightened in her chair and opened her book. "Well, happy reading!" She bent her head over the pages.

Alexander opened his volume, but his mind wouldn't settle to read. He thought of Marc Antony, who had kissed a wily slip of a girl by the Nile and lost a kingdom. Men had considered Antony weak-witted ever since, and Alexander was sure his wits were no stronger. He read the same sentence in *The Rights of Man* five times before he gave it up and glanced at Ophelia.

Her book lay at a slant in her slack hands, one page arching up between the open halves of the text. Her chin had dropped to her breast, which rose and fell quietly. As if she felt his scrutiny, she started, coming upright with a little jerk.

"Oh dear, I'm afraid I nodded off."

"Do you want to lie down?" His voice came out hoarse and low.

"This is a ploy to get me into your bed."

"It is."

She shrugged. "Lucca cannot be much longer."

"Will you lie down, then?"

She nodded. They stood, moving awkwardly around each other, as if negotiating the few feet to the bed required an intricate dance. Alexander shed his coat as Ophelia climbed into the bed. She stretched out on her back, leaving room for him, and he lay down beside her.

All sleepiness vanished. Ophelia fixed her gaze on the ceiling, as if she could find some distraction there, but its smooth plaster surface without even the novelty of swirls was no help. "I've never shared a bed with anyone," she said. "Is this how it's done?"

She felt Alexander move beside her, crossing his arms above his head.

"There are different schools of thought, I suppose," he said.

"And this, lying side by side on our backs, would this be the marble tomb effigy school of thought?"

He laughed.

"What else is there?"

He turned into toward her, grabbing her waist and rolling her to face him. "There's this."

"Like two halves of a mussel shell, very cozy."

He gave her a quick kiss that started a fluttering in her stomach and rolled her away from him. Immediately he rolled the other way so that they were back to back.

"What would you call this?" he asked.

"The bookend school of thought, and I'd say it is most likely used by those who've quarreled."

In a swift reversal, he turned and seized her waist and pulled her tight against him. "This is the approach I like best," he said. "Nesting spoons."

"Oh." Ophelia couldn't think of anything else to say. She wondered fleetingly whether Father Leonardo would speak in Italian and whether she would know when to answer and decided her heart would know.

While she pondered it, Alexander's hand slid up her ribs and opened over her breast, and he made a low sound of pleasure in his throat. His fingers played gently over her, and the tips of her breasts drew hot rivulets of sensation from his touch that trickled down through her torso

and limbs to her most intimate center, pooling
there in liquid heat. She stretched to give him
access, pressing against his taut length.

With his fingertips Alexander made tight circles on one tiny bud. He wanted to bare her
breasts to his gaze, but that would have to wait.
For now it was a sweet delight to have her open
to him, arching to his touch, unafraid. He
pressed his lips to the back of her neck, breathing
a scent like blossoms.

His breath grew ragged at her ear, and he
pressed his aching groin against her hips. Where
was the priest? He dragged his hand down her
side and up again, sliding the light muslin of her
day dress over her skin, feeling tiny tremors
shake her. His hand came to rest on her belly.

"Do you think it will be long now?" she asked.

With a groan he rolled onto his back. His chest
rose and fell with his uneven breaths. He was so
close to possessing her now, his Sprite. The priest
was coming, and he trusted her, but sprites were
elusive; one didn't really possess them. They appeared at a whim, inviting one to drop cares and
duties for play, and disappeared into the woods
and hills or the night sky. He, who had clung to
duty and denial for years, hardly expected to
hold a night fairy.

The separation left Ophelia feeling suspended,
her muscles straining for something she had
been denied. The bar of sunlight had moved up
the wall to light only the last corner of the ceiling.

"Does the spoon approach work the other
way?" she asked.

Without waiting for a reply, she turned toward

him, nudging him onto his side, facing away
from her. Boldly she kissed the back of his neck
and ran her fingers through his hair. Then she
snuggled against him and put her arm around
his chest. It seemed natural to rub her palm in
lazy circles, exploring the flat, ridged shape of
him. Under her hands the beat of his heart told
her things about desire that she had not realized
before.

Abruptly he grabbed her wrist, stilling her
hand, his body taut against hers. She waited, un-
sure what to do, aware only that his whole person expressed some urgent longing. With a low,
ardent sound, he pressed her palm to his heart
and dragged her hand down the silky surface of
his waistcoat, over the tiny buttons and the
waistband, past his belly, lower still to his man's
part. He held her hand there, unspeaking, and
Ophelia, understanding only that he needed her
touch, closed her fingers around him.

A shudder passed through him, and she kissed
his cheek. With no idea of what might please, she
drew her fingers down the length of him and up
again, then squeezed gently. He sat straight up
in the bed, swinging his legs to the floor. His
breathing was shallow and labored, as it had
been after the fight in the alley. He pushed himself up on shaking legs and staggered to the
mantel, resting his elbows there, leaning his head
in his hands.

"Majesty?" Lucca's hesitant voice came from
the hall. "Father Leonardo can't come today."

Alexander pressed his head against his arms.
He had only to summon his resolve, to walk out
the door and down the stairs, to find some dis-

traction and exercise restraint, as he'd done before. She would not escape. There was no danger he would lose her again. Neither his aunt nor Castlereagh could prevent this marriage. But his limbs refused to obey any command to move away from her. It required all his will to cling to the mantel when in his mind he was already pressing Ophelia under him in the narrow bed.

Ophelia came up on her knees, her hands in her lap. After a few minutes she heard Lucca's footsteps going down the stairs.

"We don't have to stop this time, do we?" she asked.

"What?" The word came out as a croak.

"You were going to tell me once about the fourth stage of love. Haven't we reached that?"

Alexander pushed away from the mantel and turned to her. "I don't want to dishonor you."

"You won't dishonor me, if you act from love." Her eyes were dark and knowing.

He let out a long, shaky breath. "Don't. You'll tempt me beyond bearing."

"Let this be our wedding night, these our rites of love, in this room where we can be just ourselves."

He moved before she finished speaking, reaching her in two strides and pulling her up onto her knees on the bed and into his fierce embrace. His oath was swallowed in his kiss. When they broke apart, she laughed and began unfastening the buttons of his waistcoat with a frown of concentration between her brows.

When she freed the last button, he stepped back impatiently, yanking off his neckcloth and stripping away shirt and waistcoat. He sank beside her on the bed, tugging at his boots while her fingers played up and down his back. He stood and shed his last garments.

"You are beautiful," she said, her expression solemn. "Like Raj." She ran her fingers down his sides, following the curve of his hip sockets down to his thighs. Heat raged through him like fire through a field in late summer.

"Now you," he managed through his teeth, his breath a faint whistle.

She held his side for balance, untangling her skirts, and stepping daintily down from the bed. He turned her gently and began to work the buttons between her shoulder blades, and then her stays, slowly because he had to stop often to press her to him and kiss her neck, her back, her shoulders. He was trembling when she stood before him in her shift. He lifted the edge of the dainty garment, she lifted her arms, and he freed her from bashful constraint.

As the fading light of the mild spring day washed the room in blue, he pulled back the coverlet and they joined each other in the bed, entwining limbs, sliding against each other, letting their hands touch everywhere, until they lay panting, their hearts pounding wildly.

"This is the fourth stage of love," he said, "the yielding of one's whole person to one's lover."

He rested his hand on her belly, and Ophelia pressed her lips together to keep from crying out with impatience.

"Do you know what happens next?" he whispered. "Did anyone tell you?"

She nodded. "Mrs. Pendares told us a little."

He slid his palm lower, spreading his fingers

wide through her dark curls. She drew in a sharp breath as he found the hot, moist center of sensation, and coaxed and urged her to readiness for him.

Ophelia arched and stretched, opening to his hand, and with a sudden move, he pressed her down, positioning himself between her thighs. Braced on his arms, he looked down, and in the blue of his eyes she saw hot seas of promise and love.

Alexander lowered himself into her embrace, sliding into the slick, hot center of her, where he was prince of nowhere, an ordinary man in love. With one swift thrust he broke the last barrier between them, and kissing and coaxing, he taught her a rhythm beyond the meeting of their bodies and into love.

Later, Alexander slipped into his breeches and crept down to the basement kitchen, bringing back wine, bread, and cheese, not exactly a wedding breakfast. The thought sobered him a little, but he was cheered when he opened the room and found her waltzing in his discarded shirt with his coat as a partner.

An instant's embarrassment passed over her face and dissolved into a wistful smile. "We've never danced," she said.

"I look forward to it." He concentrated on arranging their repast and starting a fire, to avoid looking at the way the thin cambric of his shirt outlined her shape. He wasn't sure when she would be ready to make love again. Passionate she might be, but she was not experienced.

She sat on the floor with her legs crossed under her, making little sandwiches of bread and cheese and offering her handiwork to him, apparently unaware of how the open collar of his shirt offered tantalizing glimpses of taut, round breasts to his view.

"Mrs. Pendares told the truth, apparently," she said, looking up at him from under her lashes.

"What?" He lifted his gaze from her breasts, trying to follow the shift in the conversation.

"She said that a man's . . . breeding instrument . . . swells and stiffens for the act of love." She looked directly at him. "But apparently it doesn't remain so."

"You peeked, didn't you?"

"I don't want to be at a disadvantage here. You have more experience than I."

"I can see I'll have to take you to Italy."

"To understand male anatomy?"

"To see the fountains." He sipped his wine. "Every town has one, and each displays the male attributes of Neptune, or Cupid, or whatever deity happens to be honored in that particular town. Of course, you may not like me so well, when you've seen more specimens."

She threw a piece of bread at him. "Tell me about Italy, about Trevigna."

He did. He was telling her about the wonders of Venice when she stopped him again.

"Your mother was from Venice?"

He nodded.

"And your parents were married there?"

"Yes. There's a church, Santa Maria dei Miracoli, a favorite of many Venetians for weddings."

"Then let us be married there." She brushed

the crumbs from her lap. "Do you want to come back to bed?" she asked.

The *Morning Chronicle* of May 7, 1816, reported, among other items, the astonishing success of the Restoration Fund, as it was called, the betrothal of Sebastian Lionel Brinsby, Earl of Cranwell, to *Signorina* Katerina Tesio of Trevigna, and the departure of His Majesty Alexander di Piovasco Mirandola and his betrothed, the Lady Ophelia Brinsby, for Italy.

Epilogue

A warm breeze blew up from the port, ruffling the dry grass of golden brown hills. Above the hills a cloudless sky darkened to a rich, deep blue with the coming evening. Ophelia leaned on the little stone balcony of Alexander's villa in a filmy white dressing gown, the only clothing she could bear in the heat. Beyond the terraced garden with its playful fountain, Raj grazed in an open field. The stallion, a gift from Jasper, had arrived two days earlier, with a note from Hetty confirming that she and Jasper and Lucca and Pet were settled in a cozy house near Solomon.

Raj lifted his head, sniffing the air, unfamiliar with the smells of Trevigna—lavender, thyme, and grapes, and dusky green trees that Ophelia didn't have a name for yet.

She liked the place, though. It was the villa from the painting in the tailor's shop. The stones were peach, rust, and cream, as if they took their colors directly from the sun. The airy high-ceilinged rooms were fitted with tall wooden shutters to keep out the afternoon heat. There had been no furnishings at first, but gradually, when people realized Alexander had come home, this or that piece of furniture arrived by cart from some village, usually with a gift of wine and olives or cheese and figs, and a note saying "this we kept for your mother," or "this for your father." Today an ancient bed had arrived. According to the housekeeper, it had been in the villa when Alexander was conceived. Ophelia had unpacked linens from deep chests fragrant with lavender and cedar and made the bed ready.

Behind Ophelia the shutters tapped against the wall as the bedroom door opened. She glanced over her shoulder, and Alexander caught and held her gaze as he came striding toward her, coatless and hatless, more golden than ever from hours in the Italian sun. She had seen the sea now and the hills and had the fanciful notion that he had been made from the very same elements that composed Trevigna.

"Everything is in order for tomorrow," he said, coming straight to the balcony and slipping an arm around her waist. He pulled her close and kissed her with a deep, slow passion, like the sun's heat sinking into her and warming her. A long whinny from Raj interrupted the deepening kiss.

The stallion cantered to the edge of the field and reared once on his hind legs. Alexander leaned on the stone parapet, his arm clasped around Ophelia's waist, and whistled to the horse. Raj answered with a snort, then, apparently satisfied with Alexander's notice, went back to his grazing.

Alexander turned to Ophelia, nuzzling her neck and sliding his hands over the curve of her bottom. Ophelia began unfastening the buttons of his waistcoat. It had become so natural in the four months of their marriage, this freedom with each other's person, this happiness.

She pushed the sides of his waistcoat apart and drew the fine lawn shirt from the waistband of his breeches. Then she had to hug him, pressing her ear to his warm chest, feeling his arms tighten around her. Her husband had a talent for hugs that began with a fierce clasp and gentled gradually to long comforting strokes up and down her back. Even in her friendship with Hetty there had been a reserve about signs of affection that had left Ophelia a little lonely and determined to show it to no one. She thought she must have been touch-starved before Alexander.

"You seem happy," he said.

"Very," she answered.

He rested his chin on the top of her head. "I haven't ignored you too much for the business of the convention?"

"No." She tried to shake her head against his chest, and the motion turned into a nuzzle. She leaned back in his arms, lifting her hands to his cravat, loosening the knot that was peculiarly his own. She grew a little solemn then and kissed the base of his throat. He tilted her head up and answered with an ardent joining of their mouths.

"I learned some useful phrases today," she told him, when they took time to breathe.

"Did you? Tell me."

"*Abbi pazienza.* Have patience."

"In your case, very useful."

She punched him playfully.

"What else?"

"And I learned that there's such a thing as an *asino calzato e vestito*, an ass with shoes and clothes."

"To whom did that apply, I wonder?" He loosened the ties of her wrapper, opening it and letting his gaze wander over her person. "You remind me of woods in springtime."

Ophelia leaned back in his arms, enjoying the rapt expression in his eyes. "Woods?"

"With dark secret places," he said, brushing her intimate curls with the back of his hand. "And plump mushrooms, pale, creamy, and so smooth." He ran his hand up her belly. "And delicate pink blossoms."

His hand came to rest on her breast and she found it hard to breathe. She pressed forward, encircling him with her arms, not giving in yet to the hunger.

"Don't you want to know who's the *asino*? One of your favorite delegates." She found the buttons of his shirt cuffs and loosened them one by one. "Are you worried about tomorrow? About the convention?"

"You think that now that it's finally come, I might be disappointed, or afraid to trust what I've put in motion? I'm not, because I have you with me."

"Me?"

"Yes." He looked at her soberly, his eyes darkening from their customary blue to a deeper shade like the sky above them. "I have all that idealism. That got them here, but they're real people. They're selfish, tired, bilious. Their feet hurt or they drink too much wine. You see that in them."

"My eye for character foibles helps you?"

"It does. I am a much more effective leader for your clear-headed judgment."

"So I suppose that means you'll keep me?"

"I will, if you'll have me."

"Well, that depends on what sort of king you mean to be." She slipped away then through the shutters. He pulled his shirt off over his head, and she tried not to look. "So far you have not been what I expected at all." She moved unhurriedly across the room to the other side of the bed, the old floor cool under her feet. The fading light barely penetrated to the bed, leaving it in a dim blue dusk.

He followed, facing her across the expanse of white coverlet. "Really?"

"No poisonings, no hired assassins, no tortures. Instead, a constitutional convention, school rebuildings, library openings. The doges of old must be wondering what's to become of Italy."

"Ah," he said. "You've been reading history."

"Yes." She drew the coverlet back slowly, her eyes locked with his. "You are a very different sort of prince, with no plans to conquer your neighbors, no schemes of revenge against all who have wronged Trevigna."

He didn't answer, and she realized his gaze had drifted down the open front of her wrapper. When his eyes came back to hers, he said, "I do have plans for revenge."

He took the coverlet in one hand and flung it back. "New bed?"

"Very old bed. Your parents', I think."

He smiled at that, slowly. Then, turning, he sank on the edge and began to pull his boots off.

"What revenge?" she asked faintly.

"On history," he said, dropping a boot. The second one followed before she had time to ask what he meant. She saw him stuff his stockings in them. Then he stood facing her again.

She clung to the edge of the coverlet. Married life had turned anticipation from a vague restlessness to sharp, specific sensations.

"Revenge on France or Austria or even Ferruci is pointless. But revenge on history, to turn Italy around, to point her toward equality and justice and freedom for all men—"

"And women," she had to add.

He grinned. "That's true revenge." He flicked open the buttons on his breeches and began to remove them. Ophelia let her wrapper fall. They stood for a moment, quietly worshipful, in the blue dusk of a dying day, then joined their bodies and their hearts in that ancient bed, making of their love something new.

Dear Reader,

Each month, Avon Books publishes the best in historical and contemporary romance. So be on watch for these up-coming Avon titles.

For historical romance fans, there's Julia Quinn's Avon Romantic Treasure, BRIGHTER THAN THE SUN. The Earl of Billingham, a notorious Regency rake, must marry before his 31st birthday or lose his inheritance. He thinks he's found the solution to his problem in marriage to Miss Eleanor Lyndon. But Ellie is more than he'd bargained for. Is it possible for this rake to become reformed?

In THE WILD ONE by Danelle Harmon, Julia-Paige — and her baby — arrive in 1776 England from America to confront devil-may-care Lord Gareth de Montforte. When Julia informs Gareth that his late older brother is the father, Gareth impulsively marries the beautiful mother. But is he truly ready to settle down and become respectable?

The romantic Scottish Highlands is the setting for Lois Greiman's HIGHLAND BRIDES: THE LADY AND THE KNIGHT. It's 1516, and Sara Forbes is on the run with a very special baby. Soon, she finds herself protected by Sir Boden, an irresistible and brave knight. But can their growing love overcome his devotion to duty?

Looking for a contemporary romance with a touch of humor? Then don't miss Barbara Boswell's WHEN LIGHTNING STRIKES TWICE. Rachel Saxon, a modern career woman, is swept off her feet by Quinton Cormack and must decide if it's time to put *pleasure* before business in this sizzling love story by one of romance's most popular writers.

Remember, each month look to Avon Books — for the very best in romance.

Sincerely,
Lucia Macro
Avon Books

Avon Romances—
the best in exceptional authors and unforgettable novels!

THE PERFECT GENTLEMAN   by Danice Allen
78151-4/ $5.50 US/ $7.50 Can

WINTER HEARTS   by Maureen McKade
78871-3/ $5.50 US/ $7.50 Can

A LOVE TO CHERISH   by Connie Mason
77999-4/ $5.99 US/ $7.99 Can

FOR MY LADY'S KISS   by Linda Needham
78755-5/ $5.99 US/ $7.99 Can

THE LOVER   by Nicole Jordan
78560-9/ $5.99 US/ $7.99 Can

LADY ROGUE   by Suzanne Enoch
78812-8/ $5.99 US/ $7.99 Can

A WOMAN'S HEART   by Rosalyn West
78512-9/ $5.99 US/ $7.99 Can

HIGHLAND WOLF   by Lois Greiman
78191-3/ $5.99 US/ $7.99 Can

SCARLET LADY   by Marlene Suson
78912-4/ $5.99 US/ $7.99 Can

TOUGH TALK AND   by Deborah Camp
TENDER KISSES   78250-2/ $5.99 US/ $7.99 Can

Avon Romantic Treasures

*Unforgettable, enthralling love stories,
sparkling with passion and adventure
from Romance's bestselling authors*

LADY OF WINTER *by Emma Merritt*
                              77985-4/$5.99 US/$7.99 Can

SILVER MOON SONG *by Genell Dellin*
                              78602-8/$5.99 US/$7.99 Can

FIRE HAWK'S BRIDE *by Judith E. French*
                              78745-8/$5.99 US/$7.99 Can

WANTED ACROSS TIME *by Eugenia Riley*
                              78909-4/$5.99 US/$7.99 Can

EVERYTHING AND THE MOON *by Julia Quinn*
                              78933-7/$5.99 US/$7.99 Can

BEAST *by Judith Ivory*
                              78644-3/$5.99 US/$7.99 Can

HIS FORBIDDEN TOUCH *by Shelley Thacker*
                              78120-4/$5.99 US/$7.99 Can

LYON'S GIFT *by Tanya Anne Crosby*
                              78571-4/$5.99 US/$7.99 Can